MATT

MW01503518

DUNKS

outskirtspress

DENVER, COLORADO

Outskirts Press, Inc.
http://www.outskirtspress.com

ISBN: 978-1-4327-8653-3

Outskirts Press and the "OP" logo are trademarks belonging to Outskirts Press, Inc.

PRINTED IN THE UNITED STATES OF AMERICA

This book is dedicated to my family: Mom, Dad, Mike and Moya

Chapter 1

At around 6:45 am, on a summer Monday in 2008, Duncan Lipton looked at himself in the mirror, slowly shook his head, and said aloud, "I cannot fuckin believe I'm me." That had a lot to do with the huge pile of hundred-dollar bills scattered all over the floor at his feet. It had even more to do with the fact that he had no idea how the pile had gotten there.

Duncan's best friend, Matty G, was passed out on the floor behind him. Glancing at the bottom of the mirror, Duncan could see his hard-sleeping friend with a little bit of drool dangling out of his mouth, inching its way toward the carpet. He was curled up in the fetal position, still wearing the same clothes that Duncan had seen him in the previous afternoon, just before he left the Lipton house to go home for dinner. They had planned to meet back up after Matty finished eating with his mom, but Duncan had no recollection of doing so. In fact, Duncan had no recollection of doing much of anything after Matty left.

A few minutes before parting ways, they had each swallowed two two-milligram Xanax pills, which they referred to as "zanny bars". Duncan remembered that much, little more, except that the two of them had also taken three quick shots of Jack Daniels whiskey to wash the pills down and amplify their effects. He had then unwrapped a new bar of Irish Spring, turned on the shower, and waited for the hot water to create heavy cloud-cover in his bathroom. Once the mirror had fully fogged, he drew a smiley face on it, and then… *blank.*

When he woke up the next day, he groggily got out of bed to go take a piss. On his way to the bathroom, he looked at himself in the full-length mirror attached to his open closet door. He looked shot-out, he thought, his eyes droopy and his hair a sloppy mess. He then took notice of the money pile at his feet, and verbally declared his astonishment for the simple fact that he was himself. However unlikely it may have been to find a massive heap of money on his bedroom floor, this was hardly the first time that he had found himself in extraordinary circumstances. And it would hardly be the last.

Duncan's bladder pulled him into the bathroom. As he relieved himself, he looked to the pile on his right and reveled in the fact that there were Benjies all over his floor. *One hundred dollar fuckin Benjies all over the fuckin floor! I am about to ball outrageous!* he thought, immediately making shopping plans with himself, failing to care where all the money had come from. But while he may not have *cared* how the money had gotten there, he was nonetheless curious. *Maybe G'll know*, he thought.

Duncan zipped up, step-hopped over the pile, and walked over to his apparent partner-in-crime. Leaning down, he whispered, "Yoooooooo, G, you awake, doggy?"

"No," said Matty G.

"Dude," Duncan said, "did you see this fuckin pile?"

"What?" Matty G croaked. He grunted as he lifted his head to look at the pile of money. "Oh shit, Dunks. It's real?" He was floored. "Man, I woke up at like 5:30 to yak and I saw it. I was so fuckin wrecked, it kinda just fit in there. If you hadn't said anything just now, I prolly woulda thought it was a fuckin dream."

This is *a fuckin dream*, Duncan thought. *Has to be. But it feels pretty real though.* He gave himself a moment to process the surreal nature of the situation, then continued his internal monologue. *Yeah. I'm definitely awake. Oh shit. There's really a huge pile of money on my fuckin floor!*

And there most definitely was. This was not a dream. There was a huge pile of money sitting on his floor. Somewhere else, someone was definitely very upset at this fact; Duncan knew that for sure. But he would cross that bridge when he came to it... if he ever did. He knew that it would be a blown-to-shit, road-hazard of a bridge. But, for the time being, that bridge lay too far down a champagne-asphalt covered road for him to care.

Hundreds and hundreds of fucking Benjies! he thought. *Maybe more.*

Right on cue, Matty G, now fully awake, said, "Let's count. There's gotta be at least, like, a thousand of these Mr. Franklins, I bet."

"Probably even more," Duncan replied.

Matty G started to count while Duncan went to the kitchen, where his mom kept a big jar of rubber bands. He grabbed a handful and walked back to his room, where G was sitting on the floor, meticulously laying out the bills in stacks of twenty, each stack totaling two thousand dollars. By the time Duncan returned to his room, Matty G had already laid out ten stacks. Twenty thousand dollars. And that didn't even scratch the surface. Their rough, hung-over estimation was clearly paltry compared to the reality of how much money was lying on the floor.

They decided to wrap rubber bands around the bills in twenty-thousand-dollar increments because that was what was already conveniently laid out, and, after consolidating the ten original stacks into one, they agreed that the fatness of each folded-over stack looked pretty badass.

Within ten minutes of careful counting, they were more than halfway done: fifteen twenty-grand stacks. Three hundred thousand dollars. They looked at each other, eyes wide, mouths agape. A guilty smile creased Matty G's lips while Duncan's mouth remained hanging wide open. They briefly paused their counting to stare at the money and absorb the massive sum that lay before them. Making eye contact with his accomplice, Duncan's lips formed a guilty smile to match the gleaming white, ear-to-ear one on his best friend's face. They laughed and resumed counting. When they were done, 25 stacks lay before them: an even five hundred thousand dollars.

Yup, Duncan thought. *Somebody's pissed.*

Chapter 2

Tessa Moya woke up at seven am on the dot, like she did every day, to the sound of loud techno music blasting out of her cell phone. She hated techno music, with its throbbing pulse, dramatic synths, and auto-tuned vocals, which were often seemingly affected by helium inhalation. It easily ruined her peaceful sleep. Trying desperately to turn the painful music off was the shock she needed in order to get out of her soft, comfortable, very pink bed, and get ready for work.

Tessa loved her bed and its restorative powers, but, thankfully, she also loved her summer job, teaching tennis lessons to five through eight year olds at the Wesson Tennis Center. That always made having to leave her fabulous bed a little easier in the morning than if she were getting up to go to school. Teaching cute little kids how to play tennis out in the sun was pretty much her idea of a good time. As far as jobs went anyway.

In general, Tessa Moya had a sweet deal. No complaints. She was seventeen years old, tan, beautiful, athletic, employed, and in love. Life was good.

She climbed out of her bed, then out of the XL Billy Joel t-shirt that she had slept in. She wrapped herself in a clean red towel and went to her bathroom to take a shower. Opening a small box containing a pink bar of Dove soap, then making the shower-water hot, she considered the likely predictable day that lay before her. As usual, it looked like it was going to be a good one.

As she stepped out of the shower, wrapped again in her red towel, she heard the familiar beep of a missed call from her cell phone. She walked over to the phone lying on her bed to see who could be calling so early. The screen informed her: 'Duncan Lipton'. The phone beeped again to inform her that he had just left a message. That was good. *It should be an apology*, she thought. She didn't want to talk to him now anyway, so it was good that he had left a message.

Tessa was angry with Duncan for the way he had acted while having dinner with her family the previous Friday night. He *knew* that her parents were die-hard Republicans. And yet, he had still engaged in political verbal warfare with them, in support of his man-crush, Barack Obama's bid for the Presidency of the United States.

Tessa pressed her cell phone's '1' key, 'Send', and then typed in the pass-code for her voicemail. Duncan's voice sounded excited. Though not the apology that she had hoped for, his message was intriguing enough to prompt her to call him back: "Baby, you're not gonna fuckin believe what happened. You are not gonna fuckin believe it! Oh my god! I can't even say over the phone. Call me back as soon as you get this. Love ya. Bye."

Tessa's curiosity put her anger at Duncan on the backburner, at least for the moment. She went into her phone's contact list, found 'Duncan Lipton', and then hit 'Send'. Duncan picked up after the first ring.

"Babe, you're not gonna believe this! Get over to my house *ASAP!*"

"I'm still pissed at you, Duncan. Don't forget that."

"I know, I know. We can talk about it when you get here, okay?"

"Fine. What's the big deal anyway?" she asked, irritably.

"I can't say. You gotta come over and see for yourself, baby."

"Fine. Gimme a half hour."

"Cool. Love ya, babe. You're the best."

"Uh huh," she said, her voice tinged with a little sarcastic cool. "See ya soon." She hung up and looked at her phone, making what she knew to be a half-smile of forgiveness, and shook her head. Even though she was upset with him, Tessa loved Duncan to death, and she was willing to readily accept an in-person apology from him for this relatively minor transgression. And besides, now she was also too curious *not* to go over and find out what was going on. She had just enough time before work that she could spend about fifteen minutes over there.

Tessa put on a lime green bra, with matching thong, and pulled on a tight baby blue t-shirt that matched her eyes, followed by a pair of black three-quarter length tights that made her awesome butt look even nicer on her 5'5" frame. She ran a comb through her long, wet, brunette hair and gave herself two quick sprays of Polo perfume, Duncan's gift to her for her seventeenth birthday. She put on her Nikes, then looked herself over in the mirror on her wall. She liked what she saw.

Tessa was smokin' hot and she knew it. She took great pride in her looks and put much effort into styling herself out. She loved being Duncan's prize. She felt that *he* was definitely *her* prize, so she wanted everyone in school to know that Duncan Lipton was going out with the hottest girl in Eastfield. Accordingly, she made a point not to leave the house without looking sexy, whether sporty, dressy, or preppy. It contributed to Duncan's status as the coolest boy in school and she liked it that way. She felt like she *should* be going out with the most popular boy at Eastfield High, and she enjoyed the social status that their relationship afforded her. She was the most admired and "popular" girl in school, in the high school sense of the term. To say that she was actually the most *liked* would probably not be quite accurate.

One of the pitfalls of being the most "popular" girl in school was that she was also the most hated. Mostly, it was jealousy that inspired bad feelings and shit-talking behind her back by other girls. She had it all. The looks. The brains. The clothes. The family. The sports trophies. The most popular boy in school around her arm. She was even really nice. To a lot of other girls, that just didn't seem fair, and, without ever exchanging a cross word with a single one of them, Tessa was loathed by many of her female classmates.

Usually, it was feelings of inadequacy regarding one's attractiveness that inspired bad feelings towards her from her male peers. Before she began dating Duncan, boys whom she considered unworthy of her affection (and yet-to-be-taken virginity) had hit on her countless times. Unfortunately for their egos, she responded to most of their approaches by curtly rejecting them. She usually brushed them off with a smug "Not interested" or an aloof "No thanks", as she casually walked away. She knew that she *could* be nicer. But she didn't want to leave any ambiguity. More or less, the only times that Tessa Moya wasn't a smiling sweetheart, were when she was being blatantly hit on.

She had just been waiting for the right guy, and for a long time she thought she had known who he was. But she and her crush, Duncan Lipton, had remained only passing strangers in the hall, occasionally making eye contact and quickly looking away, each embarrassed at being caught staring. They had finally run into each other at a house party hosted by a mutual friend-of-a-friend, whose wealthy, swinging parents were on vacation somewhere in the Caribbean.

Thanks to a few hits from a circulating blunt and a little liquid courage (courtesy of a $6.99 bottle of Jaegermeister and a keg full of cold Yuengling), Duncan managed to say a few words to Tessa in mid-exhale: "Damn, this is some *good* shit," he sputtered. It wasn't his most charming opener ever, true, but the weed *was* good. And though not usually one to be timid when it came to talking to girls, Duncan couldn't help but be made nervous by her, in a way that no girl had made him feel in his roughly five years of sexual awareness/experience (which had begun when he got laid by his chubby, brace-faced, acne-afflicted, fifteen-year-old babysitter, Betsy, when he was only twelve and still curious and naïve enough to have not yet developed *anything* resembling standards).

There was just something about Tessa that intimidated him, something *beyond* how hot she was; it was some intangible quality that he couldn't quite put his finger on. If Duncan had to put a word to it, he thought that *smooth* would be apt. Every possible connotation of the word, from her looks to her manner to her movements, to her... whatever. All seemed to apply rather accurately. The chick was definitely *smooooooth*.

Duncan's feelings of intimidation, however, evaporated as soon as she met his eyes, smiled, and responded with an enthusiastic and charmingly goofy, "Fuck yeah!" to his praise of the weed they were sharing. They had both burst out laughing, causing Duncan to cough on the thick blunt smoke for a few seconds, which prompted Tessa to laugh that much harder. After the blunt was finished, the two of them, giggly high, found a seat on a couch, where they sat talking to each other for five hours straight, completely forgetting the others partying around them. Since then, they had been more or less inseparable.

On her way out of her family's house, Tessa stopped in the kitchen to grab a banana for breakfast, as well as a large thermos of ice water. She had recently learned that potassium (which bananas were apparently loaded with) prevented cramping, and being in the hot sun all day long, running after tennis balls, sometimes led to her feet and hamstrings cramping up. The thermostat read 88 degrees Fahrenheit, and it was looking like it was going to be another day in the high 90's, so it seemed that eating the banana would be a good idea. Potassium deficiencies and dehydration are some of the leading causes of cramps in hot weather, so she was coming prepared.

She walked out to the driveway that ran along the right side of her family's house and got into her silver VW Jetta, turned the key in the ignition and blasted the A/C on high. She peeled the banana, then shifted into Reverse and eased out to the street, munching as she drove.

Duncan's family's house was on the north side of Eastfield. Tessa lived on the south side, about four miles away. Since it was early in the day, there was very light downtown traffic, and it took her a little less than fifteen minutes to get to his street after she hung up the phone.

Just as she turned onto Candace Place, the small cul-de-sac of eight similar, brick-face "McMansions" that Duncan's family lived at the end of, a black Corvette lurched out of the Liptons' driveway. The car was *flying,* moving about 70 mph by the time it passed Tessa's Jetta. Looking in her rearview mirror, she could see that the driver clearly had no intention of obeying the rapidly approaching stop sign at the corner of Candace Place and the perpendicular Harley Street.

When the Corvette flew through the intersection, Tessa's universe all of a sudden seemed to move in slow motion, as she witnessed the front of a navy blue Ford Explorer, appropriately cruising around forty-five mph on Harley Street, meet the passenger-side door of the black Corvette at a perfect ninety degree angle.

The Explorer immediately tipped over onto the driver's side and skidded about thirty yards further down Harley Street, spinning and wobbling like a top until it flipped completely upside down, eventually coming to rest at the end of a river of shattered glass, which glistened as it reflected the early morning's brightening summer sun.

The Corvette, however, was not so lucky.

Chapter 3

Tessa Moya's eyes opened wider than they had ever opened. Her jaw hung lower than it had ever hung. She held her breath longer than it had ever been held. Staring into the rearview mirror, she saw the craziest shit she had ever seen.

By the time the black Corvette reached the intersection, it must have been going about 80 mph, maybe even 90. Incredible pickup. Whereas the Explorer tipped over, wobbled, and skidded while staying on the ground, the black Corvette went completely *airborne*, flipping half a dozen times before it hit the ground. Pieces of it flew *everywhere*. What had been a beautiful automobile only seconds earlier, was now a flying hunk of scrap metal, spraying pieces of its former self hundreds of feet in all directions.

The Corvette hung in the air for what seemed, to Tessa, like a solid minute, though it was probably more along the lines of three seconds. And then it landed. And then it exploded.

After several moments of being frozen in pure shock, Tessa picked up her cell phone and made the first of the two 911 calls that she would make in the next five minutes.

Before the 911 operator could even finish the first syllable of his greeting, Tessa started screeching, "Oh my god! Oh my god! There's a huge car crash! Oh my god!"

"Where are you, ma'am?" asked the operator.

"Oh my god. Woah. *Woah*. Oh my fucking god!"

"Ma'am, where are you located? Please tell me so that I can have dispatch send help for you as quickly as possible."

"Sorry, sorry. I'm on Candace Place, right by the intersection of Candace and Harley," she choked out. "Hurry!"

"Have you been injured ma'am?"

"No, no. I'm fine. You gotta send an ambulance now though! Oh my god! Like *now*! There was a crazy car accident. One of the cars exploded. It's burning right *now*!"

The black Corvette was indeed burning. It had landed on the large front lawn of 454 Harley St., three houses from the corner, and then tumbled violently, flipping three times and sending debris everywhere. It finally came to rest on the lawn of 456 Harley St., next door to where it landed and four doors down from the corner. To say that it came to *rest* wouldn't be entirely accurate though. The black Corvette stopped moving, but it continued to burn like an inferno, smoke pouring from the wreckage.

"Ma'am, we will get there as soon as we possibly can," the 911 operator attempted to assure Tessa. "Ma'am?" But she had already hung up.

Tessa suddenly remembered where she had been going when she had gotten, to say the least, distracted. *Whose car was that?* she wondered.

She sped up the Liptons' driveway at the end of the cul-de-sac, and pulled around back to the garage entrance. When she got out of her car, she immediately ran to the code box next to the garage and tried to type in 1-2-3-4-Enter, the combination needed to raise the door. Her hands were shaking as she tried to punch in the numbers. It took her three tries and then, the third time being the charm, the garage door rumbled and began to rise.

As soon as it was high enough that she could bend over and slip herself under the rising door, she sprinted through the garage and flung the door open that led into house. She ran through the laundry room, which opened into the kitchen, shouting Duncan's name twice at the top of her lungs. But when she reached the precipice of the kitchen, she was suddenly frozen in her tracks by the most horrible scene she had ever witnessed. Things did not look good for Matty G.

Chapter 4

Eastfield was a predominantly white, upper middle-class/wealthy suburb. There were, however, a number of black kids who went to Eastfield High, all of whom lived in one small area known as Hightown.

The Hightown Projects were a series of three nearly dilapidated tenement buildings. Near it were about 3 acres of land with 37 houses, lining four streets: Washington St., Lincoln St., Jefferson St., and Roosevelt St. Though the surrounding area's houses were not a part of the Hightown Projects, when one referred to "Hightown", it was usually implied that the whole area, including the 37 houses, was to be taken into account. The disparity in wealth and resources between this area and the rest of Eastfield was a discouraging and sore topic in the local political arena.

If a white kid said that he was going to Hightown, chances were good that he wasn't going into the projects themselves; he was probably heading to one of the houses around the area to play X-Box, buy some bud, or play basketball. The actual projects were almost entirely a white-free zone. The only white people who ever really went there were social workers and crack-heads. And Duncan.

Though neither a social worker nor a crackhead, Duncan was frequently present (and always welcome) at the Hightown Projects. Duncan was *that* whiteboy, a neighborhood celebrity deemed an honorary resident by the close-knit, completely black community of the building where Matty G lived with his mother.

Duncan and Matty G had been playing basketball together since they were four years old. Their dads, buddies from rec league at the Y, had decided to train their sons to be devoted ball players, ultimately with great success. Being that Matty G and Duncan were always the two best players on all of the rec, travel, all-star and school teams they had been on, including Eastfield High's varsity squad for all three years of high school that they had attended thus far, the two had built a strong bond of mutual respect and admiration. And ever since the first time they had played ball at the Y together with their dads and went out for ice cream afterwards, they had each been the other's best friend and closest confidante.

Matty G, who Duncan had sworn to secrecy, was, to this day, the only person who knew that Duncan had had sex with his ugly babysitter Betsy when he was twelve years old, proof enough to Duncan that his best friend was a trustworthy soul. That story, told to Duncan's twelve-year-old peers, would have been sensational. And definitely in a bad way. But Matty G never said a word, and Duncan was spared the humiliation.

Matty G also had what he considered to be concrete proof that Duncan was *his* ace. Time and again, Duncan had had his back, always looking out for his skinny, marginalized best friend who, as a scrawny pre-pubescent member of the very small African American minority in Eastfield, was subject to more than his fair share of bullying at a young age, at the hands of the offspring of some of Eastfield's abundant racist whites. One time, in sixth grade, Duncan had strolled into the gym locker room to find two white eighth-graders cornering Matty G near the showers, pushing and taunting him, calling him a nigger and a pussy. As soon as the early-blooming Duncan (already just under six feet tall and pushing 165 pounds before he was thirteen) heard the forbidden 'N-word' directed maliciously at his friend, he had single-handedly kicked the shit out of both older boys and spent the next week suspended from school for fighting.

That was the last time Matty G had ever been picked on. He was able to float on Duncan's protective cloud for a while, but then, about six months after the locker room incident, he began a *massive* growth spurt of his own. By the time the boys began seventh grade, Matty G no longer required Duncan's assistance to avoid being preyed upon by bullies. His body, seeming to grow exponentially, said more than words ever could to his former tormentors' intentions of harassing him.

When they walked through Eastfield High School's doors for their first day of ninth grade, Duncan was 6'1", and weighed around 190 pounds, having filled out his once rakish, lanky body. By junior year, his growth had slowed and he had settled to around 6'3" with 215 pounds of sinewy muscle.

Matty G, however, had turned into a different person altogether. By the time he was fifteen years old, he was still growing rapidly and already stood 6'7". Regularly eating massive amounts of protein and whatever else he could get his huge hands on, he weighed about 250 pounds of mostly brick muscle that kept expanding from his daily regimen of push-ups, sit-ups, pull-ups, and as many hours as possible of basketball at the Hightown courts. By junior year, he had grown to almost 6'10", and, after shedding all of his baby fat, weighed about 270 pounds, no longer just *mostly* brick muscle, but now made completely of steel. Undeniably, the boy was a total powerhouse.

Three games into Duncan and Matty G's freshman season, it became patently clear that Eastfield was going to be the new state super power in high school basketball. This was owed to the fact that the two of them, particularly as a duo, were utterly amazing. Individually, they were spectacular in their own right, but together…watch out! They were completely dominant.

Duncan and Matty G were well-raised, respectful kids, who knew to abide by their coach's rules and regulations. Although they were man-children, they were still only fifteen years old at the time of their varsity debut, and had been implored by their parents to respect their elders.

Their coach, Donny Stager, was beginning his fifteenth season at Eastfield and had yet to have a losing season. Eastfield was a big town with lots of basketball courts and numerous leagues for kids of all ages to play in, so there was a solid talent pool coming in each year.

Stager was a talented and creative coach who liked to pull the strings on his ball-playing marionettes. But he had been sick the previous summer with a spinal infection, called vertebral osteomyelitis, and was still rehabilitating from surgery when the season began. He lacked most of his usual energy, and was unable to design new plays for his squad to effectively incorporate his new stars. It wasn't that he didn't know how good Matty G and Duncan were; he was just alternately in immense pain or doped up on painkillers that made him nod in and out and caused him distressing itchiness. Coaching didn't meet his top-priority list when the activities of wincing and whining in pain, or relentlessly scratching himself, had to be attended to.

Consequently, old plays were used from when Duncan and Matty G's positions (shooting guard and power forward, respectively) were occupied by the previous year's seniors. Neither starter at that time had been a particularly strong player and Coach Stager had designed plays based more around the team's 6'9", 310 pound center, Ike Eze, who was now a senior himself. But Easy, as his friends and teammates called him, had injured his knee, jumping off the dock at his friends' lake house before anyone informed him that the murky water below was only six inches deep. He twisted his right knee pretty badly and the cumbersome knee brace that he had to wear contributed to the slowness that the pain itself was causing. His defense was horrible. His offense was lackadaisical. He pretty much sucked and had become a liability.

Usually, because this was high school ball, Easy was taller than most of the centers that he played against, so his jump hook was relatively effective, and his muscular and husky frame allowed him to overpower much of his significantly lighter opposition. But he was no superstar, and Eastfield played in the state 1A league, the highest level for public high schools. The competition was no joke, and Easy's slow pace was hurting the team, particularly on defense where the other teams' centers dunked repeatedly, once they realized how easily they could exploit the injured big man's lack of speed. Consequently, they started out 0 and 2, and an uneasiness gripped the locker room.

And then came the third game of the season. Eastfield played Mountain Top High, the second ranked team in the 30-team 1A league at the beginning of the season. Easy was visibly suffering. Because Matty G was needed at power forward to defend against Louis Patterson, Mountain Top's best player, he couldn't, with the current system, get the ball down low on offense. At halftime, Eastfield was down by 12, and the team cheerlessly settled into the locker room to take their 15-minute rest period and listen to Coach Stager's standard halftime pump-up speech. Stager, however, was nowhere to be seen.

With about five minutes left in the intermission, Duncan got up to take a piss. He went straight to a stall, bypassing the urinals. Duncan always had a thing about urinals. He just didn't like them. He liked being able to stand over the toilet with his dick out in the air, without worrying about standing too far away and attracting unwanted attention, or standing too close and getting rebound-spray all over himself. He regularly made a point of averting the awkwardness inherent in pissing with too much distance between himself and the urinal, coupled with the presence of another individual, by utilizing a stall whenever possible. In a word, he valued his privacy.

Duncan opened up the door of the first stall. There he found Coach Donny Stager passed out cold on the toilet with his pants at his ankles and the Business section of the New York Times in his lap. "Coach? Hey. Coach," Duncan whispered. No reply. He tried louder. No reply. "Coach!" he shouted.

All doped up on Percocets and thinking that he was still at the hospital being woken up by his enormous, bald, black nurse, Paul, Coach Stager shouted, "Leave me the fuck alone, Paul! I'm trying to sleep, man!"

Wow, thought Duncan. *That's a new one.*

Duncan went back to the locker room, giggling like an idiot, and found the team's assistant coach, Lawrence Curran, a chill guy in his mid-30's who had once been the star of Eastfield's varsity basketball squad and now worked as a social worker for the state's Division of Youth and Family Services (DYFS). "Yo, Coach," Duncan said. "You gotta come see this, man."

"What's up, Lipton?"

"You just gotta come, Coach."

"Oooookay," Curran sighed, as he rose from his seat. He and Duncan walked to the bathroom and Duncan opened the stall door. Curran immediately burst out laughing hysterically. Duncan hadn't seen *that* coming and started laughing his ass off right along with his assistant coach. "OK, buddy," Coach Curran said, regaining his composure. "You go get Nurse Jesse. Do it with the quickness. She's sitting in the third row of the home-side bleachers. Hustle up."

Duncan ran out and got Nurse Jesse while Curran kept an eye on the assed-out Stager. Once she arrived, Duncan and Curran returned to the locker room so the temporary head coach could address his team.

As they left the bathroom, Duncan noticed Curran and Nurse Jesse exchange a furtive glance which hinted to him that his assistant coach had his own personal reasons for knowing where the pretty young woman had been sitting. Those reasons, he guessed, probably had little to do with the team's medical necessities. Duncan smiled knowingly at Curran who shot him a wink and gave him a playfully light punch on the arm before they reentered the locker room.

"Boys, listen. Coach Stager got sick. He's with the nurse. I'm taking over for the rest of this game. Now, frankly, what's been going on so far this season has been a bunch of straight-up bullshit. Easy, you're a fucking mess, kid. Stay down low on D and try to stand your ground the best you can with your good leg. You're a big motherfucker. Just stay down low and the intimidation factor alone should significantly reduce their ability to get these *easy motherfucking dunks*.

"Now…" Curran paused for effect, "I've been waiting to see something since I first happened upon *these* two gentlemen, right here." He pointed to Duncan and Matty G, who were sitting together in the far corner of the locker room. "I saw these two little fuckers play in seventh grade and I've never seen anything like it. You two still do that *craaazy* shit? That Woops and Oops, or whatever?"

Curran was referring to the unofficial name for the two-man show of Matty G and Duncan Lipton making the game of basketball look easy. Duncan had made up the nicknames Woops and Oops for himself and Matty G, respectively, after a game in seventh grade during which he had thrown the first of what would, over the next few years, amount to countless ally-oop passes that he would toss to his best friend, like a quarterback to his favorite receiver. He had executed an ankle-breaking crossover on his defender to the left, stopped on a dime, then crossed him up to the right. The kid had actually *fallen down*. Duncan had then tossed up a perfect lob that Matty G threw down, seemingly without effort, a true rarity for *any* thirteen-year-old, as the boys were at the time. After that, every time Duncan crossed someone up, his trademark saying as he blew by the defender was, "*Woops*". And because of Matty G's grace in flight and uncanny ability to turn Duncan's ally-oop lobs into five or more vicious dunks every game, he became Oops.

When they heard their coach's question, Matty G and Duncan looked each other in the eye and shared smiles not all that dissimilar from the guilty ones that they would wear a few years later as they counted Benjies on Duncan's bedroom floor. The looks implied unapologetic guilt. They were about to get a lot of touches, and some of their teammates would probably be pissed because Woops and Oops were about to hog the shit out of the ball. *Oh well*.

Duncan looked over at Curran and said, casually, "Yeah, Coach.

We still do that shit." The whole locker room laughed nervously, the collective consciousness wondering, *What the hell is going on?*

Coach Curran was big on cursing. He felt that a few dirty words helped to open up the lines of communication between the youth and the aged, as he had begun to only half-jokingly consider himself, with his consistently sore knees and back and his persistently receding hairline. A little mutual swearing between young men and an adult was often a surprisingly powerful way to bridge the generation gap, and, to illustrate the point, the positive energy in the locker room became palpable.

"Alright, gentlemen," Coach Curran said. We have about three minutes until we go back out there, so let me tell you about the new game plan. It's called "Woops and Oops." As you've seen in practice, Lipton and G are obviously very good players. But they're freshmen, so you obviously, at least most of you, haven't really seen them play before."

"I have," said Scotty Hershorin, the team's faithful towel boy.

"Good. So, you know the deal, Scotty?"

"They're fuckin amazing!" the diminutive sophomore shouted.

"Scotty, watch your fuckin mouth!" hollered back Coach Curran, sharply. Scotty, a small, bookish, nerdy type with a touch of ADHD was taken aback, his pulse immediately spiking. But the raucous laughter from the team and the broad smile that broke out on the coach's dimpled, friendly face made him realize that the snap had been a joke, and he nervously giggled along with the others.

"Basically, boys," Coach Curran continued, "the rest of this game is going to be the Lipton and G show. We clearly don't have enough time to draw up any new plays and, frankly, we're down by too much for me to find a way to get you guys cohesive enough to pull this off. So, this is how it's gonna go: Duncan, you break some fuckin ankles out there. Then, G, you catch the oops. I don't want any shots from anyone else. We can't afford to be missing opportunities right now, so all I want for the rest of the game, pretty much, is G dunking. Unless you have a *very* easy lay-up, I don't wanna see any of you fuckers shooting. Absolutely no jumpers. Understood, gentlemen?"

They understood. Some of them may not have particularly liked the idea of having nothing to do with the offense, but none of them had ever heard any kind of hype like that before and they couldn't help but be curious. "Alright, fellas, bring it in," Curran shouted with enthusiasm. The team grouped around their coach and they did the whole psych-up, go-team thing and ran back out to the court.

The game was a success, to say the least. The play-by-play is unnecessary. Duncan embarrassed the defense over and over with crossovers, spins, and drives, most of which led to Matty G slamming it home *twenty-two* times. Eastfield won by twenty-six points and began an era of complete domination over its division. They lost only two games in the three years that the Woops and Oops combo had played thus far, not including the losses in the first two games of their freshman season. The other two games that ended in defeat were, not coincidentally, lost while both Duncan and Matty G were unable to play.

The first game that they missed, during their sophomore year, was because of Thanksgiving. Matty G had eaten over the Lipton house and Mrs. Lipton had made a chocolate mousse that used raw eggs. Because she was on a diet at the time, Mrs. Lipton's avoidance of her own dessert creation meant that she was the only one at the table who, the next day, found herself without salmonella poisoning. So, Matty G and Duncan were forced to spend a day simultaneously shitting liquid and vomiting instead of playing ball.

The second game that they missed, during their junior year, was because they had both gotten whiplash when Duncan, buzzed on Jack and smoking a blunt with Matty G in the passenger seat, crashed into a telephone pole. The injuries weren't severe and Duncan had made up some reasonably believable excuse for the accident so as not to get caught for driving under the influence. But, consequently, they had to miss their next game while being checked out in the hospital, and Eastfield lost out on a perfect season two years in a row.

And that's how it was with Duncan Lipton and Matty G. Always doing everything together, taking turns as angel and devil, pushing one another to the limit, laughing 'til it hurt, playing basketball, smoking blunts, talking, listening. Best friends. And that's what broke Tessa Moya's heart, as she spoke these words to the 911 operator, as clearly and precisely as she could, so as not to waste any time: "Ma'am, please listen to me. There isn't much time, if there's any at all. I'm at 16 Candace Place in Eastfield," she said, saying the address extra slow and clear. "My friend, Matty, is bleeding badly. I think he was just shot in the head."

Chapter 5

Duncan told the police this: Two black guys had walked in through the open back door of the Lipton house. He had no idea who they were. They wore masks. They demanded money. Neither he nor Matty G had any. The first one who walked in the door raised a silver handgun at Matty G's face and said, "Money now, nigga. Now, motherfucker!" Though they had begged and told the assailants that they had no money, the angry robber pulled the trigger and shot Matty G in the head. Duncan had then wailed at the seemingly guaranteed loss of his best friend's life and fell to the floor in tears. Through his sobs, he heard the slam of the closing back door and the firing-up of a powerful engine in his driveway. After that, nothing but gushing tears and the feeling that his chest was caving in. He had lain on the floor, sobbing, until his girlfriend showed up and called 911.

Considering Duncan's legitimate grief, he surprised even himself that he could come up with such a believable story to tell the cops. Here's what really happened: Duncan and Matty G were having a swig of some of Duncan's parents' top-shelf rum to toast their sudden increase in cash flow. Prior to the pile of Benjies appearing on his floor, Duncan had been broke, catching the occasional twenty from his mom for various sundries and his activities of choice (other than basketball, of course), going to movies, smoking weed, and doing things with Tessa.

Startled by a knock at the back door, Duncan reflexively threw the liquor bottle in the garbage bin; he *was* only seventeen, and always did his best to avoid getting caught drinking by any persons of authority. His parents were already at work. He knew it couldn't be them. Maybe it was his next door neighbor, Mrs. Pearlmutter. Mrs. Pealmutter and the Liptons shared a fence with a gate that she frequently marched through to show up at their backdoor and complain about something to Mrs. Lipton. This was, on average, at least a daily occurrence. Probably something along the lines of a visitation rate of 1.2 visits/day. The woman was out of her mind, always angry about something or other, and Duncan's mother was just too nice and too good a listener to tell her to leave. Luckily, Mrs. Pearlmutter was not a lingerer. She just needed to spit some vitriol, blow off some steam, and then she'd politely thank Mrs. Lipton for listening. She'd then walk slowly back through the gate, always closing it gently, and go back home to be alone with her beef with the universe.

When Duncan turned to the backdoor window, he had not seen Mrs. Pearlmutter or any other "adults" per se. He had seen Keary and Judney. *Shit*, Duncan thought. Keary held what Duncan knew to be Keary's favorite "piece". It was a Desert Eagle .50. It was a big, silver handgun. Shiny. Mean.

Judney had no weapon in his hands. His very dark face was smushed up against the glass, distorting his features and exposing his wet, very pink gums. Both of his hands were pressed against the glass too. This boded well, Duncan had thought. Judney was the funniest person that he and Matty G had ever known; he was pretty much the funniest person that anyone who'd ever met him had ever known, and it was comforting that he was goofing around at a time such as this, when five hundred thousand dollars was resting in the closet upstairs, and a lighter-skinned, not-so-happy-looking Keary was glaring through the window, holding a Desert Eagle... *point* five O. (Keary's favorite movie was the English Guy Ritchie-directed *Snatch*. His favorite character was Bullet-Tooth Tony. Hard as hell. Tony carried a Desert Eagle... *point* five O. "*Point* five O" was to be said in an English accent.)

In Hightown, you stayed strapped. Duncan had seen Keary's full collection of artillery before; it was impressive, and, in that neighborhood, the guns were not just for show. The surprise had long since worn off, but Duncan never failed to be amazed that a community such as Hightown could exist within the confines of Eastfield. The threat of gang violence hung in the air like smog in LA, and was just as constantly present. Regular robberies. Regular Rapes. Regular day.

Matty G had never gotten caught up in any of the gangs that had been a Hightown staple since the early seventies. Ever since he was a little kid, he had always been too busy playing ball and hanging out with Duncan, either spending time in Duncan's upper middle-class neighborhood or hanging out at the Hightown basketball courts.

Because Matty G was so nasty at basketball, he was considered by many to be *the man* in Hightown. And because Duncan was nasty at basketball and a seemingly color-blind, cool *white boy*, and because he was the best friend of the king of the Hightown courts, he was *the man* too in his own right.

The prevalence of gang involvement among the youth of Hightown was outrageous, with more than half of the high school age kids living there affiliated with one gang or another. Hearing thunderous gunshots was to be expected, at least, weekly, around the projects. Though gang members fought constantly, carried Tec 9's, Mac 10's and sold crack outside the 7-11, they never messed with Matty G and Duncan.

Although Duncan and Matty G knew what their neighbors and peers were getting into, they weren't ones to judge. They were friends with the whole neighborhood. So, it wasn't the scariest thing that Duncan had ever seen when Keary displayed his Desert Eagle *point five-O* at his backdoor. He had been, upon first seeing Keary and Judney at the door, relieved that an adult hadn't shown up to catch him drinking.

"Keary, why the fuck are you carrying an unregistered firearm out in the open at my fucking house?" Duncan inquired. Judney laughed. Hard. He always laughed really hard. That was one of the things that made him the funniest person that any of them had ever known. He'd start laughing at something and then you'd start laughing because he was laughing and then in a little while your sides were split and you wouldn't have a clue what had been so funny to begin with.

Judney was laughing then because he loved the way Duncan spoke, splicing his many different linguistic influences to form his own unique hybrid of different versions of the English language. There was something about using the word *firearm*, instead of gun, piece or Desert Eagle… *point* five-O that just killed Judney and made him keel over in laughter.

"Nigga, shut the fuck up!" Keary was livid. The shout was directed at both Judney and Duncan. Judney stopped laughing. Duncan, caught off guard by Keary's sudden aggression, was also silenced.

"What's the deal, ma nigga?" said Matty G, trying to be calm as Keary pointed the weapon at his best friend. "What's the beef?"

"You know what the beef is, nigga. Where's the fuckin money?" *Shit*, thought Duncan. *Shit*, thought Matty G. The jig was up. Blown-to-shit road-hazard of a bridge: uncrossable.

"Relax, dude. It's upstairs. I'll go get it. Just chill and let us explain," Duncan said. This calmed Keary down considerably, knowing that the large sum was soon to be back in his possession. Duncan ran up the stairs and got the shoebox that he was stashing the money in. When he got back downstairs he said, "Bro, we took maaad zannies yesterday afternoon. Neither one of us remembers a fuckin thing from yesterday. I don't know how the fuck all this money ended up on my bedroom floor, but, on behalf of my associate and myself, I'd like to extend my most heartfelt apologies for inconveniencing your black ass."

Judney couldn't take it. He started laughing so hard that all four of them ended up in tears. It had seemed that the situation was cleared up. No free money. Oh well.

Unfortunately for all parties concerned, Keary was still holding his gun while he was laughing his ass off. Accidentally, while doubled over, ribs on fire from laughing so hard, Keary had squeezed the Desert

Eagle's trigger. The gun was pointing in Matty G's direction, and the bullet hit him in the head. A copious amount of blood splattered all over the kitchen.

Keary screamed. Judney cried. They were momentarily frozen, but within a couple seconds they both bolted simultaneously through the backdoor, leaving behind Duncan, a dying (possibly already dead) Matty G, and their shoebox full of money on the Liptons' kitchen counter. They jumped into the used black Corvette that Judney had recently purchased. Judney's foot was lead.

Out of the corner of his left eye, Judney thought he saw Tessa Moya driving by. Momentarily distracted from the road by his brief recognition of Duncan's girlfriend, Judney ran the stop sign at the corner of Candance Place and Harley St. That was when the black Corvette was broadsided by a Ford Explorer.

By the time the police and medics arrived, Tessa had already made her second 911 call of the day. In that time, Keary and Judney died, if not from injuries sustained during impact, then from the fire. Their bodies had both been incinerated in the inferno that had moments earlier been a sexy black Corvette.

By the time Tessa arrived in the Lipton kitchen, Duncan was sobbing in the corner. But before she arrived, he had sprinted up the stairs to throw the shoebox back in the closet. He had a feeling that Matty G, if he didn't *die*, would be kind of pissed if he got shot in his dome and had nothing to show for it.

When he got back down to the kitchen and saw his best friend lying in a pool of his own blood, Duncan had collapsed onto the kitchen floor in pure horror and grief. He was positive that someone who looked that terrible had to be dead, positive that his best friend was gone forever. But luckily, Tessa arrived with the presence of mind to call 911 and find towels with which to apply pressure to the gunshot wound until the medics arrived. Despite what Duncan thought, there was still time.

Chapter 6

When Coach Stager first got out of surgery, he had been awoken by Paul, his huge, black nurse, and had promptly puked on Paul's scrubs. Matty G gave Paul the same pleasure when *he* woke up, coincidentally, in the same room that his coach had been taken to post-op, in the Intensive Care Unit. "All the fuckin time," Paul breathed, bowing his head and shaking it side to side. "All the motherfuckin time."

"Gross. Go throw those out, man," said Dr. Thomas Bonham, a fifty-something white man with a full gray beard and a receding hairline that led into a gray ponytail.

"Yeah. Be right back, Doc," said Paul.

Dr. Bonham lightly slapped Matty G's face a few times. "How you doin, kid?"

"What the fuck?" said Matty G. "Where the fuck am I?"

"Hospital, kid," said Dr. Bonham. "You got shot in the head."

"Holy shit. Where's Duncan?"

"Who's Duncan?" asked the doctor.

"My best friend. Is he okay?"

"I don't know, kid. But your mom is outside, in the waiting room. I'm going to go speak with her for a moment and let her know that you're awake. I'll tell her you were asking about your friend. She'll be in here in a minute."

"Thanks, Doc," said Matty G. Dr. Bonham walked out of the room.

Confused, alone, and waiting, Matty G studied the wall. A big purple dinosaur was painted on it, with a little yellow bird on its shoulder. The dinosaur was not Barney and the bird was not Woodstock, more like a five-year-old's approximation of them. But they conveyed the message that this was supposed to be a room for children. In fact, as he would later find out, the ICU had recently moved to what was formerly the children's wing when the children's wing became the new children's hospital, next door. And when Mrs. G bounded through the door and smothered her son's face and upper body into her huge breasts, Matty G felt like he was a little kid again.

"Oh ma baby! Ma *baby!*" Mrs. G cried out, in her strong, distinctly southern accent. She sobbed over his head, as he slowly suffocated in his mother's massive bosom.

"Mom!" he shouted. "Lemme go."

Mrs. G, hearing the muffled shouts, eased off of her son and blew her nose. As she wiped her eyes, she said, "You been out for thirteen hours, baby. Some crazy nigga shot you in the head. Doctors didn't know if you was gonna make it." She began to tear up again.

Wow, thought Matty G. *That's a new one.* "Where's Duncan, Mom? Duncan okay?"

"Duncan's real shook up, baby. He been cryin his pretty little white head off out in the waiting room, ever since the police finish they questions." At that moment, a knock came at the door and Duncan's eyes, puffy and red from hours of sobbing, stared through the skinny window. When he saw his best friend look over at him, he burst through the door, ran to Matty G's bed, hugged him, and cried on his shoulder.

Wow, thought Matty G. *That's a new one.* G couldn't remember having heard Duncan cry since they were little boys, so he attempted to lighten the mood. Imitating Duncan's style of speaking, what Matty G perceived to be akin to a California surfer-stoner-dude's speech, he joked, "Duuuuude. I'm cool, bro. No worries, dude-man-bro."

Duncan looked up from Matty G's shoulder. Imitating Matty G: "Ma nigga. Ma mothafuckin nigga." They both burst out laughing, though it gave Matty G a headache.

Mrs. G, eyes still puffy, but with a contented smile on her lips, said, "I'll leave you boys alone for a minute."

"Thanks, Ma," said Matty G. "I love you."

Mrs. G paused by the door and looked at her son. "I love you too, baby. I love you so much." She blew him a kiss, walked out of the room, and gently closed the door behind herself.

"Jesus, dude," Duncan said. "I thought you were dead. Cooked goose, baby boy!"

"Not yet, son. Not *me*, not *now*!" They laughed, though it again caused Matty G to wince from the pain on the side of his head. *Not me, not now* was an old joke between the two of them. There used to be commercials on TV, telling young girls not to cave in to the pressure that boys might put them under to have sex. It was *supposed* to be the hormone-suppressing teenage girls' mantra; it was now, however, a declaration of Matty G's continued mortal existence.

"So, uh, what the fuck just happened?" Matty G asked Duncan, who was still slightly bent over, recovering from their inside joke. "Well, let's *see*," mused Duncan. "In a nutshell: I woke up a little before seven; I went to take a piss; I saw a fuckin huge, messy pile of Benjies lying on the floor of my bedroom, which you, my friend, were asleep on the other side of, drooling all over my fucking carpet." They laughed. Duncan continued, "I noticed that you were still wearing the same clothes you were wearing the day before, when you left to go home and get some of your mom's fish, cause she was doin salmon, and you said you had to get in on that before you got too fucked up, 'cause we just took those zannies and drank the rest of that Jack."

Matty G remembered that. But did he have salmon with his mom? He couldn't recall. That's what Xanax, combined with alcohol, does to people. Complete memory eraser. Usually, people weren't too happy the next day when they found out what they had done, or how they had acted while on the liquor and pills. "Shit. Those fuckin things make you forget fuckin *everything*, Dunks," Matty G said, calling Duncan by his long-time nickname, which he had had since picking up his first pair of Nike Dunks, a popular model of basketball shoes, eight years earlier.

"Word," said Duncan.

"*Word*," said Matty G, emphatically.

"Anyway," Duncan continued, I woke your ass up; we counted and stacked the money, which was five hundred G's; we danced around like wild Indians for a minute or so, if I remember correctly, before we decided to have a civilized alcoholic celebration in the kitchen. Then..."

"Yeah, yeah, I remember all that shit, ma nigga. Who the fuck shot me though? I don't even remember getting in a fight with anybody. Weren't we laughing and shit?"

"Yeah, dude. Keary was laughing so fucking hard at *Judney* laughing so fucking hard, he accidentally pulled the trigger of his Desert Eagle... *point* five-O." Duncan hammed up the English accent.

"There was fuckin blood all over my kitchen, dude. It was disgusting."

"Oh, shit."

"No shit," said Duncan, who had much more tale to tell. "Alright, dude. Get ready for a ridiculous chain of events that was set into motion when Keary pulled that trigger. Check it. You got shot in the head. I couldn't say a fuckin thing. Judney started crying. Keary fuckin *wailed*, dude. He was screaming bloody fucking murder. Like a dying whale or some shit. He, like, couldn't believe it, ya know? He obviously didn't mean to shoot you. This was probably more Judney's fault than anyone else's." Matty G and Duncan both chuckled. They had played basketball and smoked blunts around Hightown for years with Keary and Judney. This was clearly an accident. "So," continued Duncan, "the three of us are just like, holy shit, no clue what the fuck to do, deer-in-headlights stunned out of our minds. Like two seconds later, nobody says shit and the two of them turn around and run out the door. They get into Judney's new Corvette. You saw his new whip, right?"

"Yeah. Black Corvette. Stylin'," Matty G said.

"It *was* stylin'. Not anymore, dude. Listen to this shit. Keary and Judney jumped into the whip and took off down my driveway. Unbelievably, who should be pulling up the street to come to my house, right at that moment? Why my faithful and beautiful baby girl, T, of course. She saw the whole thing. Check this out, son. Judney slams the gas and hauls ass down our driveway. He's *flying* by the time he gets to the corner. He, like, forgets that there's a stop sign and runs into Harley Street. A fucking Explorer was doin like fifty and completely T-Boned this motherfucker. His car was annihilated, bro. Shit flipped and flew four fucking houses from the corner and blew the fuck up, man. Keary and Judney were probably already dead by then, but if the crash didn't kill them, the crazy fire got 'em. They were, like, incinerated, dude. It took mad long for the firemen to get there, so it was a lost cause, ya know. Fuckin sucks, man.

"So, Tessa stops when she passes Keary hauling ass down the street and watches this outlandish spectacle unfold through her rearview mirror. She calls 911 then gets over to my house. She runs in the kitchen, freaked as fuck, to find you in a puddle of blood on the floor, and me, crying like a bitch in the kitchen corner, curled up fetus style. But, dude… they forgot the shoebox." Duncan stopped.

"What fuckin shoebox?

"*The* shoebox," Duncan half-whispered. A huge grin, typically guilty, showed on his face. Dealing with more pressing issues, such as the fact that he had gotten shot in the head, had made Matty G forget to think about what had happened to the money in all of this.

"Oh. My. God." He couldn't believe what he was hearing.

Duncan said nothing.

"Holy shit," said Matty G. "Keary and Judney are dead? What the fuck." They were good, old friends. Money couldn't change that. There was nothing that could be done. *It is what it is though*, thought Matty G. And it was.

"Yeah, man. Sucks, right? I'm full of absurdly conflicting emotions right now that I, frankly, cannot and will not begin getting into right now. So, anyway, right when they took off, I grabbed the shoebox, ran to my room, and threw the shoebox in my closet. I ran back downstairs, and I saw you, lying in a pool of your own blood, and I completely fuckin freaked, dude. We're so lucky that Tessa is the most clutch chick of all time. I just started bawling and curled up and cried in the corner of the kitchen. You looked completely dead. I forgot about 911 and all commonsense shit and just went crazy. Amazingly, Tessa gets into the kitchen, and, instead of freaking out, she runs to the bathroom, grabs towels, picks your head up and applies pressure to the wound, using both hands, while talking to 911 operators on her celly, tilting her head and resting it on her shoulder. Like fucking Super Woman. While I'm in the corner, crying like a fucking bitch. Sorry, bro. I couldn't do *shit*."

"Don't worry about it, baby boy," Matty G said, placing his hand on Duncan's shoulder. I would have done the same shit probably." Duncan felt relieved. His inaction had been bothering him. But Matty G understood that the sight of one of the people who matters most to you in the world, dying, maybe dead, right in front of your eyes, is crippling. He didn't know what he'd do if he saw Duncan like that. Life wouldn't make a drop of sense without Duncan Lipton in it. Not a drop.

"Tessa was *there* though, son. No harm, no foul, ma nigga. That girl is wife status, breh. Fuckin hold onto her. Who knows when I might need her clutch moves again when the shot clock's winding down, right?"

"True, true," agreed Duncan. "So, check it out, man. Basically, we've got five hundred thousand dollars in crisp, green United States currency. We've got ourselves five thousand Benjies. Five thousand Mr. Franklins, as you so eloquently referred to them the other day, my good sir. Yes, my good man, we have ourselves the equivalent of fifty million pennies. As my great grandmother used to say, "It's all currency of the realm", so we must pay homage to that fact and to her memory. We have one half of (imitatiting Dr. Evil of *Austin Powers*, with his pinky to the lower right corner of his lips) *One million dollars*! (Imitating Matty G.) We're dealin with ballin sums, ma brotha. Muhfuckin *ballin ass muhfuckin sums*. Word is bond, ma nigga. Word is bond."

Matty G, imitating Duncan, said, "Right on, bro. Righteous, dude. *Gnarly* dollars, brosef. Totally fuckin gnarly. Shred the *gnar*, bro! (Duncan never really knew how Matty G managed to clump his slow, stoneresque speech with that far-out, Cali wave-head lingo, but it was always funny anyway.)

"But in all honesty, Matthew G, you and I have become fairly wealthy members of society. This presents numerous options for us to achieve great successes in many areas of our lives. It's time to go fuckin ape and live it *up*, motherfucker! After you get your pussy ass out of this hospital bed, I do believe we need to go get ourselves a couple bottles of Popov."

"Nigga, we need to be hittin up that Grey Goose. We got *bills*, son." Popov was cheap, shitty vodka that came in a plastic jug. No baller would ball outrageous with such swill.

"But Popov makes the party *pop off*… and you know this… maaaaan," Duncan said in a high-pitched, Chris Tucker imitation. Judney would've laughed.

Chapter 7

It was the first day of senior year, 2008. Fully recovered, Matty G was excited to start school. He loved school. Despite his constant use of slang, he could easily turn on what he called his "white folks talk", speaking clearly and using "proper" grammar. Going into his senior year, he had a 4.0 GPA. His mom always made sure that he did his homework on time, usually making sure that he finished it early. But it wasn't a chore to him. He was something of a knowledge sponge, voraciously reading and rarely missing Jeopardy at 7pm. Watching Jeopardy after dinner was a ritual that he and his mom took very seriously. She was always doing her best to fill his head with knowledge, so even though she placed strict limits on TV watching, Jeopardy served the three-fold purpose of providing knowledge, a little bit of relaxation in front of the TV, and time for the two of them to bond as they enthusiastically competed to see who could get the most questions right each episode.

Matty G's dad, Ernest G, died in a car accident when he was only thirty-five. Matty G had been ten years old, certainly old enough for his heart to be broken by the death of his beloved father. Ernest G had been a good man, always faithful to Mrs. G, always doting and affectionate to both her and their two sons. They had lived in the neighborhood next to the Hightown projects, in a nicely furnished, always clean house where Matty G and Duncan would spend at least every other weekend sleeping in the basement, watching movies and eating popcorn. Whenever Ernest G didn't have to work, he would play against the boys, 2-on-1 in basketball, in the family's driveway. Matty G loved his dad to death and so did Duncan, who called him Uncle Ernie. At the funeral, Duncan sat next to his best friend, with his arm around his shoulder the whole time, trying his best to be strong for him. But the ten-year-olds cried their eyes out the whole time. Both of them would forever regret viewing Ernest's lifelessly bloated, embalmed body in the casket. That memory stuck in both their minds, and, particularly for Matty G, would sometimes pop up out of nowhere to haunt his thoughts. Duncan never understood why a viewing had to be a part of a Christian funeral. Jews didn't have viewings. He had gone to the funeral of his teammate Ben Rosen's mom when she passed away from cancer. There was no viewing. Duncan liked it that way. You could remember the life of the person, the way they looked when they had had a personality, a soul maybe, if such things existed. But the dead body did not represent the person. It didn't even really look like them.

When Ernest G passed away, the income that he'd brought in from his job as an electrician was lost, and Matty G, Mrs. G, and Matty G's little brother, Stevie G, had to move into one of the nearby apartments of Hightown.

Stevie G was a little less than three years younger than Matty G. Though he remembered his father, Stevie G didn't absorb the same kind of positive influence from him that his older brother did because he was only seven years old when Ernest G passed away. Maybe, with a positive father figure in his life, Stevie G would have been more like his brother, but instead he developed an incredible proclivity for getting himself into the kind of trouble that Matty G chose never to partake in.

As the new school year began, Stevie G was presently doing a nine-month stint in juvenile hall for selling coke to an undercover cop. It hurt Matty G, who loved his little brother too much to take his being sent to jail lightly, but he knew that "Kid Geezy" (as Stevie G was known to many around Hightown) could handle it. Matty G figured that his little brother was a streetwise and funny kid who could conduct himself appropriately in jail, avoiding fights by easily making friends with his jokes, affability and easy-going personality.

Mrs. G, on the other hand, was completely overwhelmed with sadness and disappointment with her younger son. She refused to visit him while he was locked up. Being that only legal guardians were allowed to visit their children at the facility where he was detained, Stevie G got no visitors during his incarceration. She told him that he needed to be alone while doing his time to learn his lesson, that he needed to spend his time thinking about what he was going to do to turn his life around; the truth was she really just couldn't handle seeing her baby boy in jail. She didn't want to have any image of him in his prison clothes because she knew it would never leave her head.

Although she wouldn't visit, she did write him letters regularly, as did Matty G. Twice a week, during the six hours that he was allowed out of his cell each day, Stevie G would respond to the letters and send others to friends whose addresses he had obtained during the ten-minute calls that he was allowed, weekly, from the social worker's office on his "pod" (one of the bullet-proof-glass encased sections of juvenile hall, of which there were six).

While in his cell, he spent most of his time drawing because, even though "residents" (not to be confused with one of the "prisoners" that a resident would become if he were to commit another crime after turning eighteen and landing his ass in D.O.C., the adult prison) weren't allowed pens or pencils in their rooms, they had a lenient officer, Sgt. McDougal, who would allow certain, particularly well-behaved or particularly entertaining kids to have the privilege of being able to write or draw in their "rooms" (not to be confused with the "cells" that one would find in D.O.C. It was important to the state that these distinctions were made, that juveniles should be treated in a humane fashion, so as to facilitate their rehabilitation and reentry into society.).

Stevie G had always had, since he was very young, an incredible ability to draw. If he drew a portrait of someone, even in pencil on notebook paper, it was practically the spitting image of his subject. It was effortless for him. He had gone through periods in his life when he had lost interest in drawing, basically because it was so easy for him. He felt at times that he was just going through the motions any time he drew, not really enjoying what came so naturally to him. While his skill was a novelty and mystery to most, to him it was just something that he was inexplicably able to do. He didn't really understand or appreciate the amazement that others displayed upon seeing his art. But while he was locked up, he got a new appreciation for drawing.

Because he was well behaved during his first week there, and because he had displayed his incredible talent during some time out of his room, Sgt. McDougal decided to let Stevie G hold onto a pencil. Sgt. McDougal was a wise officer; he knew that some kids were easily driven stir-crazy by so much time locked in a tiny room. It was his duty to keep his pod safe and one of his strategies to do so was rewarding good behavior. Considering the suffocating confines of the residents' rooms and the three quarters of the day that they spent locked in them, having the opportunity to draw or write was a privilege and pleasure to most residents.

Not that the residents thought in those terms exactly. Most of them hated McDougal. He was certainly gruff, to say the least, but the man was fair. His policy was simple: You break the rules, you pay the price. His game was that good behavior warranted such luxuries as pencils and books and, being that the rules in juvie were not, in his eyes, at all hard to follow, he had little sympathy for rule breakers. Although juvie's policy was not to allow residents to have these items in their rooms, McDougal's experience taught him that having something to do prevented a lot of kids from going nuts in confinement. But they had to earn their privileges. If they acted up, they got locked up, activity-free, with all the time in the world to just sit and think. And for lots of the kids at juvie, boredom relentlessly gnawed away at the psyche.

For that first week there, Stevie G had to sit in his room for eighteen hours a day and just think. He couldn't believe he'd been so stupid. So money-hungry. So trusting of the seemingly cool Dominican undercover cop in the Rocawear jacket and classic beige, high-top Timberlands. But after the first week, in which he attended all the mandatory classes, was quiet and respectful, all "yes, sir" and "yes ma'am", and managed to befriend some fellow residents, Sgt. McDougal let him have a pencil and several pieces of paper to keep in his room. McDougal's willingness to let Stevie G have the pencil also had to do with the incredibly accurate caricature that Stevie G had done of the sergeant stepping on some of the more obnoxious residents on his pod and he wanted to see what the kid would come up with next. Talent such as that shouldn't go to waste, he thought.

The first night that he had the pencil was a revelation to Stevie G. Drawing removed the monotony, boredom, and guilty, self-hating thinking from his mind and replaced it with creativity and freedom. It was the freedom to do whatever he wanted even though he was so confined. Anything he wanted to create, his pencil produced. And for the first time in his life, he was able to think of himself in terms that did not involve drawing a negative comparison between he and his incredibly talented, trouble-free older brother. It was a night of self-discovery in which he realized that he was blessed with a great talent of his own, and even though Hightown, and seemingly the whole world, valued basketball more highly than an ability to draw well, it suddenly didn't matter. That night, he knew that everything would be fine, that life would be good.

With his newly positive life perspective, Stevie G decided to turn his life around. And what did selling matter anymore anyway? He had money waiting for him when he got out, money incurred from an incredibly large drug deal that was supposed to have ended his career as a hustler. Enough money to have a good time for a long time. Keary, one of his closest friends and his "business associate", was holding onto it. Half a mil. He looked forward to getting out of jail, pursuing his newfound love of art, and spending his money. *I'm gonna open a gallery*, he thought, amazed by his own ambition to live a straight life by employing his talent. But he had almost seven months to go in his sentence. That was a lot of time. It was a lot of time to work on some pencil drawings for his future gallery, but it was also a lot of time for the prison environment, full of its gang affiliations, sex offenders, mental illness, and all-around madness, to influence and affect him. And it was a lot of time for his older brother and his brother's best friend, Duncan, who *thought* they were in possession of the late *Keary*'s money, to spend it with indiscriminate haste. Unbeknownst to Stevie G, his half-mil was being drastically depleted.

But the money wasn't really all his. He had been fronted three pounds of methamphetamine by a strange, redheaded, freckle-faced kid he met through some customers of his, from a neighboring suburban town, that he sold weed to. The kid's name was Edward Slendger, and he was a "cook", a meth producer, who wanted nothing to do with the business aspect of selling. Stevie owed him a hundred grand, which Keary was supposed to have given him. After paying the kid back, and splitting the money with Keary, Stevie was expecting to have two hundred grand.

But as Stevie's time incarcerated slowly crept by, and he sat comfortably in the knowledge that he would be rich when he got out, Edward Slendger was finding himself unable to get ahold of his dealers. As the days went by, assuming that he had been ripped off, Edward grew more and more furious. He was already a highly unstable individual to begin with, and this situation was driving him over the edge. Had he ever seen a psychiatrist, he undoubtedly would have been diagnosed with an array of emotional and personality disorders. But he had not, and lacking any kind of therapy or medication, he became utterly preoccupied by an obsession with getting revenge. Meanwhile, however, he found other destructive outlets for his aggression.

Chapter 8

The black Corvette was eventually traced back to Keary. When he and Judney went missing, it was assumed that Judney was the passenger who had died in the car wreck. The police questioned Duncan and Matty G repeatedly about who it was who had come into the Lipton house the day that Matty G was shot and the crash had occurred. The friends continued to plead ignorance, saying that they had no idea who the two assailants were. The police knew that Duncan and Matty G had been friends with Keary and Judney; the cops wanted to get out of them that they knew who it was who had broken into the house, but they wouldn't change their story and the police couldn't prove that they were lying.

One of the several reasons Duncan and Matty G continued to lie was because they were afraid that if they admitted that they knew who had done it, there would be much speculation as to the motive of two kids who were supposed to be their friends, and a big investigation might ensue. That would suck, they thought. Secondarily, they would prefer that their friends not be remembered as the guys who had broken into the Lipton house and shot Matty G. Keary and Judney's mothers deserved better than that, they thought. They were nice ladies. Football boosters. Class Moms. Keary's mom always made the best sweet potato pie. They also wanted to keep the money. They figured that if they admitted that Keary and Judney had been the ones who broke into the house, someone else would come looking for the money. But no one was coming anytime soon.

Duncan pulled up to school, for the first day of senior year, in a new silver Lexus with his beautiful girlfriend, Tessa Moya, riding shotgun and wearing a bunch of new jewelry from Tiffany & Co. that he had bought for her with his newly acquired funds. Duncan pulled into a parking spot in the student lot, pulled up his parking brake and leaned over to kiss Tessa. She reciprocated, and they continued kissing for about five seconds before someone tapped the glass on Duncan's driver-side door. It was Matty G with a huge smile on his face. "Whatup, baby boy?" he said.

"Chillin, ma dude," Duncan replied, as he rolled down his window. "What's good with you?"

"*Everything*," he said slowly and happily. He pointed across the lot and said, "Check it out." Duncan and Tessa followed his finger to a brand new, cherry-red BMW. "Not bad, huh?"

"Not at all, my good man," said Duncan. "Not bad at all. How much?"

"A little more than fifty. Not so bad."

"Not at all, my good man. Not bad at all," Duncan jokingly repeated. More than a hundred thousand dollars had now gone down the drain on new cars, jewelry and lots of new Nike Dunks. But they didn't care. It was free money.

Duncan, Matty G and Tessa walked through the back door of Eastfield High, into their last year there. There was a long hallway that stretched ahead of them and another to their left. Down the hall, straight ahead, Matty G saw one of his many female "friends". "Yo, Dunks, T-baby, I'm about to go holla at a shorty."

"Which one?" Tessa inquired with a giggle.

"Mmmm, I see Kimmy down there. She's lookin *fine*," Matty G said, snapping his fingers and licking his lips.

"Word," said Duncan. "Get some."

"Oh, you know I will, baby boy. Why you think they made that upper level in the auditorium?" Matty G and Duncan laughed as Tessa rolled her eyes. She was all too familiar with the upper level of the auditorium. Junior year, Duncan had a required art class third period while Tessa had choir. They regularly spent half of their respective classes in "the bathroom", actually convening in the upper level of the auditorium to fool around. Duncan's art teacher, Ms. Jarvis, had been kind enough to give him a C despite his abysmal attendance record and frequent bathroom breaks, for which he would be forever grateful. Ms. Jarvis was Duncan's favorite teacher and he was pleased to see on his schedule that he would be having her for art again this year, this time for his first period class.

"Peace, dude," Duncan said, as Matty G walked off towards his girl, Kimmy.

"Peeeeace, duuuuude," Matty G teased Duncan, talking in his stoned surfer-dude accent. Duncan gave Matty G a raised right eyebrow and then a wink with his left eye. He couldn't do his impression of Matty G there. There were some black kids nearby in the hallway and they usually didn't take kindly to white-boys saying the N-word, even in jest. Duncan wasn't worried about what they'd do, but it was a respect thing. It was their word. They could have it.

Matty G gave Duncan and Tessa the backwards two-finger peace sign as a farewell symbol and shouted down the hall to Tessa, "Love ya, T-baby. Don't let my boy get himself into any trouble on his first day." Tessa smiled and nodded and put her arm around Duncan's waist. Duncan draped his arm over her shoulder. The couple walked down the hall to their left, towards Tessa's first period calc class, pressed against each other.

"How you doin, babe?" Duncan asked, looking Tessa in her big, beautiful, blue eyes, as they slowly trekked down the hall.

"I'm okay. I'm a little irked that school's starting though. Other than *the disaster*, this was a pretty great summer. I just didn't want it to ever end, ya know?"

"Yeah, I know. We did have a good time. But all good things must come to an end in order for new good things to happen." Duncan always had a way of contextualizing things that comforted Tessa when she felt like the world wasn't quite right. "This year's looking pretty promising from where I'm standing," he said. "Me and G are being scouted like crazy. We're both definitely gonna get scholarships. Definitely D-1. If a school wants me, you're part of the deal, baby."

Though Duncan insisted that he would never go to college without Tessa being right there with him or very nearby, she feared what might happen if Duncan got a scholarship to a school with a top basketball program. Though she had decent grades, they might not be enough to get her into wherever Duncan would be going. He was an excellent basketball player, but she didn't know if that meant that they'd let his girlfriend into the school of his choosing. She reassured herself though that everything would be fine. A whole school year awaited them, and where they would be headed next year was far from determined.

"Oh yeah?" Tessa said, responding to Duncan's certainty with a hint of testiness in her voice. "What makes you so sure a school would just let your girlfriend in, huh? I don't think that's how it works, Duncan."

"Baby. I'm *Woops*," Duncan said emphatically, but with a hint of self-deprecating humility. He and Matty G had grown famous throughout the state by this point. Woops and Oops. Everyone loved it. It was like seeing the Harlem Globetrotters or And-1 street ball. And they were winning every game (almost). Eastfield heroes.

"Oh, you and your big head, Sir Woopsy Dunks-a-lot," Tessa teased, half-heartedly trying to give Duncan something of a level head. But he ruled the school. Everyone knew it. And Tessa was the hottest girl there, further raising his already very high stock. Duncan gave her a mockingly incredulous look and then flashed a dimpled grin that made Tessa giggle.

"Well, Mr. Lipton," she said, opening her blue eyes wide to look at his, smiling and pulling his body into hers as they neared her classroom, "I will see you later."

"Later, baby. You know I love you." Duncan lightly kissed her forehead.

"I love you too." Tessa turned away from him and walked into her classroom as Duncan's eyes followed her in. She turned around and blew him a kiss through the door's window.

How did I get this girl? Duncan silently asked himself, as he stared at her perfect ass through the white, shin-length tights that she had worn to school that day. *I cannot fuckin believe I'm me.*

Turning around to head to Ms. Jarvis's art class, Duncan saw Casey Zanorick walking down the hall and looking at Duncan with a goofy grin on his face. "Whatup, Dunks?" Casey said, as he gave Duncan a greeting of a dap and a back slap.

"What's gooood, baby boy?" Duncan asked, raising the pitch of his voice and smiling widely at the sight of his junior year biology lab partner. Casey was dressed, from toe to head, in Birkenstock sandals, long corduroy shorts with colorful patches, a tie-dye t-shirt with a giant mushroom gracing its front, a necklace made of big white shore beads, and a backwards red Yankees hat with the 50/50 sticker still stuck to the brim.

"Chillin," said Casey. "Chillin, chillin."

"*Truuuue,*" Duncan said. "How was your summer, kid? You get dirty, you dirty bird? I know you did."

"You *know* I did, son. You fuckin know I did," Casey excitedly reported. "*Ridiculous*, dude. Best time I've ever had in my life. Forreal, forreal."

"Acid?" Duncan said. Casey burst out laughing.

"Am I *that* obvious, dude?"

"Naaaah," Duncan said. "I just *know* you, my brother."

"True. I guess after hearing my daydreams about using the bio beakers to make LSD for an entire year, you pretty much figured out my idea of a good time."

"That would be the case, my good man." They both laughed.

"Oh, but Dunks, check it. I got a girl, dude. Beautiful. We been hookin up since, like, the middle of July." As Duncan considered Casey to be somewhat of a protégée when it came to picking up girls, he was psyched to hear the news. During bio class, Casey would always ask him questions regarding anything to do with members of the opposite sex. Duncan would give him advice on how to "mack bitches", as Casey would so eloquently refer to the art of seducing girls, so it was nice to know that his influence had resulted in Casey getting laid.

"Oh word?" said Duncan. "You fuck her yet, playboy?"

"Yeah, dude," Casey replied. "Every fuckin day bro. The girl is an animal. A fuckin minx, bro. Yowza."

"Right on, man. Good shit." Duncan locked hands with his baby-faced friend and said, "You have done well, my young Padawan. You are becoming a Jedi."

"Yeeeeah, you know it dude. I'm so money, baby," Casey said, paying homage to his and Duncan's mutual love of the Vince Vaughan movie, *Swingers*.

Duncan laughed and asked, "So, who is this chica, papi?"

"You probably don't know her. She's a sophomore. Her name's Becky."

"What's her last name?"

"Sheldon."

Duncan shrugged and said, "I don't know her." He maintained a straight, unassuming face as he said this, but the truth was that he *definitely* knew Becky Sheldon. On Valentine's Day, the previous year, he and Tessa had gotten into a massive fight because Duncan had run out and bought a bag of weed right in front of the Moyas' house. Tessa was furious that Duncan had done something illegal like that right in front of her family's house. Duncan had repeatedly apologized, saying that he had a brain lapse and that it wouldn't happen again, but Tessa wouldn't drop it. After she had yelled at him for two minutes while he tried to apologize, he began to raise his voice. It turned into a nasty fight with hurtful things said that shouldn't have been, by both parties, and Duncan had stormed out of her house. He had stopped at 7-11 to buy a tin of mint Skoal because whenever he was pissed he liked to drive around with a lip packed, listening to music and thinking. When he pulled into the convenience store parking lot, he had seen Becky just getting into her car to leave. He thought she was cute, so he had chatted her up and then taken her back to his house and had sex with her for three crazy hours. But nobody knew that, and Duncan wanted to keep it that way. It wasn't the only time that he had cheated on Tessa, but she didn't know that he ever had, and the less people who knew about his indiscretions, the better. Duncan also didn't want to rain on Casey's parade. Becky was a cute girl. *Good for him*, Duncan thought.

"Yeah, man. She's gorgeous," Casey said, exaggerating a bit (in Duncan's eyes, at least). "I'm pretty stoked, dude. I definitely owe you one for teaching me the one-eye technique."

When Duncan was a freshman in high school, he figured out the one-eye technique for talking to girls, or really anyone you want to hold solid eye contact with. Instead of looking at both a girl's eyes when talking to her, you are supposed to focus on one eye. That keeps your eyes from moving at all. If you look at both eyes, you have to shift them side-to-side a little bit, which can lead to you looking at other parts of a person's face. There are a few reasons why you don't want to let your eyes wander while talking to a girl. You want her to be sure that you're listening to what she's saying. It also shows confidence. And if you look all over a girl's face it might make her self-conscious, thinking about the zit that her makeup is supposed to be covering or how she hasn't gotten her eyebrows waxed in two weeks. If you're looking at her eyes, it's less likely that she'll feel uncomfortable. She'll more likely feel important. That was Duncan's philosophy anyway. It seemed to work for him. He had slept with eight girls, including his most successful conquest, Tessa, since he'd made it up, so he felt confident that the one-eye technique was a valuable tool. And he was proud of his protégée's successful use of it.

"Ooooh, sick bro! You used the one-eye technique? Shit's money, right?" Duncan asked rhetorically. "I told you that shit was butter, baby boy. Buttery biscuits, bitch!" They laughed.

"Dude, I fuckin owe you one, for real," Casey said with unabashed sincerity.

"Blam!" Duncan said, making a motion with his hands to represent his favorite made-up word, mimicking an explosion.

Casey laughed, then nodded his head at the classroom door a few paces down the hall. "Word. Blam is right. I'm goin to class, dude," he said, flashing a backwards peace symbol with the pointer and middle fingers of his right hand. "Deuces."

"Latas, playboy," Duncan said, thinking that it was nice to see his buddy doing well and being able to use his advice so successfully. He liked spreading his 17 yr old wisdom to the youngins who would listen.

He rounded a corner and walked down the hall, then felt his phone briefly vibrate in his pocket to inform him that he had received a text message. He picked it up and saw that Tessa was its sender. He flipped open his LG NV phone to read what she had sent. It said, simply, *I love you Woopsy*. Duncan smiled and responded with, *back atcha boo*, another one of their inside jokes, of which there were plenty.

He reached his locker about five minutes into first period. He twisted the dial on his padlock, one full clockwise rotation to the 10, two full counterclockwise rotations to the 28, and then another half clockwise rotation back to the 10. The lock popped and he pulled his locker open. He looked at the magnetized mirror on the inside of his locker door and checked to see how the pimple he'd popped on his right cheek two days earlier was healing. It was almost invisible, he observed, much to his delight.

Duncan closed his locker door and walked over to Ms. Jarvis's art classroom with a casual gait that conveyed how at ease he felt with the world that day. *It's all good*, he thought. *Right now, it's alllllll good.*

Chapter 9

Matty G was walking down the upstairs northeast corridor of Eastfield High when he felt his phone buzzing in his pocket. Cell phones were forbidden within the walls of the school and would be temporarily confiscated if seen by a person of authority, so he slipped into the bathroom to see who was calling. He stepped into the large, handicap-accessible stall, the closest one to the door, and looked at his vibrating phone. He did not recognize the number that showed up on the caller ID, but he was familiar with the area code. It was from the southern part of the state. He wondered who could be calling from so far away. Normally, he didn't pick up phone calls from numbers that were unfamiliar to him, but he got curious and decided to answer. "Hello?" he said.

"Yoooo, big bro. Wusgood, homie?"

"Oh shit. Stevie! What the fuck's up, ma dude?"

"Chillin, man. Doin time, ya know?"

"Yeah, baby boy. How is it in there? You doin alright?"

"Been better, ya know? But it's not so bad. I'm up in Mr. M's office, the social worker here. He's a cool-ass white-boy. How old are you, Mr. M?" Stevie G asked the social worker across the room. Matty G could hear a voice calling out unintelligible words over the phone before his brother continued to speak. "Yeah, word, he's twenty-four," Stevie continued. "Cool as fuck. He's letting me use the phone 'cause I drew him a picture of these two dickhead officers playin fuckin tummy sticks."

Matty G burst out laughing, momentarily forgetting that he was in school and was not allowed to be using his cell phone. "You're ridiculous, kid," he chuckled.

"Word," said Stevie G. "I been drawin a lot. There ain't shit to do in this motherfucker."

"True?" said Matty G. "They let you get pencils and shit in your cell?"

"They're not supposed to, but since I been actin real good 'n shit, they let me have one 'cause the officer on my pod saw a picture that I drew while I was in class. He thought it was ill, so he lets me draw 'n shit. He says my talent shouldn't go to waste."

"Ah, you're still nice with the drawing, huh?"

"Of course, big daddy. You know this."

"Of course. You was always a wiz with the pencil, ma nigga."

"Yeah, man. I stay drawin. We gotta be in our fuckin cells almost eighteen hours every day. There ain't shit else to do besides pushups and read. And they only let you get a book in your cell once every five days. So, I get one and I'm done with it in like a day, maybe two if it's a long one. The rest of the time, I just draw. Otherwise, I have too much time to think. It just fucks with my dome, ya know?"

"That's heavy, ma dude," Matty G said, not sure exactly how to respond, being that he'd never been in a situation in which he was confined to a tiny room eighteen hours a day. But, being the big brother, he knew he had something better than that to say. "Listen, Stevie. Just be strong. Simple. It's only time, baby boy. I don't mean to downplay it. I know it's whack. But it is what it is. *Just a matter of time.* And the day you get out, son, oh my god, a party you wouldn't believe." Stevie G smiled at the thought. He knew that his brother always had his back.

"Matty, I gotta get off the phone, ma nigga. My time's up. Tell Mom I love her, ya heard?

"Word, ma dude."

"Alright, peace big daddy. I love you, man," Stevie said. Matty G thought he heard his little brother get a bit choked up.

"I love you too, bro. *Just a matter of time. Just a matter of time.*"

"Peace."

"Peace." On each end, the brothers hung up. Matty G laid his head against the cool tile of the bathroom wall and said a prayer for his brother, asking the powers that be to grant his brother the strength to get through his ordeal in one piece.

But the powers that be weren't listening that day. Just about the time that Matty G was stepping through the bathroom door, back into his school's hallway, a young man was knocking at the door of Mr. M's office on Stevie G's pod. Mr. M was on the phone when the young man knocked, looking at his computer. He looked at the door and waved the young man in to come take a seat in front of his desk.

The young man was a pale, redheaded, freckle-faced, and blue-eyed 16 year old who had just been sentenced to no less than four years for burning down a neighbor's house. Miraculously, the family that lived there had been out to eat the night that he set their house on fire, and no one was hurt, but he was nonetheless going away for a long time.

The kid had just arrived on the pod, and had shown no sign to Sgt. McDougal that he was any kind of safety threat, so what he did after being waved into the office by Mr. M was virtually unpreventable.

For a new resident to knock on the door of the social work office was to be expected. Mr. M had no reason to be suspicious of the kid's reason for coming in. He continued the conversation that he was having on the phone with a clerk at a county court who clearly was a new hire and very unfamiliar with their computer system. He was staring at his computer screen, trying to discern some information from the court's website, which was full of nearly unintelligible words written in tiny print. He had to move in close to the screen and squint in order to see. As he did so, he didn't notice that the new boy was picking up a ballpoint pen from his desk and removing its cap.

Stevie G was staring at the phone on the other side of the office. He hadn't even turned around when he heard someone knock on the door.

He was trying to regain his composure after choking up on the phone. Doing time was tough, no matter how positively he portrayed his state of mind to his big brother; he needed just a moment to collect himself. But that moment was too long. Stevie G slowly turned around on the swiveling chair at which he was seated with his eyes closed. When he opened them, he saw a demonic Edward Slendger wielding a ballpoint pen like a dagger, just about a foot from his face. He had no time to shout, no time to move. Edward stabbed him as hard as he could in the right side of his neck, spraying blood all over the office and continued to stab him repeatedly as Stevie G made choking, gasping sounds, and his body violently, fitfully twitched.

Mr. M dropped the phone and screamed, "McDougal!" as loud as he could. He darted over to the two boys and grabbed Edward, throwing the boy's skinny frame as aggressively as he could with his almost two hundred pounds. Edward crashed into Mr. M's desk and lay on the floor, a strange, vacant look on his face. McDougal arrived only moments later.

"Holy fucking shit!" McDougal shouted. "What the fuck happened?"

"This crazy little fuck just stabbed Stevie with a fucking pen, man!" Mr. M screamed back, horrified at what he had just witnessed. And what he now saw, his office splattered in the blood of his favorite resident and a psychotic 15 yr old with empty eyes lying on his floor, further mortified him and elicited a pained cry from deep within his soul.

Sgt. McDougal threw cuffs on Edward, dragged him out of the office, and threw him into the cell reserved for solitary confinement when a resident received a disciplinary charge, usually for fighting another resident or threatening an employee of the juvenile detention facility. McDougal had completed the task of securing Edward Slendger in solitary by the time the other officers arrived, in response to his call for backup when he first heard Mr. M shout. He had already returned to the office within thirty seconds of first grabbing the psychotic, red headed boy. In the commotion of trying to do his job as quickly as possible, Sgt. McDougal had not been able to fully appreciate the true disaster that was the social work office. There he found an absolute bloodbath, Mr. M in tears, and the body of an unquestionably dead Stevie G.

Chapter 10

The funeral sucked, as most funerals do. Mrs G beside herself. Matty G beside himself. Duncan assumed somewhat of a caretaker role for the bereaved mother and brother who had always been a second family to him. After the funeral, Duncan went home with the G's and stayed there for three days straight, cooking, cleaning, consoling. Matty G refused to go to school, preferring to stay in bed all day. Duncan hung out in his room, watching out for his fragile friend and playing video games. Sometimes, he would hear Matty G quietly crying under his down comforter. But Duncan didn't say anything. *Sometimes you just gotta cry it out,* he thought.

After three days of Matty G's silent, withdrawn inconsolability, Duncan had to get back to school. The funeral had been on a Sunday. It was now Wednesday night.

"You gonna be alright, G?" Duncan asked. Matty G exhaled heavily. "I gotta go back to school, G. You really should go back too, dude. Don't wanna get too far behind, ya know?" In response, a long sigh from Matty G. "I mean, you gotta get on with *life*, baby boy. You know Dirty Steve (a nickname Duncan had made for an eight year old Stevie G, who had come into the G house crying, covered in mud with no explanation as to how he had come to be in that state) wouldn't want you to be lyin in bed, mopin around and shit."

At Duncan's mention of the nickname, "Dirty Steve", Matty G couldn't help but chuckle. "Yeah, man," he said. "I know." He started to choke up again.

"You got big shit to do, baby boy. Big stuff, ya diiiig?" Duncan said to try to bring a lightness to this dire situation.

"Yeah, man. You're right," Matty G said flatly, knowing that Duncan was referring to the basketball scholarship that he was guaranteed to get, due to his incredible hang-time, size, and pure numbers - his unassailable statistics. He led the state in points, field goal percentage, dunks, and blocked shots - by *miles*. Though scouts had been at almost all of their high school games, it was in Matty G and Duncan's senior year that coaches from the schools with the best basketball programs would be most interested in recruiting them. There was no way that either of them *wasn't* going to college. They were Woops and Oops. And they intended to keep that dynamic duo together, at the next level, if circumstances were to permit.

Duncan held the back of Matty G's head and, pulling his huge friend's melon down, gave him a kiss on the cheek. "I love you, bro," Duncan said. "You're my dude."

"Thanks, Dunks. Love you too, man." They hugged, did their elaborate, 11 year-old, secret handshake, and Duncan left, to go see his girl for the first time since the funeral. He needed some positive energy after this ordeal. Some love. Some sex. Some Tessa Moya.

As soon as Duncan left, Matty G walked to his window and watched his best friend pull his new fancy car out of the Hightown parking lot, then burst into heaving sobs, the kind that make you gag. He fell to the floor, curled up into the fetal position and shook. Then he threw up and went limp, lying in a puddle of his own vomit, staring at the maroon wall of his room, which was covered in almost seven years' worth of graffiti and guest signatures, the names of the countless friends he had accumulated with his charming personality, modest self-presentation and, for the hangers-on who regularly brought over blunts and 40's, his impending stardom.

He coughed violently for several seconds, then jumped to his feet and hustled to his desk drawer. In it was the prescription bottle of Xanax that he and Duncan had purchased a month earlier from a high-strung forty-something guy named Xander, who was prescribed a heavy monthly dose. Matty G flung the drawer open, grabbed the bottle, and twisted off the cap to see how many pills were left. He and Duncan hadn't taken any more of the pills since their blackout, so the bottle was nearly full. He dumped the pills out on his desk and quickly counted twenty-one of the pills. That would definitely be enough. Enough to cure the pain of the loss of his beloved baby brother. *I can't handle this*, he thought. *I can't live without Stevie. I can't do this shit anymore. Fuck it. I'm out.*

He grabbed a bottle of red, fruit punch flavored Gatorade from his mini-fridge and proceeded to wash the pills down in three big gulps, each swig containing roughly a third of the twenty-one two-mg zanny bars. Then, he lay down and cried for ten minutes until an all-consuming sense of calm, of everything being all right with the world, washed over him.

For another five minutes, Matty G stayed awake and reflected on how amazing his life was. He was a basketball superstar. A king of Eastfield High School. He had everything going for him. His mom loved him. His dad and brother were safe in God's warm, heavenly embrace. Yeah, life was good. Life was really good. Everything was cool.

Then, Matty G fell asleep and quietly, painlessly died.

Chapter 11

Duncan woke up in Tessa's bed, covered in sweat, freezing cold. Tessa was asleep next to him, gently snoring. Duncan thought that her snoring was probably the only thing about her that bothered him at all. She was perfect. He smiled, looking at her, and gently smoothed her hair. He pulled off his shirt, which was clinging to his body and grabbed another pillow. He wanted to get in another few minutes of sleep before he had to go back to his house to change, shower, and get himself ready for school.

Just as he placed his head on the pillow, Tessa's snoring ceased and her eyes opened. "Hi," she whispered.

"Hey there," Duncan said. "Good sleep?"

"Yeah. Anytime you're next to me I sleep well, baby. How 'bout you?"

"I woke up all sweaty and cold. I must be sick or something."

"Ew, don't get me sick, dude!" Tessa squealed and jumped out of bed. But Duncan didn't feel sick. Just sweaty and cold. And he felt like there was something wrong. Something permeating the air. An unexplainable feeling of negativity. He was *sad*. Everything was all right though, he thought. It was stressful being around Matty G when he was in such a state, but he wasn't hurting like Matty G and Mrs. G were over the death of Stevie G. This was a feeling unrelated to any event that he could place. He just knew something was wrong.

"Baby, I'm gonna go home and get ready for school," Duncan said, kissing her on the forehead. "I'm not sick. Just nightmares probably. I don't remember though."

"Okay," Tessa replied.

"I'll pick you up in like forty-five minutes, k?"

"Sounds good, handsome."

"Alright, babe. See ya then. Love ya." Duncan pecked Tessa on the cheek and jetted out of her room, down the stairs, and out the front door of the Moya house.

The sun was out. Cloudless sky. Light breeze. *Something's all fuckin wrong*, Duncan thought. *All fuckin wrong, man. What the fuck is going on in my head?* He pulled leaves off low-hanging branches and slowly, gently tore the leaves to bits, as he walked down the street to his car. He got in, started it up and drove home, parking around the corner from his house. He always parked his new car around the corner because he didn't want his parents asking any questions regarding how a seventeen year-old kid without a job had obtained such a fancy vehicle.

He got out of his car and walked around the corner, resuming the mindless activity of leaf-plucking and still feeling terrible. Life was really good, but Matty G's pain was *his* pain, and seeing his best friend so despondent was eating him up.

Duncan walked up the driveway to the garage and typed in the passcode to get inside. The garage door slowly rumbled and Duncan walked through, hitting the button to close the door with an open palm. He kicked his Nike Dunks off in the laundry room and walked into the kitchen. His house was very quiet. Normally, at this hour, Duncan's mom would be cooking breakfast. His dad would be eating, drinking his morning coffee, and reading the paper.

Duncan walked through the kitchen, towards the stairs that led upstairs to his bedroom. He glanced to his right, through the front parlor, into the living room. His parents were sitting there. Their faces were drawn. His mom's eyes were red and puffy; she had obviously been crying.

"Hi," Duncan said. "What's goin on?" he asked, trepidation permeating his tone.

"Hey, buddy," Mr. Lipton said. His voice sounded sympathetic.

"C'mere, pal." He patted the seat next to him. *Pal?* Duncan thought. *When the fuck's the last time Dad called me "pal"?*

Upon seeing her son enter the living room, Mrs. Lipton, though she tried to control herself, began to cry. "Oh, Duncan!" she wailed, getting up and throwing her arms around him. "Oh, baby. Oh, Duncan!" She pressed her face into his chest and drenched his t-shirt.

"What's the matter, Mom?" Duncan asked, worried and scared.

"Sit down, honey," she sniffled.

Sitting down, Duncan looked, wide-eyed, back and forth between his parents.

"Duncan," Mr. Lipton began, starting to choke up a little bit himself. "Oh man. Duncan, there's no easy way to say this, so I'm just gonna say it. Matty G killed himself last night, buddy."

A shock was sent through Duncan's body like he had never experienced before. He lost all ability to move and just sat there, saying nothing, his breathing quickening, his heart racing. "No," he said, quietly, and shook his head. "No."

"Oh, Duncan. I'm so sorry, honey," Mrs. Lipton cried, throwing her arms around him again. "I'm so, so sorry."

"No," he repeated, in a hushed voice. His voice steadily rose as he repeated, "No, no, no, no, NO!" over and over again, recoiling from his mother's embrace. He was crying and shaking, heavy sobs violently racking his body. "No, no, no, no, no, no!" He tried to stand, found his legs made of jelly, and fell off the couch, onto the white-carpeted floor, where he continued to bawl his eyes out.

Mrs. Lipton bent down and rubbed Duncan's back as he wept. "Mommy," Duncan whispered. He hadn't said that word in years. He felt broken, pathetic. She held his hand.

"Come on, Duncan, baby. Let's just relax and watch 'The Shawshank Redemption'. Duncan didn't respond to what would normally be a no-brainer when he was in a bad mood. The movie was the Lipton family common denominator. The three of them loved the movie about a banker, imprisoned for over sixteen years, for a false conviction of murdering his wife. Despite the depressing description, the movie was an uplifting portrayal of friendship and emotional endurance. The Liptons, over the years, watched it together at least once every two months. It unfailingly provided enjoyment to all of them. But it would not heal this wound; it wouldn't even slow the bleeding.

Duncan's dad was already running late for work, and now that he had told his son the worst news the kid could ever imagine, he had to leave his wife in charge of making sure that he'd be alright. "I'll be back later, buddy. We'll get some Sicilian pizza and chill out when I get home, alright?"

"K, Dad. I'm gonna go lie down and read 'Musungu Jim' for a while, okay?" 'Musungu Jim and the Great Chief Tuloko' by Patrick Neate was Duncan's favorite book. He had read it six times, regularly using it as his going-to-sleep book. The story of the wayward 18 year-old, Jim, going to the fictional African nation of Zambawi, to teach English, always took him away from his racing thoughts. Reading it was the only thing Duncan could think of to do to help him escape from the pain that presently wrenched his heart.

"Okay, pal. I love you, Dunks." Duncan never said so, but he normally hated when his dad called him by his nickname, which was bestowed upon him by his friends. But right now, he needed his dad to be his friend, so the use of the nickname had the desired effect.

"I love you too, Dad," he said. "I love you too, Mom."

Duncan rubbed his red eyes as he walked up the stairs, very slowly to his room. When he got in, he closed the door and leaned against the wall to think. *I'm outta here*, he thought. *Gone. That's it. I'm fuckin gone. Gotta talk to Tessa first though.* He wouldn't just bounce on Tessa. He loved her too much.

Duncan called her and told her what had happened. When he made his proposal for the plan he had impulsively concocted, Tessa was predictably incapable of joining him.

"Duncan, I need to finish *high school*!" she told him emphatically.

"Please, baby. I love you so much! You know I love you so much. Please come with me. Please, please please, baby! Oh man, I have to do this. Tessa Michelle Moya..." He paused. "I can't be here anymore, baby. I just can't. I gotta get outta here."

"Duncan. Please don't go. Please, honey, *please*! You're gonna get a scholarship to play college ball. You've got everything going for you. Matty would want you to make it happen. You know that, Duncan, baby. You *know* that."

"I'm gone tomorrow, Tessa," Duncan asserted.

"Tomorrow? Why tomorrow? Wait and think about it, Dunks. Please. Wait and think about it."

"Nah. Flight's tomorrow morning at 6, baby. I'm so sorry. Please, please understand. I love you so much and this has nothing to do with you. But I can't be in this town. I can't live here without G." Duncan started to cry.

"Oh, Duncan baby. Oh, baby. You do what you need to do, honey. Please call me and send me messages on Facebook whenever you can. I need to know that you're ok."

"Baby, I swear on my life. I will write you no less than once a week. Scout's honor, baby girl," he said, his hand over his heart.

"Make it twice a week... if you can. Okay?"

"Okay, beautiful. I'm gonna go read for a while, clear my mind. You'll send me off tomorrow?"

"I'm sleeping over. I'll make sure you get up. Or maybe I'll just make sure you're up all night," she giggled. At this remark, Duncan smiled. He knew that he was getting laid a good three times before he got on the plane. *Amen*, he thought. *A-motherfuckin-men. How can I leave this girl?"* But he had to. His mind was beyond made-up.

They actually did fall asleep around 3:00am. Duncan's alarm woke him up at 4:45. Tessa was still fast asleep. He tried to wake her, but she was in a deep slumber. That last "I love you," that he would forever cherish, after their third round of making love/having sex/fucking would never be forgotten. That girl was an angel.

Duncan left a note, with an inside joke between the two of them, saying only, "I'll be back. Love, Duncan." It paid homage to Arnold Schwarzenneger's classic line in one of their odd choices for a mutual favorite movie, 'The Terminator'. He took one last look at the girl, who Chaz Palmintieri's character from 'A Bronx Tale', Sonny LoSpecchio, would have referred to as "one of the great ones," of which a man will only have three in his life. Then, he quietly, slowly walked out of the Moya house. Once outside, he called a cab to take him to the massive airport forty-five minutes from Eastfield.

When he arrived at the terminal, Duncan saw that his flight was already boarding and would be departing in thirty-three minutes. He gave the beautiful, blond, full-lipped, yet sad-looking flight attendant his ticket. She handed him his stub, shoulders slumped and forcing a smile. With a forced smile of his own, he thanked her and boarded the plane. He was ready to leave this life *behind*. He was ready to get out of Dodge.

Duncan took his seat and considered himself lucky to have ended up with that seating arrangement. Sure, he would inevitably have to climb over the other passengers to go take a piss at some point during the long plane ride. But seeing the clouds and the nearing landing area were worth the window seat. He thought it was beautiful, the descent from great heights to a rapidly approaching, desired destination. And the water would be so blue. He had only seen pictures.

He buckled his safety belt, put his seatback up and folded his tray away. He couldn't help but notice how cute one of the flight attendants was. C's. Blonde. *Niiiiice*. He considered the possibility of a casual macking session. He wasn't about to see his girlfriend for a long, long time: fact. Despite his love for her, his being faithful wasn't likely. Duncan was a charming, handsome kid and he could easily pass himself off as being in his early 20's, which often came in handy when trying to purchase alcohol without a fake ID or talking to girls quite obviously no longer of high school age. *Might as well get the ball rolling*, he figured.

The plane began to roll and made a smooth, seamless takeoff. "I'm on my way, man," Duncan said, quietly, to himself. *Wow*, he thought. *This really is really a really fuckin new one. Fuckin A, man.* For the first time since his parents broke the news, the brutal pain caused to his soul by the death of his best friend was temporarily forgotten. It was time for a new life to begin. His old life was ruined, and, as far as he was concerned, it was to be left behind. He didn't want to be around anything that felt empty without G. And that encompassed, more or less, his whole life. Basketball. School. Hangin out. Whatever. He couldn't take it. He just needed to get out of the area, out of the country. He had the money to do so because of the Xanax and Jack Daniels-fueled lost-night that had resulted in so much insanity.

Duncan had already let Mrs. G know where Matty G had stashed his portion of the half-mil. That would drastically improve her circumstances, which somewhat eased his mind. The idea of both G boys being dead and Mrs. G being left alone without them, stuck in Hightown, was too much. She was a second mom to him. He wouldn't leave her hanging out to dry.

But he had to split, and that was that. He knew he was throwing away his life-long hoop-dreams. But how could Woops play without Oops when he knew nothing else? Right now, he couldn't be bothered. He was running away.

Caribbean, here I come, he silently mused. *Motherfucking, Caribbean.* The plane began to fly Duncan Lipton to the start of his new life.

Chapter 12

The dreadlocks pointed out of the young man's head in thick tufts, reminiscent of Bob Marley's hairdo on the cover of the 1973 Wailers album, 'Burnin''. His dark complexion was much more like that of Bob's band-mate Peter Tosh though, and his eccentric, stylistic use of the color spectrum in his attire recalled the third member of The Wailers, Bunny Wailer. The dude definitely looked cool. *Authentic,* Duncan thought, not even sure what that authenticity exactly referenced.

The young man's exceptionally dark skin was beautifully juxtaposed against a particularly large and full-bodied, flawlessly white acoustic guitar. Attached to the upper-left of the guitar-body's face (from the audience's perspective) was a circular mirror, three inches in diameter, that brilliantly reflected the warm light shining on him as he played. He wore a tight-fitting, baby blue t-shirt, which had a large image of the face of Garfield the Cat pictured on its front. Under the picture of the grinning tabby were the words, "I'm not as innocent as I look." He adorned himself in all manner of jewelry: beaded necklaces, hemp bracelets, gold earrings. He also wore loose, light-colored blue jeans that had a large hole in the left knee-area. And to Duncan's delight, the styled-out islander was rockin a pair of black and red Nike Dunks.

As much as Duncan was taken in by the young man's style, far more intriguing was the music emanating from the two-foot-high stage in the corner of 'The Shanty', a small bar around the corner from the hostel that Duncan had just checked into. Playing solo acoustic guitar and singing, the young man displayed a rare passion, the likes of which Duncan had never seen live, or on any TV or computer screen for that matter. A couple hippie-type buddies of his played a little bit of acoustic guitar, but none of them could sing for shit.

When he walked into the bar, Duncan was surprised to hear Billy Joel's classic, 'Piano Man', being sung in a gravelly, heavily island-accented tenor. And the fact that the song was being played without a piano added a certain raw *je ne sais quoi* to the performance. Something about it spoke to him. 'Piano Man's" lyrical content, Duncan thought, cries out for the vocal to be accompanied by a piano. *How could the 'Piano Man' vocal have no piano? How could it survive?* But the young man had changed the lyrics and renamed the song "Guitar Man". *Clever,* Duncan thought. *Way to adapt.*

His thoughts turned then to a basketball game in which he had played as a sixteen year-old sophomore at Eastfield High, against Rollins Prep, the fourth-ranked team in the 1A division. By that time, Woops and Oops were established as the most dynamic and unstoppable tandem in the state, leading their team to win the state title and secure the top ranking, which they would never relinquish during their three-year reign. But Duncan had yet, in the eyes of many fans and critics, to prove himself as his *own* man on the court. They wondered what kind of player he would be without the incredibly large and athletic Matty G to lob the ball to, over and over again for easy flushes.

In the Rollins Prep game, Matty G had gone up for a rebound, only five minutes into the first half, and had come down awkwardly on his left ankle. It was not a major injury, but it was enough to necessitate his sitting out for the remainder of the game. At that point, the Eastfield talent pool was not terribly deep. All of the team's success revolved solely around Woops and Oops. So, without Oops, Woops had to put the team on his shoulders. Accordingly, he put on a show against Rollins that silenced all those who had any doubts about how talented he was. Duncan went for fifty-five points that day, hitting eleven three-pointers, driving the lane three times to make outrageous circus lay-ups, *dunking* three times, and making all ten of his free-throw attempts. He shot 92% as his best friend went bananas on the sidelines. Matty G accidentally fell off his seat twice when, so excited by a couple of Duncan's near-half-court three-point bombs, he forgot that he had a twisted ankle and tried to stand up, causing him to tumble to the floor. Duncan also got eleven assists (as basketball *is* a team sport), passing to his wide-open teammates, whose defenders had no choice but to double and triple-team him. And he pulled down fourteen rebounds (lest anyone forget that 6'3", while not Oops-huge, is pretty damn tall for a high school player).

To ice the cake, he added an absurd sixteen *steals*. And *nobody* gets sixteen steals. Maybe an overzealous fifth-grade gym teacher could accomplish that feat against an early-morning class of sleepy ten year-olds, but it certainly didn't happen in the state's 1A division. The old record for steals in a game had been nine, and that record was twenty-seven years old. And really, *nobody* gets a quadruple-double (double-digits in four separate statistical categories) in any league. It does happen once in a blue moon, but to say that it was a rare accomplishment would be a heavy understatement. It had never happened before in 1A. Duncan would never do anything like that again for Eastfield since Matty G remained healthy for the rest of the games that they played in together. They continued to dominate as a duo. And Duncan preferred it that way. It was supposed to be Woops and Oops. It always had been. But he had proven that he could do it on his own.

That had been a special day for Duncan. He hadn't thought about it in quite a while, but the music that he was now hearing brought him there. He reflected fondly on the beautiful, brilliant, and talented super-athlete who would eternally be his best friend. *What a fuckin guy*, he thought. *Man, what a motherfuckin guy*.

The young man ended his rendition of 'Piano Man', and the thirty some-odd people in attendance clapped enthusiastically. As the applause faded, Duncan stood up on a chair and shouted, "Thanks!"

He made the universal "Hang Loose" sign with his hand, his right thumb and pinky extended with the middle-three fingers folded down, twisting his wrist back and forth.

The young man looked up at him and smiled a set of beautifully aligned teeth, as shiny and white as the guitar he held. "Ya welcome, mon. I knowed ya need it," he said into the microphone, in a thick Caribbean accent. Above the smile, the young man's big brown eyes were serious, as they held contact with Duncan's for several seconds. "This next one fa you too, brudda. Mista Bobby Dylan." He started to strum his guitar, G, D, A minor, G, D, C, twice repeating the pattern, and then began to sing "Knockin' on Heaven's Door". Duncan, sitting by himself at an otherwise empty table, began to tear up, thinking about his fallen friend who was knockin' on heaven's door himself. But a minute into the performance, a smile cracked on Duncan's lips and he started to chuckle because he *knew* that this was a message from above. Matty G was okay wherever he was, somewhere way up in the sky. He was sure of it. And the pain of his loss became happiness and gratitude that his best friend was safe in the hands of a higher power. Duncan had never been one to believe in God, or any particular "higher power" before, but he was now experiencing a spiritual connection to the universe that simply gave him faith that there was something beyond this world, and that, whatever it was, it was taking care of his boy.

Duncan looked up at the young man on the stage, his eyes puffy and red, his cheeks wet with tears, but with a big, genuine smile on his face. The young man looked back at him and Duncan noticed that the musician's cheeks glistened with wetness and his eyes were also red, as though he was feeling Duncan's pain. They smiled at each other, and then the young man closed his eyes and finished the song, truly singing his heart out as Duncan replayed, in his mind, countless baskets that Woops and Oops had scored in their amazing run together. When Matty G got to heaven's door, Duncan knew that he hadn't even had to knock. *They must've had the fuckin red carpet rolled out for that dude already*, he thought.

"Danks, bruddas and sistas," the young man said, after the applause had died down. "Dank you so so much. It's time for da intamission. I be back on in twenty minutes… so don't go fah!" The crowd laughed and applauded, and the young man put his guitar on a rack at the back of the stage before once again leaning into the microphone and saying, "Oh yah. Don't fuhget ta tip da mudda fuckin bahtenda, mon," before hopping lightly to the floor and walking straight to Duncan's table.

"Smoke, mon?" the young man asked, sliding into a chair next to Duncan.

"Cigarettes? Nah, man. Sorry," Duncan replied, thinking that the young man was asking him for one.

The young man chuckled, "No, bwah! Not da tobacco. Da *gaaaaanja…*"

Chapter 13

"What's your name, bro?" Duncan asked, as he and the young man walked out back, behind The Shanty.

"Rennie, mon. Rennie. Plezha, brudda," the young man said, as he pulled from the front-right pocket of his loose jeans the biggest joint Duncan had ever seen. The joint was *way* bigger than even his epic quarter-ounce seventeenth-birthday blunt, which had required three Dutchies to roll. Duncan was impressed. "Wus ya own name, brudda mon?" Rennie asked.

"Duncan, man. Pleasure to meet you too. Dude, seriously, you just blew my fucking mind in there. You don't even know, bro. That was the best thing I've ever heard in my life."

"Stop it, mon. If I was a pale mon like you be, ma cheeks be pink!"

"Dude..." Duncan's voice trailed off as the two of them made eye contact. He didn't know how to express how important that music had been for him just then.

"I knowed you needed dem songs, Duncan mon. I felt you comin in befo you come in. De energy. Dem songs... dey was de *right* songs. I don't know why I knowed, mon. I just know it..."

"You couldn't have been more right, bro. You really couldn't possibly have been more on point."

"I knowed it, Duncan mon. But why? What happened to ya, mon? Why was dey dem right songs right den, brudda?" Rennie asked, as he lit the massive joint, spinning it around in his mouth like a cigar. His positive energy helped Duncan hold it together as he told a brief version of everything that had transpired in the months leading up to Matty G's death. The two of them passed the massive smoking apparatus back and forth as Rennie listened intently to how Duncan had ended up on his island.

When Duncan finished telling his pained, sad story, Rennie's face lit up with his broad, shiny smile. "You lose a brudda, mon. But now, you gain a brudda. Matty G in de aftalife, Duncan, ma brudda. In heaven wit dem beautiful babies and da bouncin bosketballs, mon. But I's here fuh you, mon. From dis day on. Dat's true, Duncan mon. Please believe."

Duncan smiled and nodded, surprised at his lack of skepticism. This guy was genuine. Duncan knew it. Rennie, embracing Duncan strongly, said, "OK, Duncan brudda. I told dem nice people I was to be back in twenty minutes. I's a little late. Come inside, brudda. I play a couple nice songs. I tink you like, pretty shaw. Sit wit dem nice people. Vibe wit dem. Dey you people, Dunks."

To Duncan, Rennie's unprompted use of his nickname didn't even register. It felt so natural.

Rennie walked back inside, striding with considerable swagger. He stepped on stage, picked up his guitar, threw the strap over his shoulder and began to play, all in one fluid motion. The set-list that he made, in honor of his new American friend, was a reggae-infused islander's take on rock n' roll, and the crowd was most appreciative of this soulfully original showcase. He played "When I Come Around" by Green Day, "Nutshell" by Alice in Chains, "While My Guitar Gently Weeps" by the Beatles, "Wonderwall" by Oasis, "Hotel California" by The Eagles, and, lastly, he finished with the most soulful rendition of "Dock of the Bay" since Otis Redding sang it himself. He sang them all, particularly the last, with so much originality and flavorful passion that he made the covers his own. They became his personal tribute to music and love and life. Duncan was floored.

After the show, Rennie invited Duncan to his home to hang out and smoke some more. Not one to ever turn down an invitation to blaze, and lacking anything else important to do, Duncan was more than willing to partake.

What a cool guy, Duncan thought. *Definitely cool.* It would be good, he figured, for him to have a new friend in this crazy place that he knew nothing about. In his old life, Duncan had had a gazillion friends; he planned on keeping it that way. Meeting this cool, styled-out, dreadlocked musician was a solid start, he thought.

Rennie drove and Duncan sat shotgun. "Nice car," Duncan said. He didn't expect Rennie to be driving a brand new Range Rover with twenty-inch rims.

"Danks, mon," Rennie responded, simply.

In the car, Rennie put on a CD of Bob Marley's greatest hits. Duncan was jammin'. Comfortably, they rode without speaking for the whole fifteen-minute trip, bobbing their heads on beat to the beautiful reggae rhythms.

They pulled up in front of a modest, one-story, brick house. "Welcome, welcome, to ma humble abode, brand-new-brudda Duncan!" They stepped through the front door, into a small, cozy front room. The walls were decorated with prints of paintings by artists including George Rodrigue, Keith Haring, Ron English, Romero Britto, and other well-knowns. There was also a bookshelf that took up a whole wall of the front room and was filled to capacity with a variety of literature. Duncan was impressed and intrigued.

"Nice spot, Rennie," Duncan said, liking the quaintness of the little house, with its Rennie-infused personality.

"Danks, mon," Rennie replied. "But wait 'til you see da *basement*, Duncan brudda. Da basement where da magic be *hap'nin*." He flashed a shiny, toothy grin and laughed out loud. Duncan wondered what kind of magic Rennie might be referring to, and he anxiously looked forward to finding out.

Rennie walked across the front room and picked up a Dutch Masters cigar box from the mantel over the fireplace. The box did not contain cigars though. When Rennie opened it, Duncan could see a numbered keypad, which looked like one in a telephone booth.

Rennie typed in some numbers that Duncan couldn't see. He then turned around, and with a huge smile on his face said, "Duncan brudda, welcome to my *not*-so-humble abode." He laughed and hit 'Enter' on the keypad.

Chapter 14

The impressively stuffed bookcase slid quietly off the wall and into the middle of the front room, revealing a staircase to the basement. Duncan's jaw dropped, giving Rennie a good laugh. He approached the newly visible staircase and saw that the stairs themselves and the walls of the staircase were a pleasant lime-green. The stairs were steep and reminded him of the cellar stairs at his family's house that had left one or two of his wasted friends with a few bumps and bruises. Duncan, amazed at the crazy sliding bookcase turned to Rennie and said, "Shit."

"Yaaaaaah, mon," Rennie laughed. "Follow me, brudda. Come see, come see. I tink you gon like dis veddy, veddy much." He motioned to Duncan with a casual wave to follow him down the stairs. "Hold onto da railin, mon," he said. "Dem some steep stairs, brudda."

"Cool, dude," Duncan said. "I'm right witcha." As they descended the stairs, a familiar aroma wafted from the basement and tickled Duncan's nostrils. "Smells like goosh, Rennie. Fuckin goosh-goosh, baby boy!" The smell of weed, with each step further down, became more and more pungent. At the bottom of the steep staircase, Rennie opened a door painted the same lime-green color as the stairs and walls. He walked through and bowed as he held the door open for Duncan. Duncan, chuckling as he watched Rennie's exaggerated gesture with bemusement, stepped through into one of the most beautiful scenes he had ever witnessed. Later, reflecting on that first glimpse of the "basement" of Rennie's house, he would decide that it was probably the second most beautiful image he'd ever seen in person, right after the first time he saw Tessa naked, a memory he would forever cherish.

Sitting there in front of him, in a shockingly huge room, were no less than five hundred marijuana plants, beautifully maintained in formal rows. *Wow*, Duncan thought. *That's a new one.* Immediately, Matty G came to mind, and Duncan badly wished that he could be sharing this moment with his best friend.

The plants had the necessary lamps hanging above them, and all other requirements to have a successful indoor harvest (tools and nourishment and fertilizer and this and that) sat in the far-left corner. Duncan's jaw, as it seemed to be doing quite frequently lately, practically dropped to the floor. Rhetorically, he asked, "What the fuck?"

"Welcome to da Hole, Duncan, brudda," Rennie said, extending his right arm out and grandly sweeping it from left to right. Duncan stared in amazement at all the plants, some growing, others hanging out to dry. He loved weed. He was in heaven.

Then he noticed The Girls with the Guns, though he didn't yet know that moniker. *Holy shit! Girls with fucking guns!* he thought. Rennie draped his right arm over Duncan's shoulder, and pulled him in tight. "Let me introduce you to dem beautiful ladies ova dere," he said, smiling that huge, bright white smile.

Although he was now twenty-eight years old, Rennie had not forgotten his horny teenage days and nights. Always one to be very particular about a female's looks, he handpicked The Girls with the Guns himself. They could learn how to use the guns later, he figured, so long as they put the Dallas Cowboys cheerleaders to shame.

There were six girls standing in the far-right corner of the massive room Duncan and Rennie had just entered. They were a mix of races: one Asian girl, two white girls, and three black girls. They all wore bikinis: red, orange, yellow, green, blue, and purple. And they all carried Uzis. (Duncan knew that the large machine guns being toted by these small, sexy girls were Uzis because he had done a ninth grade presentation on illegal firearms in the United States.) And he knew that anyone carrying an Uzi wasn't fuckin around. But Rennie's happy greeting and the excitement that the girls showed at seeing him put Duncan's mind at ease.

Rennie introduced the girls to his new friend, saying, "Duncan, mon, meet Da Girls Wit da Guns. Ladies, dis is ma brudda, Duncan. He be da king uh dis castle along wit me now." Duncan blushed. *These girls are gorgeous,* he thought.

Jessica was the Asian girl. She was in the blue bikini. Ari was the tanner of the two white girls, with wavy blonde hair, high cheek bones, and bright blue eyes. She was in the red bikini. Nicole was the other white girl. She was a strawberry blonde with freckles and an infectious smile that lit up upon Rennie and Duncan's arrival in the Hole. She was in the purple bikini. Kim was the shortest of the black girls. She was full-figured, with a big ass, big boobs, and a cute baby-face. She was in the yellow bikini. Diamond was the tallest of the black girls. She was lighter-skinned than the other two and had very light brown eyes. She was in the orange bikini. Tara's height, skin-color and weight stats were all clearly in between those of the other two. She was in the green bikini. All of them were stunning. 10's. *All six of them are 10's,* Duncan thought, *but Ari is the most beautiful girl I have ever seen in my fucking life.* Caught up in the moment and the outlandish circumstnaces, he was quick to forget about Tessa.

"Ladies," Rennie said, "please monita da cameras 'round da perimeta, and Ari, check da plant levels, baby girl, while I talk to ma brudda, Duncan, fuh a while. We be back soon." Duncan and Rennie climbed back up the stairs, and through the bookcase into Rennie's small house. "Let's walk, brudda," Rennie said, and he and Duncan walked out the back door into the backyard.

Duncan now noticed how much land was behind and surrounding Rennie's home. As they walked out into the backyard, Rennie explained to him that he actually owned twenty-four acres and that his little house was a decoy for the Hole. His house was less than five hundred square feet, all situated on one floor. But the Hole was a massive, underground mansion and weed-growing facility, which was over eight thousand square feet in all. It had a movie theatre with tiered seating. It had a pool, hot tub and sauna. It had seven bedrooms. It had living rooms and reading rooms and dens and libraries and rooms that had no particular purpose. It had a gym with weights and aerobic equipment. And it had a basketball court. "You do *not* have a fuckin basketball court, Rennie," Duncan said disbelievingly, even though he knew that Rennie wasn't lying after what he had just witnessed.

"Yah, brudda. All dis… all mine. You a balla. Right, Mista Duncan?" While telling Rennie about Matty G, Duncan had mentioned the importance of basketball in he and his best friend's relationship, but Rennie didn't know the full extent of what the sport meant to them.

"Somethin like that, dude. Somethin like that," Duncan responded. "Can I check it out?"

"Of course, brudda. Dis be your house, mon. *Your* house, fa true."

"Let's do it," Duncan said.

They walked into the house, and went through the sliding bookshelf, down the steep lime-green stairs, and into the grow room. On their way to the basketball court, they ran into Ari, as she was checking water levels for the plants. "Hi, boys," she said.

"Hi," Duncan said, somewhat sheepishly.

"Baby girl," Rennie said, bright smile shining, "How ma plants lookin?"

"Real good, Ren baby. Beautiful. Everything's *perfect*." When she said the word "perfect", it seemed like she was definitely talking about more than just the plants. *Unreal*, Duncan thought, looking at this beautiful, bikini-clad girl tending the most beautiful marijuana plants that one could imagine. *Un-fucking-real.*

"Me n' Mista Duncan gonna go play some ball, baby girl," Rennie said. "We see you lata." "Bye," Duncan said, unable to make eye contact with her. No girl had ever intimidated him in this way before. Tessa had definitely intimidated him, but this was different. This girl seemed inaccessible. Like an air-brushed fantasy out of Maxim. As he and Rennie walked away, to go play ball, Duncan couldn't help but look back. Ari was looking at him. They locked eyes. She smiled and winked. Duncan smiled and blushed, and said, "Check ya later." All of a sudden he felt like an idiot. *Why would I use Slater's shitty line from Dazed and Confused?* he thought. *I'm an idiot.*

But Ari gave him a little hang-loose sign with her right hand and said, "Later, dude." The way she said it was in a comically similar way to Matty G's impression of Duncan. Duncan laughed, and then slowly turned away to follow Rennie to the gym, when he realized that he had failed to ask him one of the most basic questions about this shockingly unexpected, surreal experience. At the precipice of the court, Duncan said, "Rennie… what the fuck is up with the bikinis and Uzis, dude?"

Chapter 15

As it turned out, Rennie and Duncan shared a mutual love of the movie 'American Gangster', in which Denzel Washington plays the kingpin of a New York City heroin ring, named Frank Lucas. In the movie, Denzel's character has it all: the mansions, the beauty-queen wife, respect, ringside seats, a bevy of naked girls cutting down his pure Vietnamese heroin. Rennie wanted to mimic that character, but to do it in a different, more positive and optimistic way. He wanted to sell something that he didn't feel guilty about selling. And he certainly felt no guilt over selling weed, the way he would if he were selling dope, which ruins lives and turns good people into depraved wasters. He considered what he was doing, on the other hand, to be a necessary service for the good of the people.

Frank Lucas introduces his younger brothers to the dope industry that he commands and blows their minds when he shows them where the dope is cut, in a room full of naked girls. He says that they're naked so that they can't steal anything. Rennie loved it. So he adapted the aesthetic of it to his own, more positive version of having hot girls scantily clad, around tons of drugs and money. He was sure that there was no reason to worry about anything being stolen. He loved his girls, and, as far as he was concerned, they could have as much weed as their beautiful hearts desired. He just wanted to pay tribute to the movie. And he loved women. As they were *his* employees, he unapologetically enforced the bikini/Uzi uniform.

But there were more important reasons why Rennie had the girls working for him. Rennie, truth be told, was the island's marijuana kingpin. Indisputably. He was the boss of the island. But no one knew... thanks to his *system*. And the Girls with the Guns. They enabled him to safely supply, more or less, the entire island with world-class-quality weed, without the police having any idea that the guitarist/singer, who regularly performed at the 'Shanty', was involved whatsoever in distribution. One look at Rennie, and anyone could tell that he smoked weed. But that is a different animal altogether than being involved in supplying it to others. And no one had ever even bought so much as a dime bag from Rennie, at least not since he was a kid.

Every transaction that involved significant amounts of weight were handled by the girls who, when doing business, wore less revealing, yet still sexy attire. As far as any buyer was concerned, this was as high on the island's marijuana food chain as he was going to get. None of his girls had ever exposed him, and he had not a worry in his mind that they ever would.

Anonymity was something that was as important to Rennie as the massive amount of money that he earned. He was not going to go to jail. No way. He didn't really worry about that considering the extremely lax policy on weed on the island. Though it was technically illegal, it was hardly treated as such, although the occasional cop would be an asshole and bring someone in for possession. But you never heard about grow operations getting busted. Basically, if the cops busted the grow operations, where the hell were they supposed to get what *they* needed to smoke? More importantly though, he didn't want any scumbags to know where his operation was. This was absolutely key for Uzi usage to remain unnecessary. Duncan accepted this explanation. Nothing could surprise him anymore.

When they stepped into the gym, Duncan was blown away by the size of the basketball court. *Under-fucking-ground,* he thought. *Un-fucking-real.* He found a ball lying on the court. Though he hadn't touched one in a few days, he could hear the ball begging him to make it go *splash.* He jogged over to the half-court line of the regulation-size court, where the ball lay. "Yo, Rennie," he shouted. "Splaaash!" Duncan dropped a bomb from just inside the half-court line. Nothing but net.

Rennie had not expected that. "Mista mudda fuckin Duncan. Damn, mon. Do it again!" he urged.

Duncan picked up the ball with a cocky smile, turned and fired. "Backboard!" he called. The ball banked against the glass and swished through the net. Rennie was very impressed. They shot around for a while and Duncan made at least ninety percent of his shots. Rennie wasn't bad either, making more than half of his. He had obviously spent a little time on his pristine court, Duncan surmised.

They shot around for close to an hour, just talking about everything from music to food to girls, until Rennie told Duncan that he needed to catch some sleep. "Let me show ya where ya con rest yer head, brudda-Duncan. Rennie guided him to one of the guest rooms. "Let me see, let me see," he said. "I tink dis one be veddy nice. Goodnight, brudda. My house – your house. Go whereva, eat whateva, do dis, do dat... just be *free*. Much love."

With that, Rennie dipped off down the hall, leaving his new friend in a state of profound amazement about what had occurred in his life since he had woken up that morning. Duncan opened the door to the guest room and turned on the light. The room was big. There was a private bathroom, a large oak desk that matched the dresser drawers and bedside tables, a thick white shag rug, mirrors on the ceiling, and beautiful art on the walls. But even more beautiful was what was lying on the plush king-size bed, rendering Duncan incapable of noticing any of the room's aforementioned features.

What grabbed Duncan's attention, so single-mindedly, was actually not a *what*, but a *who*. Ari, sans bikini, lay on the bed in front of him. "Hi," she cooed. *Wow*, he thought. *That's a new one.*

"Uh, hi." Duncan uttered. His jaw hung open, as he stared at the smooth, long, perfectly tanned left leg crossed over its right counterpart. Her chest was a work of art. C's. Perky. Her flat stomach was centered by a lovely pierced bellybutton. The piercing was all she wore. Duncan's dick stood at attention, like a soldier ready to go into battle. He felt it pushing against his jeans, begging to get out.

"C'mere, cutie." Her voice was velvet. "Have a seat."

With some trepidation, Duncan walked over and sat beside her. "What's *this* all about?" he asked.

"You're cute. I'm gonna show you a *real* good time, baby Dunks." Duncan hadn't even told *Rennie* his nickname. Ari had made that one up on her own. Being called by his nickname brought back a flood of memories. A nostalgic blast. *Sir Woopsy Dunks-a-lot*, Tessa would say.

"You know, that's my nickname back home."

"Oh yeah? *Duncan*. The shoes. I put two and two together." She giggled and stared into Duncan's eyes. Her eyes were the brightest green he'd ever seen.

"Jesus. You're one of the most beautiful girls I've ever seen, Ari."

"You're not so bad yourself, Dunks." She winked at him and started to rub his back. Then she began to kiss his neck. Then she moved down to his pants. Then Duncan had the best time since he and Tessa lost their virginity together.

Ari lit a cigarette. "Hey, Dunks, you wanna hear a joke?"

Duncan, in post-coital bliss, mumbled, "Yes… please."

"Okay," she said. "So, a chicken and an egg are lying in bed. The egg lights a cigarette and says, 'Well, I guess we know who came first.'"

Duncan burst out laughing. *Solid joke*, he thought. *Good stuff. I definitely dig this girl. Even if she's one of Rennie's "Girls with the Guns". He obviously set this shit up. But, fuck it. It was fuckin amazing.*

Duncan spoke with Ari for about half an hour before he nodded out. When he woke up, he was alone on the king-size bed. He thought, for a moment, that his fantastic sexcapade with the gorgeous blonde may have been nothing but a dream. But he quickly got his wits about him and realized that it was legit. *Way to go, Dunks,* Duncan thought to himself. "Way to go, Dunks," he said out loud. "Way to fuckin go!"

Feeling rather spritely, Duncan bounced out of bed and realized that he had no clue how to make his way around Rennie's underground mansion. He had learned from Ari that Rennie ran the island and was completely in control of the marijuana business there. He had been in charge of it for the past five years, since his father had passed away. His father had set up an empire that Rennie now controlled. *What luck*, Duncan thought. *What fucking luck. My new brudda-man Rennie brudda brudda-man is the fucking boss.* "I cannot fuckin believe I'm me," he said aloud. "I really cannot fuckin believe I'm me. I mean, really. How do I end up in these situations?"

"Fate, brudda Duncan. It is meant to be what it now is and what it surely will be, mon." Duncan was caught off guard by Rennie's response to what he thought was a rhetorical question that he was asking of himself. He did not know that Rennie was in the doorway.

"Oh shit, Rennie. I didn't know you were there, bro."

"Here I am and here I always will be, brudda." The two friends gripped hands and embraced. "Much love."

Rennie began to ask Duncan how his evening had been with Ari: "Did you have a good…" when a massive explosion rocked the house and the distinct sound of rapid Uzi gunfire echoed off the walls, coming from Rennie's grow-room. "Shit. What da fuck, mon!" Rennie shouted. "Duncan, mon, stay in da room, mon! Stay in da fucking room 'til I come back. Undastond?"

"I got it, dude."

Rennie took off down the hallway and raced up the stairs to the first floor of the basement, where the grow-room was. Duncan stopped him, calling, "Rennie!" Rennie turned around, a panicked look on his face. "Be careful, man. I don't wanna lose anyone else close to me. You're my man, dude. Be smart. Be safe."

Rennie's face lit up. "'Tis good to have someone care, mon. 'Tis real nice, Duncan, brudda." He ran slightly further down the hallway, then turned left into a stairwell and disappeared.

Chapter 16

Duncan sat hunched over on the bed he had shared with Ari the night before, his head buried in his hands. The door was locked, but fear racked his mind as his heart palpitated along with the rhythmic gunfire. He rose from the bed and began to pace around the room. "I can't fuckin believe I'm me," he said. "I cannot fuckin believe I'm me."

The gunfire continued for roughly five minutes, though fear and anticipation made it seem like hours. Then, it abruptly stopped. Silence. Duncan, heeding Rennie's insistence that he stay in the room until his return, stood stock-still and stared at the door. Since he didn't really believe in God, he wasn't one to usually pray. But, despite his usual religious ambivalence, he suddenly found himself doing just that. "Please God, let my friend be okay," he pleaded. "Please. I know I don't talk to you much, but if you're listening, please let Rennie live. He's a really good guy and he doesn't deserve this shit, man. C'mon God, hook it up for my boy. " Duncan figured that he should have thought of praying when Rennie first disappeared up the stairs, but his fear had been too overwhelming at the time for any kind of rational thought. Not that he found praying to be rational in and of itself, but he was at least able to think clearly enough to suppose that praying, however unlikely he found God's existence to be, might be a good idea if there was indeed a higher power.

After his appeal to the lord, Duncan stared at the door for about fifteen minutes until he heard a light knocking. At the sound, his heart tried to leap out of his chest. No one besides Rennie, maybe Ari, should know where he was hiding.

Though he feared the worst, he began to slowly walk to the door, his legs jellified, the hair on his arms and legs standing on end. Staring at the brass doorknob, he wondered who would greet him on the other side. This could really only go one of two ways, he figured. It would either be Rennie or Ari, there to guide him to safety, or it would be whoever it was whose presence had precipitated the explosion and subsequent gunfire. Option two was not palatable to Duncan whatsoever. He reached toward the doorknob with trepidation, not sure if he should actually turn it, when he suddenly heard a female voice behind him, urgently whispering his name.

At the sound of the voice, Duncan's heart lurched. He jumped and spun around to see Ari poking her head out of the closet, her beautiful green eyes bloodshot, her soft cheeks streaked with tears. "Duncan," she whispered loudly. "Duncan, c'mere. Hurry." Duncan ran across the room to her, his feet loudly striking the hardwood floor.

"Ari, what the..." he began to say far too loudly, when machine-gunfire started to pummel the door. Duncan didn't even bother looking back. He jumped into the closet, and Ari, as quickly and softly as she could, closed the door behind him. "Ari, what the fuck is going on?" he whispered as quietly as his voice would permit.

"No time," she said. "Follow me." Ari leapt up, tapped a small, barely noticeable knob on the closet ceiling, and silently landed back on the floor like a cat. Immediately, the right wall of the closet slid to the side and Ari motioned for Duncan to go down a hidden flight of stairs. *Holy shit*, Duncan thought. *This is fuckin bananas.* He raced past her and flew down the stairs. Ari tapped another small knob on the staircase wall, and quickly followed Duncan down. When she met him at the bottom, they turned left and ran down a long corridor. At the end of the corridor, there was a huge kitchen, and in its left corner stood a huge stainless steel refrigerator.

Ari dashed into the kitchen, past the pots and pans, knives and forks, spoons and ladles, and raced toward the shiny, metallic door. Next to it was a code panel, numbered one through nine, at which she stopped and punched a series of keys, sliding the door open and exposing a huge, well-lit room. Climbing a step, about a foot and a half high, Ari entered the room and said, "Dunks, baby, close the door behind you, please." Duncan followed her through, and, as per her request, closed the heavy metal door behind them.

With fuming, frustrated exasperation, Duncan shouted, "Ari, what the *fuck* is going on?"

"Rennie calls this the "Safe Room"," she said. "His dad put it in here, just in case something like this ever happened."

"Well, what the fuck happened?" Duncan asked. He was sweating. His cheeks were pink. His heart was pounding out of his chest.

"Tubby P's people," she said matter-of-factly, looking at the floor, offering no further explanation.

"Oh. Yes. Of course. Tubby P's people," Duncan said, sarcastically. "Who the fuck is Tubby P, Ari? I just got here, like, yesterday. Remember?"

"Yeah. Sorry, hon. This is really freaking me out too, ya know? Tubby P is the other guy, Dunks. There are two big pot dealers on this island: Rennie and Tubby P. Rennie doesn't give a shit about Tubby because he practically has a monopoly here. He has the best weed, the best prices, and the least hassle. He's got us girls doing all the business transactions for him, while he runs everything behind the scenes. That's why he's not afraid to go out and play music at the clubs." As Duncan stared at her with rapt attention, she continued, "Tubby P is the opposite. He's a crazy, paranoid, fat piece of shit who's obsessed with guns and money. Obviously, Rennie has guns and loves making money, but it's not the same. Tubby P's whole world revolves around defeating the competition."

"So, what just happened?" Duncan pleaded. "Ari, where's Rennie?"

"I don't know, baby. I don't know. Me and the girls were sitting upstairs, smoking a spliff and having a chat. All of a sudden, the door that goes aboveground gets flung open and some white guy steps in, bites the pin off a grenade and chucks it over towards where we're sitting. Luckily, Jessica, remember the Asian girl, with the blue bikini? She is *so* quick. She dives over at the grenade and grabs it and throws it back the way it came before it could go off. It exploded just before it could land back by the guy who threw it. The guy who threw it gets killed immediately, but other guys start pouring in, through the door. Me and the other girls start to fire the Uzis at them and there's gunfire going back and forth. I see Nicole get hit and she's down on the floor, bleeding so much out of her neck. She's dead. I have no time to get upset, 'cause there are more of them coming in through the door and I need to keep shooting. All of a sudden, Rennie is standing next to me. 'Go take Duncan to the Safe Room' he says. So, I turn around and run through one of the gazillion secret passages in this house, to the room where we were last night. That's the last of what I know happened to anybody, Dunks."

Duncan's jaw was on the floor. He couldn't believe what he was hearing. "So, you have no idea what happened to Rennie?" he asked.

"No idea," she said. "Oh, Dunks, baby, I'm so scared." She hugged him tightly. "Nothing like this ever happened before!" She had been so happy. Her life was so simple and so fun. As her world crumbled around her, she began to sob. Duncan didn't know what to say, so he just hugged her tightly. Then, desperately in need of an emotional escape from the nightmare from which there was no easy out, he instictively kissed her passionately. Firmly pressed together, they migrated over to one of the three beds in the Safe Room, and attempted to relieve their mutual stress by recreating the fun they had had the night before.

But, in that capacity, they were unsuccessful. While their lovemaking provided a temporary reprieve from the harsh reality of the present, once they were finished, they were forced to face the verity of the situation: they were in a room in the depths of Rennie's house, with nowhere to go, no idea what had happened to their friend, and no prospect for a resolution to the madness. They lay in the bed, tightly embraced in an unsuccessful attempt to comfort one another. The last thing Duncan heard before drifting off to sleep was the sound of Ari sniffling, as she quietly cried.

Chapter 17

Matty G flew through the air. Flew. Duncan's lob could barely be called a lob; it moved too fast and with too little arc, a laser of a pass. Matty caught the ball and threw it down so hard that the backboard continued to bounce up and down long after the ball smacked him in the back of the head as he sailed under the hoop.

The crowd went ape. It was a huge crowd, way bigger than they had ever seen in high school. The arena was massive. Duncan recognized it. The Staples Center. It was written everywhere. He saw that Matty G's jersey was yellow and purple. It said "Lakers" across the front. And it all seemed natural. Duncan *expected* to be there. He *expected* Matty G to be there, flying through the air like a bird. It was a beautiful sight, and it all seemed natural, them being there, playing in the NBA. They were the best. Of course they should be there.

"Ooooooooohhhhhh!" Matty G screamed. "Motherfuckers!"

"Ooooooooohhhhhh!" Duncan screamed. A huge smile spread across his face as he back-pedaled down the court.

Matty G sprinted back on defense, slapped Duncan five, and pumped his fist. But then, suddenly, he passed out, falling down on the court and slamming his head into the shiny wood. For Duncan, it all happened in slow motion. And not the *in-the-zone* kind of slow motion. *Actual* slow motion. And then, as soon as Matty's head smacked against the court, he miraculously bounced up like a rubber ball. And he didn't just bounce back up. He went *way* up, at least forty feet in the air, doing all manner of flips and spins.

As Matty G fell to the ground, Duncan's girlfriend, Tessa, miraculously appeared, completely out of nowhere, surfing on a giant wave in a neon-green bikini. Before Matty could hit the ground,

Duncan watched his beautiful girlfriend swoop in on the wave, and effortlessly catch his massive, 6'10" best friend in her tiny arms.

The wave that Tessa was surfing on continued to roll at Duncan, and he realized that it was going to smash into him. But just as the wave was about to pull him under, it stopped. Tessa hopped off the surfboard with Matty G still in her arms. She gently put him down, and the two of them stood before the wide-eyed Duncan whose jaw was on the floor. They both had huge smiles on their faces, and they both had their right arms stretched across their chests, index fingers pointing to the left. Duncan looked in that direction, and there stood Kobe Bryant, the best basketball player in the world, and apparently his Laker teammate. "Kobe?" Duncan said.

Casually, yet assertively, Kobe said, "Dunks, go the fuck home." "Yeah?" Duncan asked.

"Yeah, man," Kobe replied. "Fuck yeah."

Duncan woke up.

Chapter 18

When Duncan awoke, Ari was staring at him. "Hi," he said, his voice rough, after a solid sleep in the Safe Room.

"Hi," Ari said.

"So... What are we gonna do?" Duncan asked.

"Well," Ari started, "Rennie had been meaning to install camera equipment in here. But he never got around to it. Nothing like this has happened since his Dad died. That was, like, twelve years ago, and even when he was alive, nobody had broken into the basement in, like, at least ten years. That's what Rennie told me. I wish the equipment were here so we could just know what the fuck's going on in the house." She sighed heavily.

"Well," Duncan said, "I'm not waiting in this room anymore. According to this clock, I was asleep for about nine hours." He pointed at the digital clock on the desk, near the Safe Room's entrance. "I think we've been here long enough."

"No, Duncan. Rennie told us to stay here."

"Well, I think it's been long enough, Ari. If he knew that we were going to be here and he had everything under control, he would have come down already. Something bad probably happened. You know your way around the secret halls in here, right?"

"Yeah," she said. "Rennie gave me a map when I first started working for him, and I memorized everywhere there's a private path. That's what Rennie calls the secret hallways. *Private paths.*"

"Well, let's roll then," Duncan said. Ari tentatively went to the door and opened the lock. Before she could push the door open, Duncan put his arm out and held her back. "I'll go first," he said.

"Thanks," she said, and smiled.

Duncan pushed the heavy door open. Silence. "Looks clear," he said. Holding Ari's hand, he walked into the kitchen.

"Okay," Ari said, "follow me." Ari led the way towards the stairwell they had come from, but she passed by the one that led to the room where Duncan had stayed the night before. She went to the end of the hallway, then rounded a corner. She jumped up and tapped a small, hardly visible button on the ceiling, and the wall slid away, revealing yet another *private path*. This one was not a staircase, but rather a long hallway. "Come on," Ari said, and Duncan quickly followed her through the wall. Ari tapped another tiny button on the wall as they entered the hallway. The wall slid shut.

For several minutes, Duncan and Ari walked down the hallway. Duncan couldn't believe how long it was. They eventually reached a staircase at the end of the it. "This is why I wanted to stay in the Safe Room for a while," Ari said. "This is our only way out of here right now and it goes directly to the grow-room. We'll have to go through there to get to another private path. I'm just praying there's nobody in there."

"I guess we're about to find out. 'Cause I wanna get the fuck *out* of here," Duncan said. "I wanna get the fuck outta here now!"

Ari and Duncan climbed the stairs and came to a wall. Ari inhaled deeply and let out a long sigh before tapping a button on the wall. Duncan stepped in front of her as the wall slid open to reveal the grow-room. Duncan poked his head through the door and saw no one. "C'mon," he said.

Ari grabbed his hand, and they ran across the room, which absolutely reeked of weed and was full of half-burnt plants that had been torched by the grenade. Ari tapped another button, and in moments they were through the wall and into the private path they needed to use to escape from the house.

They continued to run down the long hallway and finally came to another staircase. "This is it," Ari said. "Let's go." They ran up the stairs and Ari hit another of the barely visible buttons. The wall at the top of the staircase opened up, revealing the inside of a small shack. They stepped into the shack and Ari opened the door, revealing a wooded area outside. She was wearing flip-flops and still had on nothing but her "work uniform", the red bikini. That was what she had been wearing when the attack occurred, and as there were no clothes for her to change into in the Safe Room, she had to remain half-naked throughout her and Duncan's ordeal. "Duncan," she said, "we should stay off the road. If one of those guys drives down it and sees me walking in this thing, he might recognize me and we'll be screwed."

"You're right," Duncan said. "Can we get to town by walking through the woods?"

"Yeah," she said. "But it's gonna take a while."

"How long you think?"

"Probably, like, two hours."

"That's not so bad I guess."

"Considering what we just went through, I'd walk for a month," she said.

"True," Duncan replied. "Very true. Let's move. I wanna get as far from this fuckin place as possible."

Ari and Duncan trekked through the woods, which, unfortunately for Ari, were full of brambles. Her legs were covered with an array of cuts and scrapes. But she was a tough girl. Over the course of the hike, Ari told Duncan how she had become so. She came from a family of eleven children with a very abusive father. She told Duncan how he had lined up all of his kids and drunkenly beat them with his belt after coming home drunk. This would go on several times a week, she said, all throughout her youth. When she was sixteen, she and her sister, who was only ten months older than her, ran away from home for good. They bought plane tickets to the island and had been there for the past three years. Her sister, she said, was a bartender in town. That was who they were going to see first when they got there.

Duncan had never known someone who had been an abused child, at least not someone who openly discussed it. He expressed his sympathy, but she shrugged it off and suggested that perhaps it had made her a better person, more capable of tolerating life's difficulties, such as the disaster they had just experienced. Duncan nodded in contemplative agreement. He thought of the good life that he had recently left, the supportive and loving family, the beautiful and sweet girlfriend, and the promising athletic career. *Damn*, he thought, *I've got it good.*

They continued to walk until they eventually emerged from the woods, onto a narrow dirt road. In the distance, about three hundred yards away, they could see the town. "Aaaah," Ari sighed. "There it is. Almost there." Duncan was relieved himself. He had had just about enough of their trek through the bramble-filled woods, fearing the possibility that they were being followed by Tubby P's men. Ari grabbed Duncan's hand and pulled his face to hers for a long kiss. "We made it, Dunks baby," she said. Duncan smiled and gripped her hand. But he couldn't help thinking that it was the wrong hand he was gripping.

Chapter 19

Duncan pulled open the door to The Shanty, the bar where Ari's sister worked and the place where he and Rennie had first met. It seemed like a lifetime ago. But it had only been the day before last, and Duncan could hardly believe it.

"After you," he said. Ari curtsied, and led him through the door into the low-lit barroom. Behind the bar was a stunning young woman who bore a strong resemblance to Ari. *That must be her sister*, he thought.

"Oh… my… God! Ari, what the fuck happened to you, honey?" the young woman shouted, her voice full of surprise, concern, and fear.

"Jaime, this is Duncan. Duncan… Jaime," Ari said, beginning with an introduction so as not to have him awkwardly standing there while she detailed the incredible events of the past twelve-or-so hours.

"Nice to meet you," Duncan said.

"Who the fuck is he?" Jaime replied. "What the fuck did you do to my sister, you little piece of shit?"

Before Duncan could reply with a plea of innocence, Ari angrily shouted at her sister, "Jaime, shut the fuck up! He didn't do anything! Relax. I'll explain." Jaime looked Duncan over suspiciously, but gave him the benefit of the doubt as she listened to her sister explain who Duncan was and what had happened.

After hearing what Ari and Duncan had been through, Jaime raised her jaw off the floor and said, "Oh…shit." Then she looked at the bar's entrance door and said, "Oh…shit."

Duncan and Ari turned around. Duncan didn't know who he was looking at, but judging by the tone of Jaime's voice, the very fat man standing at the door was not someone whom any of them wanted anything to do with. Tubby P himself. Holding a six-shooter with a longer barrel than any of them had ever seen. Strolling. Casual. A gold rope around his neck. Very fat. Duncan had expected Tubby P to be a somewhat portly, dark black guy. He had envisioned a chubby version of Rennie really. No. This man could not have weighed less than 400 pounds. He barely fit through the front door. And he was a black albino. So fat and so very pale. *Wow*, Duncan thought, *that's a new one*.

"Well… well… well," Tubby P said very slowly, leaving a significant gap between each 'well'. "Hello, ladies. I think you better come with me."

Jaime and Ari didn't even stop to argue. They compliantly walked towards the door. Ari turned around and looked at Duncan, with a forlorn expression on her face. She was about ten feet away. "Bye," she mouthed, silent to Duncan's ears. Duncan just stared, wide-eyed and unable to move, as the girls were strong-armed by Tubby P's men and pulled out the front of the bar. There was nothing he could have done. Tubby P's men, all three of them, were at least six-foot-four. And brawny, to say the least.

Once they were out the front door, Duncan followed. He watched as the girls were stuffed into the back of a BMW, which then peeled out and sped away. Duncan thought about the dream he had while sleeping next to Ari in the safe room. He thought about what Kobe had said. Maybe going home was a good idea. As beautiful and exciting as it was, he had had just about enough of the island.

Chapter 20

Duncan sat aboard a commercial airliner, three thousand feet in the air, almost halfway home. His eyes were closed. His head rested on a small pillow he had propped up against the cabin wall. *Wow*, Duncan thought. He repeated the word in his head over and over, rhythmically, like a mantra.

And then he started to laugh, causing the little old lady he was sitting next to to lean as far as she could from the oddly sudden outburst. What caused Duncan's laughter was that it had just hit him how long he had been away.

He had left early in the morning on Friday. He met Rennie that night. They had shot some ball. He had slept with Ari. He had slept until Saturday afternoon, and then the attack occurred. Saturday night he and Ari had spent in the Safe Room. Sunday morning, they escaped the underground mansion and trekked through the woods. That same morning, the girls had been kidnapped.

Sunday night, Duncan took flight.

"Hello?" Tessa Moya said, not recognizing the number on her cell phone.

"Hi, baby," Duncan said, from the airport payphone.

"Oh my god!" Tessa shouted into the phone. "Oh my god, Duncan, are you alright? I've missed you so much." When you're seventeen, a weekend can seem like an eternity. But then, who knows what can happen on any given weekend? Strange enough circumstances can make a few days seem like an eternity to anyone.

"Yeah, babe," he replied, "I'm fine."

"Where the hell *are* you?"

"I'm at the airport, babe. Can you come pick me up?"

"Of course," she said. "I'll be there in a half hour. Where should I pick you up?"

"I'll be outside Terminal C."

"Okay, baby. I'll be there."

"Thanks, babe," he said. "See ya soon."

Tessa put down the homework she had been working on when Duncan called, and dashed out the door. She got into her silver Jetta and backed out of the driveway. It took her just about the half hour she had estimated to get to the airport. She pulled onto the off-ramp for Terminal C and there he was, her love. She hadn't expected to see him for a long time. The thought, as painful as it was, had even crossed her mind that she might never see him again. She could barely believe that he was back so soon. But there he was.

She pulled up to the curb, jumped out of the car and ran to Duncan, throwing her arms around him and kissing him as hard as she could without hurting him or herself. "Oh, baby," she said, "I thought I would never see you again." She was crying.

"Don't cry, babe," he said. "I'm right here."

"You didn't respond to any of my Facebook messages!" she said, pouting.

"I didn't even see a computer while I was there," he replied.

"Well, you should have found one! And, by the way, where the hell did you go anyway?"

"You know what, babe? I'm sorry, but I really don't even wanna talk about it. I'm here now. That's all that matters."

"Okay, baby," she said, though she had every intention of squeezing the information out of him later on, at some point. After all he'd been through, with Matty G dying, she wasn't about to press him for information. She was a good girl like that. Her respect of his privacy was something that Duncan loved about Tessa. And the complex story of his trip contained aspects that he was not prepared to discuss.

Although he could surely have told her most of what had happened, he was not about to talk about Ari. And Ari was an integral part of what had happened.

Tessa was respectful of his privacy, but she was also a jealous girl. Duncan was a star in high school, and plenty of girls would gladly steal him from her. She wouldn't have described herself as being suspicious of him, but she had her doubts about his fidelity. Duncan was usually faithful to her, except for a few encounters, but, in his mind, he was pretty much a good boy. And, truth be told, he had had no intention of coming home anytime soon.

Anyway, he was home now, and he couldn't have been happier to see his girlfriend, who obviously was as ready to pick up where they had left off as he was. Upon seeing her, he realized how in love he was with the girl. As hot as Ari was, in Duncan's mind, she could never light a candle to Tessa.

Tessa brought Duncan home. She gave him a kiss, and asked if he would be in school the next day. "Yeah, babe," he said. "I'll be there."

"You gonna pick me up?" she asked.

"You know it."

Chapter 21

"Duncan!" Mrs. Lipton screamed. "Oh, Duncan!" She threw her arms around her beloved son. "Oh, Duncan, where have you been?"

"Nowhere, Mom. I just had to get away for a few days."

"Nowhere? That doesn't sound too exciting." Mrs. Lipton smiled.

"It wasn't," he replied.

Mrs. Lipton incredulously looked at her son. "Okay, honey," she said, still sympathetic for Duncan's loss of his best friend. She wasn't about to start a fight with him about the specifics of where he had gone. She understood. She was a cool mom like that. She seemed to always understand. She didn't press him for information that he didn't want to give. Duncan knew that he could tell her anything, and, for the most part, he told her most of what was going on his life. But when he didn't want to say what was happening, she didn't insist. "Doug!" she shouted, to Duncan's dad, who was upstairs.

"Yeah, hon?" he hollered back.

"Doug, Duncan's home!" Immediately, Duncan heard his dad hustle down the stairs. He appeared in the doorway, and stopped still for a moment to look at his only son. He and his wife loved their son to death, and they didn't know when they would see or hear from him again. He had just disappeared, a very un-Duncan thing to do.

Mr. Lipton broke out in a huge smile, opened his arms wide, and walked over to Duncan, wrapping him in a strong embrace.

"Hi, Dad," Duncan said.

"Hey, boy. We missed you."

"I missed you too."

"Where the fuck did you go, kid?" Mr. Lipton casually inquired, a curious smile on his face.

"Nowhere really."

"Nowhere, huh? How was the weather?"

"Ha-Ha," Duncan said, as he rolled his eyes and half-smiled. "The weather was fine. I really don't wanna talk about it though. I just needed a couple days."

"Alright, boy, alright. Just glad to have ya home, you crazy son-of-mine."

"Yeah, I'm glad to be here too."

Always one to be a stickler about her son's education, Mrs. Lipton said, "You're going to school tomorrow, right, honey?"

"Yeah, I'm goin."

"Good," she said. "Well, it's past eleven. You oughta get to bed."

"Yeah," Duncan replied, yawning, at the mention of sleep. "Yeah, I'm gonna go to bed. I'll see you in the morning."

"Okey-dokey. I love you, honey-pie," Mrs. Lipton said, wrapping Duncan in a powerful hug. "I love you so much."

"I love you too, Mom. Love ya, Dad," he said, and pulled his dad into the bear hug. For relatively small people, they had produced a pretty big son, and his arms easily encircled the two of them.

Once in his room, Duncan stared at himself in the full-length mirror, on his closet door. He thought about what he had seen in that mirror the morning he and Matty G had woken up to find all that money on the floor. He couldn't believe what he'd seen since that day. "What... the... fuck?" he said, quietly. "I mean, really, what the fuck?" He shook his head and turned from the mirror. He stripped down to his boxers, climbed into bed, closed his eyes, and said, quietly, "I cannot fuckin believe I'm me." He fell asleep immediately.

Chapter 22

"You've got your whole future ahead of you," Kobe said. "It's time to step it up, man." Duncan knew that Kobe was right.

Chapter 23

Duncan picked up Tessa and drove to school. They walked through the door, as usual. They kissed as they parted ways, to go to their first period classes, as usual. Duncan felt as though he'd lived a lifetime in the past half-week, but no one at school knew anything of it, so no one had thought particularly much of his being gone. He had only missed school on Friday, and anyone who knew him chalked that up to the fact that his best friend had just died, so *naturally* he didn't want to go to school. Of all places, for God's sake. That was definitely reasonable, and it was reason enough for no one to bother him about what he had done that past weekend. So, the island remained his own little secret.

Over the course of the day, Duncan sat with a bemused smile on his face. He knew what drew near. *'Twill be mine rebirth,'* he thought, doing some corny old-English speak in his head, thinking about what he was about to do to his teammates, at the tryout after school. Duncan had decided that he was going to dominate. Simple as that. He knew that he didn't need Matty G. He could get it done himself. And this was his chance. This year. It was October, and it was game time.

The tryout started at 3:30, with a swish from Duncan. His shot was from halfway between the half-court line and the three-point line at the top of the key. He held out his arms in a "Who, me?" kind of way. His teammates, and potential teammates laughed and shook their heads. And it didn't stop there. Lay-ups. Dunks. Mid-range J's. Whatever. Even hookies. Why not?

And so Duncan was unanimously voted team captain. And so he dominated that season. Broken ankles. Buzzer beaters. Crazy angles. Lobs and lasers. He averaged forty-five points a game. Sixteen assists. Eighteen rebounds. Five steals. Four dunks. Three blocks. Great stats. That's that.

And, as Eastfield played in the state's most prestigious division, that made Duncan the best player in the state. And that made his life a recruiting circus. He heard from all the big coaches. This guy. That guy. And the other guy too. He liked his options.

He had heard from some other coaches too. Coaches who weren't supposed to talk to him. Coaches in the NBA. It seemed he was a lock to be a first-round draft pick. But not at this year's draft. The rules, by this time, forbade eighteen-year-olds from joining The League, which meant that Duncan would have to play one year either in college or overseas. Duncan, being Duncan, decided to go overseas. To play pro in the Netherlands. In Amsterdam.

Chapter 24

"So, where do you wanna go?" Duncan's new agent had asked. When the recruitment circus blew up, Duncan knew that he was going to need an agent, so he got one, a shark named Lee Bernstein.

"I don't know. Amsterdam?" Duncan laughed. It was flippant, just a joke. He doubted that they even had a pro league in Amsterdam.

As if reading Duncan's mind, Lee said, "Yeah, they've got a league there, buddy boy. You want me to make that happen?"

"Um, yeah, I guess, I mean," Duncan thought aloud, trying to give an immediate answer to a very important question. "I mean… fuck yeah. They've got that red-light district. And weed's legal, right? These are good things."

"You're an idiot," Lee laughed. He smiled and picked up the phone. He saw much of himself in young Duncan Lipton. *Nice kid*, he thought, as he made the call.

The team was called the Blue Devils. There would be no tryout necessary. Duncan's game video spoke for itself. And now he would be making a cool hundred thousand dollars for this one season abroad before he was eligible for the NBA. His parents had encouraged him to go to college, saying that it was a once-in-a-lifetime opportunity to get a good education and broaden his horizons before going pro. But Duncan thought his horizons would be plenty broad over in Amsterdam, getting paid to play basketball, smoke weed legally, and poke around the red-light district a little bit. Just to see though. Tessa was coming too.

After his fiasco on the island, Duncan decided that he was really in love with Tessa, so there was no way he was going to be without her.

Tessa wanted to go to college, but she figured a year off couldn't hurt. Being in Europe would be a great experience, she guessed.

The two of them got an apartment on a street called Lijnsbangracht. They rented it from a cool guy named Kjetl (pronounced Shyetull), who was thirty-five years old, and in the middle of building a giant winged suit for the Burning Man Festival in Nevada, which he was planning on attending in a few months. He lived in the apartment beneath them.

The apartment was fully furnished, had two flat-screen TV's, and all the amenities. The fridge was even full of some delicious wheat beer. Duncan always particularly liked sweet wheat beer, and the Netherlands was chock-full of the stuff. Kjetl also had a number of musical instruments. He had an electric guitar, two acoustic guitars, an electric bass, an acoustic drumset, an electric drumset, and a beautiful baby-grand piano, all of which he kept in his small, one-car garage. This made Duncan very happy. In addition to his basketball prowess, Duncan could also play musical instruments reasonably well. His parents had pressed them upon him since he was five years old; he was a decent pianist and dabbled with all the other instruments at Kjetl's apartment. This would provide him with much entertainment during the seven months that he would be playing in Amsterdam. But there would be much more entertainment than that. He was damn sure of it. This was Amsterdam. *Fucking Amsterdam*!

Kjetl had a crazy neighbor named Herman who lived next door. Herman, who was sixty-five years old, grew beautiful marijuana plants on his roof, and spent much of his day researching conspiracy theories on the internet and making anti-Semitic comments about how the Jews were responsible for the world's financial woes. But although Duncan didn't share Herman's outrageous belief system or his faith in the net's conspiratorial accuracy, he enjoyed jamming with the older man, who was a very talented guitarist. And the weed that he grew on his roof was like nothing he had ever seen (outside of Rennie's basement). The purples and reds completely overwhelmed the green. *Wow*, Duncan thought, when he saw the copious amount of bud nearly ready to be harvested. *I hope Rennie's okay.*

Duncan, Tessa, Kjetl, and Herman smoked a giant spliff (not like Rennie's, which was the most outrageous concoction Duncan could imagine, but still huge nonetheless), and Duncan sat down at the electric drumset to jam with Herman on guitar and Kjetl on bass. It was the best jam Duncan had ever been involved in, crisp, tight, melodic, and in the pocket. The two older men were impressed with young Duncan's skills. He was clearly a renaissance man. Great athlete. Talented musician. Nice kid. And the girlfriend. She was the kind of girl who makes old men nostalgic for a past that never existed. Kjetl and Herman definitely took a liking to Duncan, and Duncan liked them (as long as Herman kept his conspiracy theories to himself). Life was looking good.

After the jam, Duncan said to Tessa, who had been casually dancing to the jam in the corner of the garage, "Babe, you wanna go for a walk? Do a little exploring of this lovely city?"

"Sure, baby," she said.

They said goodbye to Kjetl and Herman and began a walk down Lijnsbaangracht. "You hungry, babe?" Duncan asked.

"Yeah, kinda," she said.

"Cool, let's hit up this place," he said, pointing to a spot on the corner that had a lamb roasting in the window and a sign that said "Shwarma".

"Okay," she agreed. They walked in and ordered two shwarmas, whatever that was. It turned out to be one of the most delicious things that either of them had ever tasted, sort of like a sloppy joe, made of saucy, chopped, roasted lamb on warm pita bread.

After they ate, they continued to walk down the street, holding hands, smiling and laughing at their good fortune. Amsterdam was composed of streets that lined canals, branching out from its circular center, like rays from the sun. The city's layout could make it a difficult place to navigate, due to its one-way streets and lack of a practical grid. Luckily though, there were few cars. Transportation basically, for most people, consisted of bicycles. The streets were lined with them. As it was legal to smoke weed, and space was allocated for hard-drug users to legally inject away from other citizens, crime was minimal there. The main source of crime was bums stealing bikes. The city had the friendliest vibe that the young couple had ever seen, and they couldn't have been happier to be there.

English was very prevalent in Amsterdam, though Dutch was the country's official language. Catering to heavy tourist trade, many stores had English names. As they walked, Duncan and Tessa came upon a store called "The Spot". It was a head shop, full of bongs, and other smoking apparatuses. And they didn't have any of those stupid signs that they have in American head shops that say that the products there are explicitly for smoking tobacco. Laughable. Who smokes tobacco out of a bong? In Amsterdam, they didn't beat around the bush.

Duncan and Tessa went inside the store and poked around. Duncan looked around at the bongs while Tessa checked out the heady jewelry, all hemp and stoner symbols. She saw a bunch of marijuana leaf earrings that she thought were cute and might be fun/funny to wear occasionally. They seemed appropriate in this place. Duncan saw hookahs that were the biggest he'd ever seen and some clever smoking devices, including bukkets (accordion-like contraptions meant to simulate a gravity bong, a conceptually simple, yet overly complicated, smoking device that gives you such a big hit that the head-rush wraps your brain in a thick cloud after just one rip) and gas-mask/bong combination pieces that would have looked more appropriate in a war zone than on a pothead's face. *Wow*, Duncan thought. *That's a new one. Fucking gas-mask bongs. Jeez.* This thought was immediately followed by the rhetorical thought: *Did I actually just think the word Jeez? Jeez.* Jeez.

But then, something much more interesting caught Duncan's eye. Under the glass countertop, by the register, were boxes of "magic mushrooms". Back home, his friends called them 'shrooms or boomers. "Magic mushrooms" was an archaic term of an older generation of heads. But, apparently, in Amsterdam, the marketers of the product liked to keep it old school. Duncan had tried 'shrooms twice, eating an eighth of an ounce each time. One time, he wrapped the disgusting, dried mushrooms in a peanut butter and jelly sandwich. The other time, he wrapped them in a slice of pizza. He hadn't thrown up either time, but he largely failed at his mission to make the ingestion process tolerable.

Duncan also hadn't found himself tripping in the least, either of the two times that he had taken them. He thought that maybe he was immune to mushrooms or something. However, these wet, interesting-looking mushrooms, being sold in eighths, quarters, halves, and ounces, were worth a shot. *Hell*, he thought. *We're in Amsterdam. I gotta go for it.* They didn't have anything particularly important that they had to do that day, as Duncan didn't have to go to a practice yet, not for another two days, and Tessa's schedule was as wide open as it could possibly be. *Fuck it*, Duncan thought. "Baby, look at these crazy boomers," he said. "Let's get some and go to the park."

Something about Tessa: she was, in every sense of the term, a "down-girl", as in she was down to do anything. She liked to smoke weed, get into whatever trouble her boyfriend was getting into, and even was down with going to Amsterdam for seven months, while Duncan played his one professional season overseas. Why not? Life was short, she figured. She was all about experiencing what the world had to offer. And if she didn't go with him, there was no way that she and Duncan could have possibly stayed together. It was worth it to her to postpone her continued education for the time being because she wanted to try and make sure that their love didn't die at the hands of *the curse,* the one that belies the disintegration of so many long-distance relationships.

Basically, as Tessa had been down to go with Duncan to Amsterdam, she was down to experience the place the same way he was. So, off they went to a little park near the area just off Lijnsbangracht that had the little head-shops, convenience stores, and boutiques. They each had a quarter-ounce of 'shrooms. They each had shwarma. The shwarma's strong and spicy taste, Duncan hoped, might overpower the grotesque taste of the mushrooms.

Unbeknownst to him, there was a fact about his girlfriend that he had heretofore never really paid attention to: she was a *huge* mushroom enthusiast. As a food, that is. In soup. On pizza. As a sauce enhancer. Whatever. She loved mushrooms. But she had yet to experiment with the psychedelic kind.

Tessa ate her quarter-ounce in about thirty seconds, and, to Duncan's amazement, actually seemed to genuinely enjoy them raw. It took Duncan, however, nearly fifteen minutes to get his down. He had ordered his shwarma particularly spicy, to kill the mushroom taste, and it had been a rather successful strategy. It just took a little while. The spiciness was making him sweat, and eating his meal required quite a bit of water and more than a few napkins, to clean the messy hands and face that generally accompany the otherwise delightful meal. The napkins were also necessary for him to dab at his beading forehead.

As it had taken Duncan longer than Tessa to get the 'shrooms down, and she was only slightly more than half his weight, she started tripping fifteen to twenty minutes before he did. But that fifteen to twenty minutes, preceding the start of his own trip, was a trip in and of itself. Tessa was "shroomin' something fierce, and Duncan wasn't sure what to do with his bugged-out girlfriend. *Shit*, he thought. *She's losin' it. My girlfriend is fuckin' bananas.* Because he was busy dealing with Tessa, and because he had never succeeded in getting high from 'shrooms before, Duncan barely noticed the warm, happy feeling building inside his body. Had either of his two previous attempts to trip on mushrooms been successful, he would have had a frame of reference on which to base his own mental state and just how out of touch with reality he was rapidly becoming.

That unawareness, however, was short-lived. Within a couple of minutes, there was *no question whatsoever* as to whether or not the mushrooms were, for once, taking effect. Definitely *no question whatsoever*. But had there indeed been a question as to whether or not he was feeling the 'shrooms, Duncan's answer would have been that he was straight fucked off his ass. As everything started to change, and he began to experience the "magic" for the first time, he began to feel a bit overwhelmed by the power-packed vegetables with which he had just supplemented his shwarma. What they were doing to him, visually and aurally, was no less than rocking his world. The madness he was now experiencing prompted the recurring thought that, of late, had seemingly taken a permanent residence at the front of his mind and a summer home on the tip of his tongue: *Wow*, Duncan thought. *That's a new one.*

Chapter 25

Tessa was speaking out loud, a little *too* loud, in AOL or text message-style abbreviations as she laughed hysterically at the fact that she was doing so. "OMG!" she shouted. "LOL!" she barked, after she was already "laughing out-loud" (what the acronym stood for). The fact that she was already laughing only served to increase Duncan's belief that Tessa had in fact gone bananas. She was yelling out all of the standard acronyms that she could think of. "BTW", she said, "WTF?", "LMAO", "LMFAO", "SMDB", all the classics, etc. Haha. Lol. ☺

Wow, Duncan thought, as he watched his girlfriend act like a 14 year-old, albeit harmless, lunatic. *That's a new one.* But ten to fifteen minutes later, Tessa's ridiculous display was lost on him, as he himself slipped into the mind-state that made the moniker "magic mushrooms" suddenly altogether seem to be the most appropriate name for the foul-tasting, psychedelic fungus, straight from the womb of mother earth, rather than a lab of mad scientists he thought were hell-bent on forcing an epidemic of addiction.

Green. Everything was green. Tessa was green. There were many different shades, but everything was definitely straight up green. *Going green*, Duncan thought. *Hilarious. Get me a fucking Prius!* Actually, Duncan shouted that out loud. A green family stared at the tall, cackling American. Duncan stared back. "Jolly green fucking family," he laughed hysterically.

The green mother covered the ears of her young, green daughter. "Fucking asshole!" she shouted in a Dutch equivalent. But Duncan didn't hear her, not that he would have understood her words anyway, although he probably would have gleaned the sentiment. However, he had moved on to staring at some surprisingly hot girls, who were sexily defying the fact that they were green. Duncan was impressed. And *his* greenness was just as potent as everyone else's. He was no exception, and so he decided that he ought not be judgmental. He wouldn't want to be a self-hating green.

Shit, Duncan thought. *Where the hell is Tessa?* While soaking up the sights of this unfamiliar green world, he had forgotten all about his girlfriend as he lost track of time. He had in fact not seen her for ten to fifteen minutes. Were she sober, Duncan knew, he would not have to worry for his resourceful, intelligent girlfriend to make her way back to Linjsbangraacht. However, Tessa was not sober. She could be anywhere. *And she's fucking green*, Duncan thought. *Fucking green! It's illegal to be green!*, he said to himself. *Wait a minute. I have no fucking clue what the fuck is going on. Did I take shrooms? I'm buggin'. Where the fuck is Tessa? Where are my shoes? Where are my shoes?* "Where the hell are my fucking shoes!?!?" Duncan shouted out-loud, in frustration.

"On your *fookin* feet, you fookin Yank *wanka!*" a huge, testy Scotsman, with bright red hair and beard, informed him. Duncan looked down at his feet. Nike Dunks.

"Why, thank you, kind sir," he said cheerily, as he, at that moment, realized that nothing was green anymore and that he had the good fortune of still having his shoes, despite his never having taken them off in the first place. The big, red Scot nodded. Suddenly, the huge man melted and transformed into the Wicked Witch of the West, from *The Wizard of Oz,* right before Duncan's baffled eyes.

Well, I'm just out of my fucking mind, aren't I?, Duncan rhetorically asked himself. He knew the answer. *I think I ate too many of those 'shrooms.* Then he puked. Shwarma everywhere. And everything was green again. And Duncan was convinced it was St. Patrick's day, so he bowed to the disgusted Scotsman, and took off, setting out with the purpose of getting as much green beer as he could get his hands on and capturing a leprechaun. It was, after all, a once-a-year occasion.

This was the sequence of absurd thoughts that went through his head. He knew he was a mess though; that was good. Forgetting that you are on 'shrooms and thinking that you are in a normal state of mind, when you're really toe-up and out of touch with reality, is a huge problem and can get you into a lot of trouble.

Tessa Moya, for instance, trying 'shrooms for the first time (and particularly good 'shrooms at that, legally purchased and potently grown) had no idea that she was high. All she was thinking about was how it was bullshit that people said that unicorns don't exist when there was a family of five of them sitting right in front of her. *God, people are so stupid and ignorant*, she thought. She meant it. Because of the family of five right before her eyes. She decided to share this incredible information with Duncan.

Tessa looked to her right. No Duncan. She looked to her left. Still no Duncan. She spun around. Duncan was gone. She called out for him. He didn't answer. Completely overwhelmed by the powerful mushrooms, Tessa sat down on the grass and cried. The unicorns had disappeared and there were red and yellow swirls rotating all around her. She closed her eyes, only to find vivid visuals, this time purple and green swirls dancing behind her eyelids. She felt like she was sinking, and she had never felt so alone in all her life. *Duncan, where are you?* she thought.

Chapter 26

While Tessa tripped balls, and cried herself to sleep on the park grass, Duncan found himself getting onto a bus which, according to a very old, hunchbacked man, would take him to a liquor store where he could buy all the green beer that his heart desired.

He stepped onto the bus and looked at the driver. The man was green, and his head was about five times bigger than his head should have been. "Woah," Duncan said. The driver said something in Dutch that Duncan didn't understand, although, even in his hallucinatory state, he knew that the driver was asking for the fare. He took out a scrunched up wad, paid the driver, and received some coins for change, which he stuck in the back pocket of his jeans. He looked down the length of the bus, at the fifteen or so passengers. They were all as big-headed as the driver. "Woah," Duncan said. "What a bunch of fucking heads." The passengers, who were in fact a bunch of normal-looking people with normal-sized heads, all looked at Duncan suspiciously. The collective thought was more or less: *What in God's name is this guy on? Mushrooms?* Good guess. The Dutch know what's up.

He plopped down in a seat and rubbed his eyes. Colors swirled behind his closed eyelids. *Where am I going?* he thought.

"To the store," said an enormous-headed old woman.

"Why thank you, madam," Duncan said, in a posh English accent.

In reality, like the rest of the passengers, the old woman sitting on the bus was not big headed. Nor for that matter was she old. Nor female. It was actually a young man in a suit. The young man looked at Duncan and said, in Dutch, what was easily interpretable as "Excuse me?"

"Thank you, madam," Duncan replied, "for reminding me of my

destination." Again he was speaking in his jokingly British accent to the sharply dressed young man, who Duncan was positive was actually an old woman with a dome the size of a Georgia watermelon.

In Dutch, the young man said, "What the fuck are you talking about, asshole?" He was pissed.

However, Duncan, in his stupor, did not recognize the anger in the young man's tone of voice, or the look on his face. The old woman with the big head was babbling something unintelligible, as far as Duncan could tell.

The bus pulled to a stop, and the young man in the suit lunged at Duncan, grabbed his shirt, and hauled him off the bus. Before Duncan could react in any way, the young man threw a vicious haymaker at Duncan's face. Duncan dropped like a sack of potatoes, and his assailant jumped back on the bus, just as the doors were closing, with a Dutch shout of, "Go fuck yourself!"

For about ten minutes, lying next to the curb in front of the bus stop, Duncan was knocked out cold.

Chapter 27

"What'd you do last night, Dunks?" Kobe asked. He and Duncan stood at the bus stop.

"I had a crazy night, dude. Crazy night. Me and my girl took 'shrooms. I got on this bus 'cause I just wanted to go to the liquor store, and I ended up getting lost 'cause I had no fucking idea where I was. When I got on the bus, everybody was green and they had giant heads. Some old lady got really mad at me and punched me in the grill and threw me off the bus. That's all I remember."

"What about your girl? Tessa, right?" Kobe asked.

"Oh, shit," Duncan said. *What happened to Tessa?* He didn't know. He got punched, and then immediately he was standing next to Kobe Bryant at the bus stop. The sun was shining. Had Tessa made it back to Lijnsbangracht? Duncan had no idea.

"You seen Matty G?" Kobe asked. "I ain't seen him since yesterday, man."

Duncan was silent. He knew that his best friend had died. At the same time, he knew that G was alive. He was confused. "G died, dude," Duncan said. "He died a while ago."

"Nah," said Kobe. "We were chillin' with him in the Red Light District yesterday. You don't remember? I mean, I knew you were kinda tipsy, but I didn't think you were gonna black out like that. You're kind of a lightweight, rookie," Kobe laughed.

Baffled by what Kobe was saying, Duncan said, "Yesterday? What the fuck? Kobe, I am so fucking confused, bro. Where do you think he is?"

"I don't know, man," Kobe said. Maybe with the rest of the team at the hotel. Maybe he's still with Ari.

"What team?" Duncan incredulously asked.

Kobe laughed. "You stupid, kid."

"No, really, Kobe, what team are you talking about? And who is Ari?"

"The fuckin' *Lakers*, you crazy fool. Fuckin' rookies, man," he sighed. "And Ari's that chick you met on that island. She's here, man".

"Where?" asked Duncan.

"She's here, bro," Kobe said, pointing to his heart. "But... she's also *here*," he said, spreading his arms out wide, slowly making a 360 degree turn, looking all around. "We left Matty G with her, so he could smash. That was the last time I saw him myself." Kobe shook his head.

Duncan stared at Kobe, his mouth wide open. What the fuck was happening? Matty G was supposed to be dead. Ari was supposed to be kidnapped. And here was Kobe *fucking Bryant*, telling him that neither of these certainties were in fact certain.

Duncan suddenly got nauseous. "I think I'm gonna be sick, man," he said, clutching his stomach, bent over and cringing.

"Nah, Dunks. You cool, baby boy," said Kobe, chuckling.

Duncan looked up, just in time to see Kobe fade away and disappear. Then he threw up. Then he woke up. Then he threw up.

Chapter 28

When Duncan came to, there was no one at the bus stop besides him. The streets were empty. He had a headache. Something smelled like vomit. It was his shirt.

The jostling that his brain just endured had somehow eliminated the effects of the 'shrooms. Despite the pain, he could now accurately perceive his surroundings, without hallucinating. Back in touch with reality, he could now think clearly. *Shit*, he thought. *Tessa!*

Unfortunately, Duncan really had no idea where the bus had taken him. *Where the fuck am I?* he thought. He looked at the schedule posted at the bus stop. There was no English translation. He looked up to the star-pocked sky and slowly whispered, "Whaaat the fuuuck?" He put his head down and rubbed his eyes for a few seconds. *This is ridiculous. She's gonna kill me*, he silently lamented.

When he picked his head back up, he turned to his right, to look down the street. Nothing. Duncan then turned his head left, and saw that walking towards him was a young man, probably in his early twenties, wearing loose blue jeans and what Duncan referred to as a "butter shirt", an old, very soft t-shirt, which was green and said "Playin Hookie" across his chest. Around his neck, he wore a dog tag on a silver chain, and two beaded necklaces, one with a small, wooden cross dangling between the shirt's two words. He was a thin, tan, handsome guy, about six feet tall with a head of fairly long, strawberry blond hair.

To Duncan, the guy looked friendly enough, kind of the stoner/surfer type, like a number of his friends from Eastfield. Hopefully he would be able to assist him in locating his girlfriend, who was unfortunately out of her gourd on mushrooms, in the middle of a city, in a foreign country, where the native language was not English.

As the young man approached, he smiled and said something to Duncan in Dutch. "Sorry, man. I only speak English. No Dutch," Duncan replied.

The young man gave him a funny, quizzical look, and tilted his head to the side. His facial expression said that he hadn't understood what Duncan said. He looked confused. But a few seconds later, the guy cracked a smile and said, "Just fuckin with you, bro." He started to laugh. Duncan couldn't believe it. The guy spoke English. In an American accent. *So fucking convenient*, he thought, as he joined in with the young man's laughter.

"What's up, man?" the guy said. "You look a little dazed, bro. You lost or something?"

"Oh shit, man," Duncan said, as the two of them locked hands and tapped one another's backs. "Fuck yeah. I'm lost as *balls*, doggy." They shared another laugh. The young man asked Duncan where he was trying to go, and Duncan told him the name of the street that he and Tessa were staying on. He knew that where he had left Tessa was not actually on Lijnsbangracht, but he could remember how they had initially gotten to the area where the head-shop and the small park, where they had eaten the 'shrooms, were. Conveniently, he and Tessa had been completely sober at the time of their walk, so he had a vivid memory of the route they had taken from the apartment and what the area looked like. *If* he saw it, he was certain that he would know where he was. The only problem was getting there because Duncan simply had no clue where the hell he was now.

"I've never heard of that street, dude," the young man said. "But I do know that if you wait at this stop, there's a bus that comes by every forty-five minutes or so. It follows the same route in the opposite direction."

Duncan found this information to be quite a relief. "Wow," he said. "Thanks, man. I don't know what the fuck I would've done if you hadn't just shown up out of left field to bail me out."

"Don't mention it, my man," the young man laughingly replied. "It's my pleasure to help a fellow countryman in need."

Although the bus ride that brought him to this point had been full of enormous heads, swirling colors, and a violent exit, Duncan knew he'd recognize his destination. Unfortunately, he also knew that he wouldn't recall a damn thing from along the way. At the time, the mushrooms had created too much madness inside the bus for him to divert his attention out the window. Nonetheless, he was now the sober and grateful recipient of some much-needed assistance. God only knew what kind of mess Tessa was in, and he needed to get back to her sooner than soon.

"So, what's your name, bro?" asked Duncan's late-night godsend.

"Duncan, man. You?"

"Jon, dude. Jon Read. Pleasure to meet you." Jon reached out, and he and Duncan exchanged a firm handshake, the kind that Matty G used to call "The Shake of the Business Hustler". "I swear, man, I feel like I've seen you somewhere before," Jon said. "Where do I know you from?"

"I don't know," said Duncan. It didn't seem likely that he would run into someone he knew in Amsterdam.

"Holy shit!" said Jon. "I know who you are. You're Duncan fuckin' Lipton, aren't you?"

Duncan, shocked, couldn't believe that this guy, in the middle of the night, half the world away, knew who he was. "Wow, dude. Yeah. How the hell do you know who I am? That's fuckin' crazy."

"I'm a big basketball fan, man. I was reading some on-line scouting reports for next year's NBA draft prospects. You're in, like, everybody's top twenty, dude. I checked some of your high school highlights out on YouTube. You're a monster, bro. Broken ankles *all day*, baby! I can't believe I'm meeting you right now. In the middle of the fucking night. In the middle of fucking Amsterdam. What a world, right?"

"What a fucking *world*," Duncan replied in amazement. This was just too much. His agent, Lee Bernstein, had already made it abundantly clear that he was a lock to be drafted next season, but Duncan hadn't given any kind of thought to the possibility that he was already somewhat of a celebrity. He had never been recognized on the street before, and no one had ever asked for his autograph or anything like that. He had just been a high school star. Sure, people knew who he was back home, if they followed high school ball at all. He was the best player in the state. But now, here he was, being recognized in a foreign country. *Wow*, he thought. *That's a new one.*

"What are you doing here in lovely Amsterdam, Dunks? That's what they call you, right? Dunks? They wrote up, like, a bio on you and stuff. Says you always wear Nike Dunks." Jon looked down at Duncan's feet for verification. Sure enough, he was wearing a green and white pair of his trademark sneakers.

Duncan laughed. "Yeah, man, that's what they call me."

"And, uh, oh shit, what's your other nickname. I forgot. You and your boy have rhyming nicknames, right?"

Duncan looked at the ground as he suddenly felt a swell of emotion. He automatically started to sniffle and tear up at the mention of Matty G. "Yeah, man," he said, choking back an oncoming sob. "Woops. That's what they call me. Woops."

Jon was confused. "I'm sorry, bro. Did I say something wrong? Are you alright?"

"Yeah, yeah. I'm sorry, man. Yeah… Woops and Oops. That was me and my best friend, Matty G. But G died. That's why I just got choked up. I'm sorry. Sorry about that." Duncan used his shirtsleeve to wipe the tears out of his eyes.

"Oh, brother, I am *so* sorry to hear that," Jon said sincerely.

"It's all good, dude," said Duncan. "It's been a while now, but I just can't seem to get over it, ya know? He was my best friend… *is* my best friend, I mean."

"Hey, dude," Jon said, "I've known and lost some great friends and family in my life too. I know how you feel. Believe me, I really do. No need to trade sad stories though, right? So, hey, let's just roll on some positive wheels right now, yeah? We gotta keep our domes on straight if we're gonna get your ballin ass back where it needs to be. Ya *diiiiig?*"

"Yeah, man," Duncan chuckled. "Absolutely."

"So anyway, homeboy, back to my question," Jon said. "What the hell are you doing in Amsterdam? You didn't wanna go play a year of college ball before you go into The League?" The NBA, a few years earlier, had changed the minimum age requirement to play pro from eighteen to nineteen because they wanted to encourage players to experience higher education, rather than enter the pros as immature recent high school graduates. At eighteen, you could go and get yourself blown to bits in Iraq or Afghanistan, but you couldn't play in the NBA. Go figure.

"Nah, man. Fuck that. I've had it with school," Duncan said. Just tryin' to get a li'l pro experience, make some dough, have an adventure. I'm playin' for the Blue Devils. You heard of 'em?"

"Why, as a matter of fact, I have, my friend," said Jon, smiling as he spoke in a jokingly formal voice. "But I'm a Blitz fan, personally. However, I think that I just may have to convert, and become a follower of the Blue Devils," he laughed. Blitz was another pro team in the Netherlands, kind of the Blue Devils' archrivals. "The Blue Devils were *ass* last season though, Dunks," Jon continued. "You think you can help? I don't wanna be changin' my allegiances and then have to repeatedly suffer the pangs of defeat. I get very attached to my teams. I'm kind of a super-fan. But now that we've met, I don't see how I can possibly route against you. So, ya know, I'm counting on you, playboy." Duncan was always fond of calling, and being called by others, "playboy". *Thank you Flava Flav.* Jon grinned and gave Duncan a soft jab on the arm.

Duncan flashed a cocky smile and said, in a formal accent like Jon's, "Yes, my good man, I do believe that I shall be able to provide a most valuable service to my constituency."

"That's what I like to hear, brother. That is what I like to fuckin *hear*!" Jon whooped. At the top of his lungs, he shouted, "Gooooo Bluuuuuue Deeeeeeevils!!!!" and the two of them burst out laughing.

Then, less than a minute later, bright lights poked out of the darkness down the street. They were headlights. It was the bus. It was time to go. Duncan stopped laughing. *Shit*, he thought. *Tessa*.

Chapter 29

Duncan and Jon boarded the bus. They sat down across the center aisle from each other, each taking up two seats. "What do you do, Jon?" Duncan asked.

"Ah shit, man. I don't know. A little this. A little that. I get by, ya know?"

"Cool, man. Do what you do." *No need to press any further*, Duncan thought.

"Thanks," said Jon.

The bus stopped, and two passengers boarded the bus. The first one to come on was an old Asian man, early-seventies Duncan figured. The second was a rail-thin, bearded white guy, wearing a denim jacket and jeans with no undershirt, carrying a stick roughly a yard long. Mid-thirties.

The Asian man sat three seats away from the front of the bus. The skinny white guy with the stick went to the back of the bus, several seats away from where Jon and Duncan were sitting. As soon as he walked on the bus, he was rapping unintelligible lyrics, quietly to himself, with a huge pair of green headphones on his head.

Out of nowhere, he started swinging the stick and hitting the bus's windows with it. It came dangerously close to Jon's head. "Hey, watch it, you fuck!" Jon shouted.

The guy stood up. "What the fuck did you say, motherfucker?" He was American.

"I said that you better get that stick the fuck away from me, son."

"I'll do whatever the fuck I want, bitchass motherfucker."

"Oh, *yeah*?" said Jon, imitating the guy's style of speech. "Well, not today, shithead."

Duncan couldn't believe what happened next. Jon did a lightning-fast roundhouse kick straight at the guy's jaw. It broke. Blood and teeth all over the place. Bearded guy passed out, and tossed into the gutter, just like Duncan had been shortly before, at the last stop. "Good riddance," said Jon.

"Amen," said Duncan.

Then, as they approached the next stop, Duncan saw it. The little square with the little park that he needed to get to. "Jon, it really was a pleasure meeting you. My everlasting gratitude for helping me find my way back. This is my stop. Feel free to holler at me on Facebook." He jumped off the bus, tossing up a backwards, two-fingered peace sign. "Deuces," he said.

Startled by Duncan's sudden departure, Jon sputtered out a, "Uh, um, peace, dude. Be smart. Be safe." The doors closed, the bus rolled away, and Jon was gone.

Duncan raced into the square. He saw the little park, and jetted over as fast as his feet would carry him. There she was. Curled up in the fetal position, fast asleep on the grass. He began to sprint towards her, but before he could reach her, he encountered an unexpected obstruction.

"You Duncan?" An old man stepped in Duncan's path.

Duncan was startled. "Who are *you*, man?"

"Ted."

"How do you know my name…Ted?" Duncan asked irritably.

"Well, the girl curled up on the ground kept saying your name over and over again in her sleep. I was sitting in the park when she started bawling, right over there on the bench," he said, pointing. "I didn't want to go talk to her. I didn't want to scare her. But I decided to keep an eye on her. She just curled up and cried herself to sleep. Then, when she was passed out, she kept mumbling, 'Duncan, Duncan, Duncan', over and over again. So, call it an educated guess. I just saw you sprinting towards a passed-out girl, so I wanted to make sure you weren't some fucking murderer-rapist-thief."

"Oh, ok. Well, thanks for watching my girl, Ted," Duncan said sincerely, as he realized that the guy was body-guarding for Tessa, rather than being the creep that, at first glance, Duncan had presumed Ted would be. "I gotta go check on her. Excuse me. I really appreciate this. You're a good dude, Ted."

Ted stepped aside, and Duncan ran to his sleeping girlfriend. "Tessa. Tessa. Baby. Wake up. Tessa-baby." After a minute of gentle coaxing, Tessa stirred. *Fuck*, thought Duncan. *She's definitely gonna kill me.*

"Duncan?" Tessa said, blinking her eyes open. "Is that you?"

"Yeah, baby, I'm here," Duncan said. "I'm so sorry."

Tessa sat bolt upright. She was really awake now. "Duncan," she said, "what the fuck? Seriously. You're a fucking asshole. A fucking *asshole*. I really cannot believe you."

"I know, baby. I am. I am a huge asshole. I really didn't mean to leave you."

"What do you mean, you didn't mean to leave me? You just disappeared. Were you kidnapped? Did someone give you roofies? You better give me a *really* fucking good excuse for why I was left alone in a park, in the middle of fucking Amsterdam, crying my fucking eyes out, seeing fucking unicorns, wondering where my fucking boyfriend, who is supposed to protect me, is!" She was yelling now.

"It was the mushrooms, baby," Duncan told her. I was seeing crazy shit, and I got lost. I ended up like ten miles away from here. You have no idea what kind of shit just happened to me while I was trying to get back to you.

This excuse simply was not going to fly. Tessa was livid, her blood boiling, her heart racing. Anxiousness was overrunning her fragile psyche. She had been scared and alone, in the middle of a foreign country, where she didn't even speak the language. "Duncan," she said slowly, "you know, you put me through some shit sometimes. You left me after Matty G died. I let you go away without a fight, and it broke my heart. I just knew you were hurting so bad that I didn't want to get in the way of you trying to sort out your feelings. I don't know why you came back so soon, but I know you didn't want to. You just won't tell me what the hell happened on the island while you were gone for those few days that made you leave and come back home so quickly."

Duncan obviously knew she was right, and it made him feel worse and guiltier than he already did. He didn't know that Tessa could read him so well.

She continued, "You fight with my parents over political bullshit, which always pisses me off. You take drugs too much, and I bet you and Matty G taking drugs was what started off that whole chain of events leading to him getting shot in the head." Tessa was really on point, and as bad as he felt about what she was saying, he couldn't help but be impressed by her perceptiveness. But he kept that to himself.

"I don't know what the hell is wrong with you, Duncan," she said. "It's not your fault that I got all fucked up on these mushrooms. I won't blame you for that. I wanted to take them. And I know you didn't intend to lose your head and leave me here. But Duncan…," her voice trailed off, as she stared at the ground. "Baby, I love you. Do you love me? I really would like to know. 'Cause you put me in these situations, or at least have an influence over my own decision-making process, which leads me into all sorts of bullshit. I don't think that's how you affect someone you love. I think you're just infatuated with me. I think you like having me around to keep you company, suck your dick, and make you look cool to your friends who think I'm hot. But, ya know what, Duncan? I've had enough. I'm scared of you. I'm scared of what just happened, and I can't risk my wellbeing for this anymore."

"What are you saying, Tessa?" Duncan was scared himself. He thought he knew where this was going. And he was right.

"I'm saying, Duncan, that until I tell you otherwise, we're through.

I really do love you, but you're not good for me right now. I think you need to figure out your own shit. I don't care that you're the best at basketball and that next year you're going to be a gazillionaire. That's not what this relationship is about to me. It's about us loving and comforting and being there for each other. And after tonight, I realized that I don't think I'm getting what I want, no, what I *need* out of our relationship.

"I'm going home, Duncan. When we get back to the apartment, I'm going on-line and buying a ticket for the earliest flight I can get tomorrow, and I'm going home. I fuckin love you, honey. I really do. But I have to look out for myself. I want to make something of myself. I want to go to school. I don't want to be your tag-along. I want to be my own woman, and I think that being with you is going to get in my way. So, for now at least, we're broken up, Duncan. And that's that."

Duncan had seen his dumping coming. He had not, however, expected her to say so many things that she found wrong with their relationship and with Duncan himself. He didn't realize that this incident had more or less been the straw that broke the camel's back. *Fuck*, he thought. *I should've stayed on the bus.*

Tessa speed-walked onto Linjsbangracht, and Duncan followed her at a brisk pace so that he could prevent anyone who might try to accost or assault her, or something like that. But he didn't want to get close. Tessa meant *everything* she had said. Duncan felt it. This was no angry tirade. These were her honest feelings, and he was going to have to accept the painful fact that he was now, for the first time in his life, a dumping victim. And he was now single. At that moment, he couldn't appreciate the benefits of that fact because his heart was badly wounded by Tessa's words. But he would get over it. He knew he would. He had to.

The next morning, when Duncan woke up, there was a note next to his head on the bed. It said, "Duncan, I love you, and I'm sorry that I have to get out of here and go back home, but that's the way it's gotta be. I'll see you when I see you. Good luck with basketball season! I know you'll be great. You always are. And please don't hate me, Duncan. I need this for *me* right now. I hope you can understand. — Love Always, Tessa XOXO." There was a postscript as well: "Stop taking drugs so much. Look what they've done to you. You're better than that."

Duncan treated himself to a good two to three minute crying session, followed by a half-hour-long shower of body-scrubbing, hair-shampooing, tooth-brushing, and self-reflecting. When he got out of the shower, he toweled off and dressed. It was his last day before Blue Devils practice was to begin, and he wanted to make the most of it. He thought about where he should go and what he should do; he didn't have to think for long.

He went downstairs and knocked on his new friend/landlord's door. Kjetl answered it, groggy from being woken up before noon, which was the earliest he ever really got up. But he was friendly, courteous, and more than happy to supply his new tenant/friend with his desired directions. When Duncan left the apartment, he carried a piece of paper in his right hand, on which Kjetl had provided all the pertinent information that he would need to get himself where he wanted to go. His pleasantly accommodating landlord had hand-drawn a simple map in black ink for him. The drawing used hastily sketched arrows to show a route that began on Lijnsbangracht. Duncan was to follow the arrows leading away from Kjetl's place, to his destination, which was marked with a large X, appropriately written in red pen.

The arrows were intended to guide Duncan to his self-selected destination. It was a place where foreigners, visitors to this incredibly entertaining, comfortable, and unique city, would find themselves compelled to *at least* visit, if not frequent. And, to Duncan, it was nothing less than an unprecedented world of wonder. It wasn't the kind of place you'd bring your grandmother for brunch, or send the little ones Easter-egg hunting, but it was undeniably *something else*, something amazing. Whether one is a visitor with an innocent curiosity, or a frequenter with a healthy carnal appetite and little fear of disease, ninety-nine percent of those who have taken in the sights while strolling the streets there, would undoubtedly say that you'd be hard-pressed to find anyplace in the world as surreal as Amsterdam's greatest tourist attraction: *The Red Light District*.

Chapter 30

Kjetl's map was perfect. In no time, Duncan was there. Just as he arrived at the Red Light District's perimeter, he decided to have a quick stop at a coffee shop called Ciullo's. He just wanted to grab a small cup of black before he perused, what Kjetl would call, the "merchandise", referring to the area's working girls.

This was his last free day before the start of the season, and Duncan was trying to make the most of it. Just as he had been on the island, he was again alone in a foreign land. But this was different. In Amsterdam, instead of running away from something, as had been the case on the island, where he went in an attempt to escape from everything that reminded him of his late best friend, he was now running *toward* something. *Starting tomorrow*, he thought, *I am really going to be a fucking professional basketball player, aren't I?* He asked himself the rhetorical question silently. Out loud, he answered it: "I am going to be a fucking professional basketball player tomorrow."

At this point, he was inside the coffee shop, next on line. Not paying any attention to his surroundings, he mused on the fact that his major life goals and dreams were coming to fruition. He was just one year away from the draft. Just one year.

When he finally looked up from his reverie, the girl at the counter and the old man in front of him gave him quizzical looks. He smiled and apologized for the outburst. His apology was readily accepted. He was in a great mood and his positivity was infectious, despite the oddness of his outburst. The old man even said, "Good luck," to Duncan in a thick Dutch accent. Duncan smiled and said, "Thank you, sir. I'll do my best." *I need to keep my thinking-out-loud to a minimum*, he thought. *But then, whatever. Who cares? Jeez. Wow, what's up with me and the 'jeez'?* He had found himself randomly saying and thinking the word with a surprising frequency. *I'm such a geek. Jeez.*

Duncan ordered his black coffee from the pretty girl behind the counter, who looked like she was probably about twenty, twenty-one, twenty-two at most, a couple years older than Duncan, who, by this point, was eighteen. When she gave him the coffee, she said, in English with a slightly Dutch-flavored accent, "Would you like to see the menu?"

"No thanks," Duncan said. "I'm not really hungry yet. Maybe later."

The girl laughed. "Not *that* menu, silly boy. I meant, the *menu.*"

Duncan had absolutely no idea what she was referring to. After he and the girl stared at one another for a few seconds, she giggled and just handed over the menu to him. "Thanks," Duncan said, and he looked down at the single laminated page. Quietly, to himself, he said, "Oh... my... fucking... god. This can not be real."

Again, the girl giggled. "Where are you from?"

"I'm from the US," Duncan replied. "How about you?"

"I'm from right here," she said, waving her right arm back and forth across her body several times, signifying that Amsterdam was her airspace, even though she had a much more American accent when she spoke English than a Dutch one.

"Well, your city is the best place I've ever been," Duncan said. "I seriously can not believe what it's like here. Beautiful canals. Hardly any cars. Just bikes everywhere; I love that. Let's see... hardly any crime other than bike theft, I hear. And my personal favorite: legal weed."

The girl laughed. "You didn't know about the coffee shops?" she asked.

"No," Duncan admitted. "No, I did not. I knew weed was legal, but this...this is over the top."

"Well," the girl said, "now you know. So, what can I get for you?"

Duncan didn't know how to answer that question. He was overwhelmed. There were more than twenty different kinds of pot listed on the menu. There was Silver Haze, Super Silver Haze, Black Widow, Strawberry Haze, Sour Diesel, Durban Poison, and Blueberry Kush, just to name a few. He was absolutely blown away by the coffee shop's vast selection of legal marijuana. There were descriptions of the kind of high that you would get from smoking a particular strain of weed, right next to beautiful photos of whichever kind was being described.

Duncan read some of the descriptions, but just couldn't decide which one he wanted. He was just about to ask the girl what she recommended when his eyes fell on a particular strain of weed at the bottom of the page. Again, he was compelled to say the exact same thing that he had said when he first realized what the menu was, "Oh… my… fucking… god." The last strain listed on the menu was called Da Piff. There was no longer a need to look at the menu. He knew what he was getting.

There was no weed like piff. And as soon as he told the girl that that was what he wanted, she winked at him and said, "Great choice." She reached under the counter and pulled out a plastic Tupperware container. It was full of close to a quarter-pound of the dankest piff Duncan had ever seen. The container reeked of that oh-so-distinct piff smell. It was like a skunk drank some gasoline, took a shit, and then sprayed it with bug spray and citrus Febreeze. As vile as that may sound, it was a delightful smell that tickled Duncan's nostrils and made his heart thump with anticipation. The thought of smoking legal piff at a quaint little coffee shop, instead of buying it from the rough hoods who obtained it from Harlem by way of Florida, was a concept that briefly overwhelmed him with the practicality and beauty of it all.

"Wow, um, wow. Okay. Sure, I, uh," he couldn't stop bumbling, "I guess I'll, um, yeah, I think I'll take, um, like, ummmm. I'll take a quarter. Yup, that'll be good."

"No problem, cutie," the girl said. Duncan then *really* looked at the girl for the first time. He had been out of it, not paying attention to her face at all, while he was staring down at the menu, transfixed. The fact of the matter was that the girl was gorgeous, and Duncan was a little bit dumbstruck. He couldn't believe that he hadn't fully appreciated her good looks earlier. They had been talking for a couple of minutes, and somehow he had not managed to even lift his head up to look at her. It wasn't his way to be discourteous, but his excitement at going to the Red Light District and discovering this whole coffee-shops-with-weed thing had put his mind elsewhere.

Now that Duncan had decided on Da Piff, there was no more need for his bumbling stutters. He immediately switched into his 'talkin'-to-girls mode', a style that he had cultivated with the pure confidence that came with being the best athlete and most popular guy in his high school. *Game time,* he thought to himself.

"So," Duncan said, "you said you're from Amsterdam, but I am definitely hearing an American accent. A little Dutch flavor, but definitely American."

The girl laughed. "Yeah, I've been here so long now, I kind of forget the states, ya know? I'm originally from Vermont, if *that's* what you're asking." Her tone was flirtatious.

"How long have you lived here?" Duncan asked.

"I guess it's been about six years now," she said. "Wow. Seems like forever."

Although Duncan's mother had taught him to never ask a girl/woman her age, Duncan was curious, and accordingly inquired as to what the girl's was. "I hope you don't mind my asking, but how old are you?"

"Didn't your mother ever tell you not to ask a girl her age?" the girl asked, giggling.

"Yeah, she did. But I'm curious," he said. "Can I guess?"

"Why not?" she sighed, clearly pretending to be annoyed.

"Hmmm, I'm gonna say... twenty-one?"

"You're sweet," she said, "but I'm twenty-five."

"Well, old maid, you look good for your age," Duncan said, laughing. The girl leaned slightly over the counter and gave Duncan a playful punch on the arm.

"Well, how old are you, young man?" she said.

"Take a swing," Duncan said.

"Hmmm, let's see. I'd say you're about twenty-two?"

"Oops," he replied, "not quite. You and I were both four years off."

"Oh," she said. "You're twenty-six? You look a little younger."

"Nah," Duncan said. "I just said you were four years off."

"Oh wow, you're only eighteen?" Duncan nodded. "You look older. Maybe you just seem older 'cause of how you talk and stuff. I don't know."

"Yeah," he replied. "I get that sometimes. I haven't shaved in a while though. If it was fresh-shave-day, you might think a little differently."

"Okay, Mr. Eighteen, what's your name? We've been doing all this chatting and we don't even know each other...yet." Duncan liked how she said *yet*. She was definitely implying that they were *going to* get to know each other, and she was sending him the signals. The age difference didn't seem like it was going to matter much.

"I'm Duncan," he said. "Very nice to make your acquaintance."

"My, so formal," the girl said, laughing at Duncan's jokingly posh accent and choice of words.

"Thank you, milady. And what is your name?"

"I'm Kara," she said.

"Nice to meet you, Kara."

"It's nice to meet you too, Duncan," she replied. They shook hands, and held their grip for about five seconds, locking eyes. "Listen, Duncan," she said, "that's a lot of weed you just got there. I don't know if a youngin' like yourself can handle that batch of Da Piff without someone to keep an eye on you. Maybe you should wait 'til

I get off work, in about forty-five minutes, and I can make sure you don't get yourself into any trouble. What d'ya say?"

"I'd say that you are severely underestimating my smoking prowess, Kara," Duncan replied, smiling. "But, if you're asking me to hang out and smoke some of this beautiful weed with you, I think that would be nice."

"Good," Kara said. "Meet me back here in about forty-five minutes, k? I'll be waiting."

"Cool," Duncan said. He gave Kara a smile, and walked out of the coffee shop. As he walked out, he turned around to look at her. She was watching him leave the store. He smiled again and gave her a wink. She giggled, and turned around to make a fresh pot of coffee.

With forty-five minutes to kill, Duncan decided to go window-shopping...for hookers.

Chapter 31

When Duncan left the coffee shop, he turned left to walk towards the area where one could find "the merchandise". After meeting such a nice young lady, he wasn't particularly interested in getting himself a Dutch hooker, but he was dying to see what all the hype was about.

Almost immediately upon exiting the coffee shop, he saw his first red light. It was horizontal, probably four feet wide, and sat above a glass window. What was behind the glass window was one of the most surreal sights that Duncan had ever seen. He had heard about the famous Red Light District and its hookers behind glass doors, but to actually see them was another thing altogether.

The first girl Duncan saw was a thin blonde in a nurse outfit; it was the kind that college girls wear on Halloween, for an excuse to dress like a slut for one day out of the year. *Wow*, he thought, *that's a new one. She looks like a mannequin.* But the girl was definitely real. She was wearing dark red lipstick, heavy blue eye shadow, and had her hair tied back in a ponytail.

Duncan stood about ten feet away from the glass window. He could barely believe his eyes. He hadn't even smoked yet, but he was already seeing some trippy shit. The mannequin-nurse-girl stood up from the stool she had been sitting on. She was wearing five-inch heels. They did not look comfortable. Sexy maybe. But certainly not comfortable.

As Duncan stared at what he could hardly believe was a real person, the girl moved forward and touched the glass window with her left hand. With her right, she pulled the zipper down on the front of her uniform-costume-thingy and pulled out her bombs. She looked down at them, then lifted her head, smiling. With her right index finger, she beckoned to Duncan, who gave her the "Who? Me?" face. She nodded, and, slowly, Duncan walked towards her, looking left, then right, to see if anyone was watching him. This felt dirty. Embarrassing. But he was sucked in by her seductive lips and her enticing tits. Forget American conventions, etiquette, and norms. This was Amsterdam. And there were titties in the window.

"Holy shit," said Duncan, as he approached the window. The window was a door. The mannequin-nurse-girl opened it. "Hi," Duncan said.

"Ooooh," said the gorgeous prostitute. "American boy. I love American boys. Discount, yah?" Duncan was completely overwhelmed by the situation. He had plenty of money. And he had a date in less than forty-five minutes. And this was only the first girl he had seen. What if the whole Red Light District was full of this? What if there were better? *Fuck it*, he thought. *Once in a lifetime.*

"How much?" he asked.

"For you, mmm, sixty-five Euros."

"Okay," he said. Those were the last words he would speak for the next forty-some-odd minutes.

Not a word was spoken between the hooker and Duncan as she bathed him in the shower, hidden behind a red curtain, that she sat in front of all day, behind her glass door, to hawk her wares. After bathing him, the hooker blew Duncan for about fifteen minutes. They then had sex for the remaining twenty-some-odd minutes. Luckily for Duncan, who did not have a condom on him, it is standard practice in Amsterdam for hookers to keep a solid supply of a variety of condoms in their place of business. Duncan chose ribbed and lubricated. He had fun. No worries.

When he was done, he paid the hooker and gave her a twenty-euro tip, just for the experience that she had just provided him with. It was now time for his date with Kara, the coffee-shop girl. He felt a bit guilty about just having had sex with the hooker across the street and then going on a date with Kara, but hey, she and he hardly knew each other. He didn't have to feel guilty about anything. He smiled as he strolled across and up the street, to the coffee-shop, where he was to meet a beautiful American girl from Vermont. He was excited.

Chapter 32

Kara was wiping down the counter. Lunchtime was just ending, and she needed to get the place ready for the first-shift workers to start running the show in the morning. Duncan walked up to the counter. "Hello," he said. She looked up and smiled.

"Hey, Duncan. Just gimme a minute. You want some coffee?"

"Ya know what, I never even got the black coffee I intended to order before. I was too mesmerized by the weed. I forgot all about it."

She laughed. "Well, sir, I'll get it for you right now."

"Thank you kindly," he replied.

"No problem." She smiled and winked quickly at him, returning his earlier one.

Kara brought Duncan the coffee, and told him to just hold on a minute while she finished cleaning up. Duncan gladly sat and sipped the strong coffee, enjoying his good fortune on such a lovely day in Amsterdam.

When Kara was done cleaning up, she walked over to the table where Duncan was seated and said, "Okay, Mr. Duncan. Are you ready to go check out the Red Light District or what?"

"How did you know that I was here to see the Red Light District?" He hadn't said anything about it.

"Well, let's see: You're eighteen years old. You have little reason to come to this area, as a newbie semi-tourist unless you're here to see what it's all about. And, to be honest with you, I saw you go into Elsa's nurse's station over there."

Fuck, thought Duncan, as his lips formed a sheepish grin.

"It's okay. I go there too sometimes." She giggled a little nervously at divulging such personal information. "I'm not a lesbian. I just like to mix it up sometimes."

Duncan was knocked out. And he got an idea. *But*, he thought, *that'll have to wait 'til late*r. So, he just stared, his mouth agape, as was his customary expression of surprise. Then, he let out a "pheeew," relieved that his date wouldn't be ruined by being caught messing around with a hooker.

"So," said Kara, "you wanna go poke around?" The Dutch flavor to her accent was fading more and more as their conversation continued.

"Lead the way," Duncan said.

Kara led Duncan through the Red Light District, and Duncan felt that a more surreal experience he had never been witness to. And he doubted that he would ever bare witness to such a magical place as this. There were hookers *everywhere*. There were bars, canals, locals, tourists, food, drink, gaiety…but the hookers dominated the scenery. They all stood behind glass doors, displaying themselves in all manner of lingerie, costumes, leather, you name it.

Kara led Duncan down streets where specific ethnicities dominated. There was a black street. An Asian street. A Hispanic street. Then, she led him to the holy land. Down one small alley, were the hottest girls in all of Amsterdam. Duncan rarely had seen such beauty as that that was ubiquitous in this small alley. And now, here was Kara, tugging at his arm towards one of the doors. "This is where I wanna go," she said. They walked to the door, and smiled and waved to the gorgeous girl. She came to the door, and opened it up. "Hi," she said. Her accent was American. Her face was familiar. It only took Duncan a moment to realize who the beautiful girl lying beneath the makeup was. And just at the moment that he recognized her, she too recognized him. She leapt into his arms, and hugged him tight. "Oh my *god*," she said. "Oh, Dunks, baby, I was sooooo worried about you!"

Chapter 33

"*You* **were worried** about *me?*" Duncan said. "Last time I saw you, you and your sister were getting dragged away by fucking Tubby P! There was nothing I could do. I wanted to stop them so bad. But I couldn't move. They had guns. I was frozen." It had been almost nine months since Duncan had last seen Ari.

"Oh, Dunks," Ari said. "Oh, baby, it's okay. There was nothing you could do. I hope you haven't beaten yourself up over this. I'm okay."

"What about your sister?" Duncan asked. "Is she okay?"

"She's *fine*. She's on the closest island. About fifteen miles from where we were. Not far at all. She couldn't leave the area. She loves it too much. And she's not all tied up with Rennie like I am. I can't be around there."

"Why?" Duncan asked.

"Tubby P's got people all over the islands. Rennie had to get out of there. Tubby P is dead-set on running the island. So he ran Rennie out." Duncan enjoyed her play on words. There was something about her that Duncan had really connected with, back on the island. He couldn't believe that she was a prostitute now. He knew there had to be some kind of crazy story behind this. But before he heard it, he needed to know something much more important.

"Do you know where Rennie is?" Duncan asked Ari.

"He's here, honey," she said. "He's at the coffee shop right down the block, toward that bridge going over the canal. It's called Bella Café."

Duncan turned to Kara, who he had nearly forgotten about. "Tomorrow," he said. "Tomorrow. Are you working at your coffee shop tomorrow, Kara? I've got something really important to do. I need to go, like, right now."

"Yeah," she said. "I'll be there. Just come in. Good luck with your friend."

"Thanks," Duncan said, and gave Kara a kiss on the cheek.

Turning to Ari, he said, "I'll be back soon. Don't go disappearing again. I have much I wanna say. There is much I wanna hear. There is much I wanna know. These answers, I need clear."

"Cute, Dunks. Very cute," she said, giggling.

"Thaaaanks," he laughed, as he moved the curtain aside, and stepped out into the alley where all the slamminest, banginest, hottest chicks in Amsterdam, maybe even the world, were hawking their wares. His jaw was on the floor as usual as he exited the alley. How outrageously hot these girls were, combined with the fact that he was about to see his *brudda* had his mind on overload. Utter, absolute, unprecedented overload.

Duncan reached Bella Café, and looked through the spotless glass front window. There, reading a paperback novel, with a neon orange front and back cover, was a very dark young man, with sprouting dreads and a gleaming white acoustic guitar at his side. He wore an eclectic mix of beaded jewelry around his neck and wrists, a heavily worn *butter* t-shirt (most likely 80's vintage), and a beautiful set of sparkling white teeth that were on full display as he looked out the front window and saw his best friend.

There he was. *In da flesh*, Rennie laughingly thought. *Brudda Duncan heself. Fuckin Brudda Duncan. God is good.* Duncan had, in less than two days, become a better friend to Rennie than nearly anyone ever had before. He had felt compelled to do anything he could for him, and expected absolutely nothing in return. It was just an inexplicable vibe between the two. They needed each other at that moment in time. The formation of their friendship was like a good birthday present, when you get something you can't live without but never knew you wanted in the first place.

And here they were. Each of them had thought that they would never again cross paths. Neither would have been surprised if they had heard that the other one was dead. The last time they had seen each other, Rennie had disappeared into a war zone, in his own home. Now, here they were, a massive smile creasing Rennie's lips that made his cheeks sore, and radiated the most intense warmth, relief, happiness, and love. It was the kind of smile that could only be put there by Duncan Lipton.

Rennie and Duncan just stared at each other for a funnily disbelieving fifteen or twenty seconds, smiling huge, genuine, goofy, and relieved smiles. Then they ran into a bear-hug embrace, lasting a solid, wordless two minutes.

When they finally broke apart, Duncan said, "Rennie, ma dude, talk to me. What the fuck happened?"

"Oh Duncan, brudda. Oh, oh, oh, brudda. Who will *tell* dere *tale* first, mon? Each one of us has nine mont to account foh, mon. Nine fuckin mont, mon! So, Dunks, brudda. You say who say what when, yah mon?"

"Rennie," Duncan said, "*you*, my man, are telling *me* what the fuck happened to *you* first. 'Cause I thought, for sure, like…shit, man! I thought you had to be dead."

"Okay, mon, I'm wit choo. I'm wit choo. Check me out, brudda…"

Chapter 34

Nine months before Duncan and Rennie's joyous reunion:

"Rennie!"

Rennie turned around, a panicked look on his face. "Be careful, man!" Duncan shouted. "I don't wanna lose anyone else close to me, doggy. You're my man, dude. Be smart. Be safe."

Rennie's face lit up. "'Tis good to have someone care, mon. 'Tis real nice, Duncan, brudda." He ran a short distance down the hallway, outside of the room where he had just left his new best friend, his new *brudda*. He hoped beyond hope that he would be back shortly, to get Duncan the fuck out of that room. But who knew what kind of disaster was going on upstairs. He had to find out. He had to take control. It was his house, and he himself would not run and hide from intruders. But he had to keep Duncan safe.

He was stuck between a rock and a hard place.

Rennie could defend his home, and risk leaving Duncan in the room by himself. If he were captured or injured, Duncan would have nowhere to go, and would surely, eventually, be found by the intruders. Who knew what might happen to him if whoever was breaking in were to find the defenseless white-boy. Ach, mon. That was one shitty option.

The other option was to go with Duncan through the private paths, the house's system of secret corridors, between walls, which were built for this very reason. They made escape in a dangerous situation beyond feasible. It was easy. But Rennie didn't yet know what the situation was, and as it was his house, he felt obligated to take control of the situation in his castle. Furthermore, there were the girls to think about. Only a shameful, heartless coward would leave them behind. And if Rennie was anything, he was not a shameful, heartless coward. Because Duncan did not know the private path system, he would not be able to escape on his own. In a panicked moment of confusion, Rennie had forgotten to quickly explain to Duncan how he could get out of the room if need be.

I am getting back fo brudda Duncan, Rennie thought, and confidently forced himself to believe it to be so. But, unfortunately, it was not meant to be, and instead, it was what it was.

Who knows what might have happened had Ari not popped up out of one of the private paths and saved Duncan, but for the first six months after that morning, Rennie thought that he had put Duncan in harm's way, and that his new best friend had probably been killed because he had foolishly brought this naïve boy to what he knew to be a potentially dangerous place. He now felt careless and selfish that he had done so. He hardly had given it a thought that anything like this would happen, but the chance, he knew, still existed, and yet he had not paid heed to that possibility, however unlikely it may have been. Rennie just liked the kid, and wanted to hang out with him after they had bonded so strongly at The Shanty.

On the flight to Amsterdam, Ari had told him about she and Duncan's ridiculous saga of private paths, treks through the brambly woods, and the kidnapping of her and her sister, leaving a perplexed and vexed Duncan frozen in place with his jaw below his knees. Though they still had no idea where Duncan was at that point, Rennie's mind was put much at ease by the revelation that Duncan had not in fact been captured by any of the intruders.

The day of the attack, Rennie, however, had been captured himself by his rival, Tubby P, and his henchmen.

He and Tubby P were not the friendly, "Hey, let's play a game of HORSE", kind of rivals. They were the kind of rivals who would each be more than willing to pull the trigger on the other.

Fact was, Tubby P and Rennie had known each other for as long as either one of them could remember. They had gone to school together. They had even, as babies, been in *daycare* together. But, they had *always* disliked one another.

Tubby P's father and Rennie's father were the two wealthiest black men on the island. Rennie's father, as the weed kingpin on an island booming with business, was a multi-millionaire. At certain points, particularly when the stock market was low, and the wealthy whites on the island were keeping a keen eye on their portfolios, Rennie's dad was the richest man on the whole island, white or black.

Tubby P's father though, was not in the same category of wealth as Rennie's. Unlike Rennie's father, Tubby P's father's source of income was legal. He was the best contractor on the island, and when the stock market looked flush, there were homes to be built for those reaping the rewards of the boom. The island was a beautiful place, and, over the years, land there had become very valuable. Its crystal-clear, blue ocean waters, white-sand beaches, beautiful women, copious amounts of ganja, and fantastic food/drink/nightlife made it a prime tourist destination.

Rennie and Paul (Tubby P's given name) going to daycare was unusual for black islanders' children. A dismal percentage ended up going to school at all, for modern U.S. standards of educational attendance anyway. But this was the island. Not the U.S. So, in the particular grade that the two boys were in, they happened to be the only black boys. Being amongst all whites created an interesting dynamic between the two. They could have been best friends, and leaned on one another for support. It might seem logical to want to have that kind of support system in one's life, no matter how small. But that's not how these two interacted. Instead, they had been rivals for as long as they could remember, regardless of the endeavor, though on Tubby P's end there was always something for him to try and prove. More often than not, Rennie, by high school, couldn't even be bothered, as he was too busy hanging out with his friends and operating his successful family business. But Tubby P, already embarrassed and ashamed by his albinism, always wanted to one-up his only peer of African descent, who always seemed to get the better of him.

The rivalry started in *kindergarten*. That far back. Tubby P had just begun putting on the weight that would lead Rennie to dub Paul Williams, "Tubby". All the white-boys joined in although it was childish and cruel to make fun of the boy's weight. The others didn't really mean it as maliciously as Paul took it. He hated that fucking name. Tubby. But there really was no way around it. Within a week, no one called him Paul. Within a year, no one even knew what the P stood for.

Tubby P never forgave Rennie for inventing the derogatory moniker that came to define him. Not long after everyone started calling him Tubby P, he really had no choice but to just own the name. He made the best of it. As far as most of his peers were concerned, he was a cool guy. He had lots of friends. He would get his balls busted a little about his weight sometimes, and occasionally his pale complexion, but he seemed to take it in stride. However, deep down, he harbored a serious grudge. Inside, he felt that Rennie had reduced him to little more than the inches of his pants' circumference. Consequently, Tubby P was always hostile towards Rennie.

The thing was that Rennie didn't really even give much of a shit about Tubby P's opinion of him or actions toward him. He didn't know why the guy had such a bad attitude. The truth was that he didn't even remember bestowing the nickname upon him, and had someone told him that he was the one who had come up with it, he would have been genuinely surprised. For God's sake, it was in kindergarten! Who remembers kindergarten? But Tubby P remembered. And Tubby P never forgot. So, when he got the chance, he seized the opportunity to fuck Rennie up. *Gettin even for a valid reason,* he thought.

Rennie went up the stairs. When he reached the top of the stairs, he hit a button on the wall, and walked through a sliding door. He then immediately had his legs kicked out from under him. The gun he was holding, one he had grabbed off the wall in the private path, flew out of his hand and across the room. Tubby P's henchmen stood over him, wearing the evil smiles of a kid with a magnifying glass, on a sunny day, when there are plenty of ants around to fry. These were predators of the weak. And Rennie was in the unfortunate position of being outnumbered and being at an uncomfortable vertical disadvantage. *Shit*, he thought.

Rennie was picked up by three of the henchmen, dragged across the room, and pulled up the secret set of stairs that led from the massive "basement" to the modest house upstairs, where Tubby P was waiting. Rennie was tightly held in front of Tubby P, who was laughing. "Well, well, well," he said. "Muddafuckin' Rennie. Ma old nemesis."

"Nemesis?" Rennie said. "What da fuck you doin, mon? What I do to *you*, Tubby, mon?"

"Fuck you," Tubby P said.

Rennie was baffled. He had no idea why his old schoolmate was after him. Sure, they'd always had beef, but nothing to warrant this. His expression showed utter confusion at the reason for the attack. He hadn't seen Tubby P in god-knows how long.

"You cause me much pain, Rennie mon. Now I give it back."

"What the…" Rennie wasn't given a chance to finish. Tubby P lifted his fat leg, and in a surprisingly athletic move kicked Rennie in the stomach. He and his henchmen then proceeded to beat Rennie senseless. As Rennie lay on the floor, ribs cracked, arm broken, and face mashed, he looked up at Tubby P, who was laughing hysterically.

"We no even, mon," Tubby P said, "but dis good enough fuh me. Now, you get da fuck off ma island, and ya don't come back, mon. Neva. If I catch you here, next time you dead, mon. Fuhreal. Undastond?"

Rennie meekly nodded. "Tomorrow, you gone, mon," Tubby P said. "Gone." He then walked out the front door of the house, his chuckling henchmen in tow.

Rennie pulled himself up, and hobbled to the kitchen, where he kept a first-aid kit. He disinfected and bandaged his wounds, then went to survey the damage. He gingerly hobbled down the stairs to the "basement", where he found, to his horror, a bloody massacre. Every one of his "Girls with the Guns", except Ari, lay on the floor of the grow-room, dead from gunshot wounds. Three of Tubby P's men were also dead.

Tears sprung in his eyes as he took in the horrifying sight of the carnage. As quickly as his broken body would allow, he hobbled downstairs to find Duncan. His new friend was gone. Without a clue as to where Duncan might be, he felt hopelessly lost and guilty. Crying, he packed a few things, grabbed his guitar, and left his house. He found his Range Rover destroyed, all windows bashed in, tires flattened. He went back into his house and called a cab. Seeing Rennie so badly messed up caused the cab driver some trepidation in allowing him into the car. But when Rennie flashed a hundred-dollar bill and handed it to the cabbie, any apprehension was lost, and any questions as to the cause of Rennie's wounds were silenced.

Of all the places Rennie had ever visited, Amsterdam was by far his favorite, and he decided that that was where he was going to go. But first, he had the cab driver take him to a gaudy mansion, about ten miles from his home. "Stop here," Rennie said to the cabbie.

"You got yourself some fancy friends, eh mista?" the cabbie said.

"Sometin like dat," Rennie replied. "Just wait here." He opened the trunk of the car and pulled from his bag something wrapped in an XL sweatshirt. "Don't go anywhere," he reiterated to the cabbie.

"I'm here, mon" the driver said.

"Good." Rennie limped up the long driveway, holding his sweatshirt, in which was wrapped a surprise for Tubby P.

After they beat Rennie, Tubby P and his henchmen went to The Shanty to get Ari and her sister, where they had left Duncan standing, slack-jawed. Since they had no idea who Duncan was, they had simply assumed that he was just some kid hitting on Ari.

Tubby P took the two girls back to his home, where he intended to hold them hostage, and let his henchmen have their way with them. The screaming girls were dragged to separate rooms, and they were each stripped of their attire. Tubby P planned on defiling Ari first. He followed his henchmen to the room, where she was being pinned down on the bed. "Rennie's favorite girl. I gon have fun wit dis one," he chuckled. "Much fun."

"Much fun," were the last words that Tubby P ever spoke. Rennie had walked right into the mansion, the front door being unlocked, and gates nonexistent. No one stood in the front parlor, as all the henchmen were with the girls, ready to have their way with them. So, with his rage blocking out his pain, Rennie threw the sweatshirt on the floor, revealing his surprise for Tubby P. The surprise was an Uzi.

When Rennie heard the girls' screaming, he found the hallway containing the two rooms where they were about to be raped and beaten. He opened the door to the first room, and found Tubby P standing over Ari as two of his henchmen held her down. Rennie mowed them down with the Uzi, splattering blood everywhere.

Shouts came from the next room, where two other henchmen held Ari's sister. Rennie ran over as fast as he could. When he opened the door, he found two thugs with their pants at their ankles, guns momentarily inaccessible. Taking care not to shoot Ari's sister, Rennie mowed down the other two henchmen as well. Then he and the girls had gotten the hell out of there. There was no time for the girls to dress. They ran, as fast as they could to the cab, where they found a speechless cab driver.

After Rennie had snapped the cabbie out of his trance, that he was put under by the two sexy naked white girls in his backseat, they took off. They stopped at a large drugstore to grab a few articles of clothing for the ladies, and then drove to the airport, where they got on the next plane to Amsterdam.

Chapter 35

"And now you're here," Duncan said. "And now you're fuckin *here*. This is a crazy small world, dude. What the fuck…"

"'Tis so, mon. You and me, mon, we supposed to be tuhgedda. Da powas dat be, dey make it so," Rennie replied.

"They do make it so, my dude. They do, don't they?"

"Truly, dey do," Rennie said. "Truly dey do."

Suddenly in the now, Duncan recalled that he wanted to know what the hell Ari was doing as a prostitute in the Amsterdam alley of the super-hotties. "Rennie," he said, "What the hell is Ari doing as a prostitute in the Amsterdam alley of the super-hotties?"

The left corner of Rennie's mouth turned up, forming a smirking smile. "Ari, she be a woo-mon of, shall we say, dubious morals."

"What does that mean?" Duncan asked.

"Well, she a *nympho*, mon. I heard de expression in a movie sometime," he chuckled. "Girl con't get 'nuff a da dick to keep her satisfied. So, she figguh, if she gon fuck all da time anyway, why not make a dolla?"

Shit, Duncan thought, remembering his several unprotected sexual encounters with Ari. *I better get tested.* Upon meeting Ari, for some reason, he had made a foolhardy assessment of her as being some kind of virginal beauty, offered up as a kind of gift from Rennie. But no, Ari had made the decision herself to pursue Duncan for the night.

"Yah, mon," Rennie said, "Ari a fuckin slut, mon. Fuhreal, serious." The happily reunited friends laughed wildly at the keen observation.

Rennie then bombarded Duncan with questions. For starters, he had no idea what Duncan was doing in Amsterdam. The answer, that Duncan was playing pro ball for the Blue Devils, blew Rennie away. As soon as he met Duncan, he knew that there was something special about the kid that deeply connected the two of them. They had not discussed Amsterdam at all when they had hung out, yet now here they were, in the coolest, chillest, most shwarma-packed city in Europe, their reunion a product of a little luck, a little perseverance, and, perhaps, a little bit of fate. Rennie mused that the powers that be had brought he and Duncan together because they were both *bosses*, but of different businesses, and so there could be no rivalry. Only mutual respect.

After they had spoken for about an hour and a half, Duncan told Rennie that it was time for him to go back to his apartment to rest. His first game was tomorrow, and he wanted to properly represent himself and the Blue Devils. There was a lot of hype.

Duncan told Rennie that he would leave two tickets at will-call. One for Rennie. One for Ari. He said that he'd try to get them seats as close to the court as possible, underestimating his own status in the organization and his ability to get all the courtside seats he desired.

So, it was a pleasant surprise to Rennie and Ari that the tickets Duncan left for them were courtside, allowing them an unobstructed front-row view of the Woops show. The show seemed unlikely to disappoint.

Chapter 36

Of the twelve players dressing for the Blue Devils' first game, two were French, one was Canadian, and only three were actually from The Netherlands. The other six, including Duncan, were American. The coach, Max Waleson, was Dutch, but he spoke English well, as did the three Dutch players, so English was spoken almost all of the time, even between the Dutch players and coach. Waleson didn't want any of his players ever thinking that there was some sort of Dutch conspiracy against them to avoid passing them the ball, rob them of playing time, or talk any kind of nonsense behind their backs (right in front of their faces). So, English was the common denominator on the court.

In a thick Dutch accent, Coach Waleson gave an impassioned locker room pump-up speech, and the team trotted out onto the floor for the pre-game shoot-around. Duncan was *wet*, making almost all of his warmup shots. He shot from far outside NBA range. He shot mid-range J's. He shot free-throws. He shot threes with his toe right outside the line. He shot from the wings. He couldn't miss. *Wet!*

Duncan's teammates marveled at the masterful, effortless stroke of their new point-guard. This season, everyone thought, would be the one. After Duncan knocked down fifteen shots in a row, from all over the court, the buzzer sounded for the game to begin.

The center, Mike Naha, a black, 6'11", 21-year-old American, tipped the ball right to Duncan, who began to dribble up the court. Like one of his idols, Steve Nash, Duncan licked his fingers as he dribbled, and raised his hand to signal a play for the small-forward, Ryan Cahill, to make a backdoor cut. Cahill rolled off his man and Duncan lasered a pass to him, which he caught for an easy layup. The Blue Devils' fans cheered raucously, as the team trotted back on defense. The opposing team's point-guard carried the ball up, and passed off to the shooting-guard, Duncan's defensive assignment. The shooting-guard went to pass inside to the center. But Duncan was too quick. He tipped the ball forward, and grabbed it for a breakaway at the basket. He sprinted far ahead of the other teams' players, who were futilely trying to catch him, and finished with a vicious dunk and an emphatic, primal yell.

The rest of the game went much the same way. Duncan had a double-double, scoring 36 points and getting 14 assists. On top of that, he added eight rebounds, five steals, and three blocked shots, an all-around spectacular performance for his first day on the team. The fans, coaches, and other Blue Devils could not have been more pleased with their new star, and Rennie and Ari could not have screamed louder for their friend. Not only was he a scoring machine and the quickest player on the court, he was also unselfish with the ball, as evinced by his fourteen assists, which was a new Blue Devils record.

After the game, Rennie took Duncan and Ari out to dinner to celebrate Duncan's stellar performance and the Blue Devils' season-opening win. They went to an Italian restaurant, with outdoor seating and heavy foot-traffic passing by. The hostess guided them to the outdoor section, and within minutes, the three of them had drinks in hand, and were laughing like only the truly fortunate can.

Ari, Duncan noticed, looked even more beautiful without all the make-up on her face. When he had run into her in the super-hotties alley, she had looked, literally, unreal. Seeing her standing in that window had been a surreal experience. In fact, just being in the Red Light District at all had been surreal. Window-shopping for beautiful women was not exactly a common occurrence in the life of Duncan Lipton. But seeing Ari dolled-up that way was a different experience in and of itself, as, in the brief time that he had known her, she had basically been sans makeup, let alone the heavy load of it that she wore in her job as an Amsterdam hooker. However, despite how obviously gorgeous she was, Duncan found the fact that she was now sleeping with men for money to be extremely unattractive. He noted to himself that he was not interested in rekindling their sexual relationship.

After a nice dinner, the three of them sat, enjoying after-dinner drinks and watching as people passed by. After about half an hour of talking about Duncan's game and reminiscing about his short time on the island, Rennie called for the check, and the three of them left.

The plan was to go back to the apartment where Rennie was staying, smoke some weed, and chill out while Rennie played some music. The plan, however, changed when, as they slowly walked the cobblestone-paved Amsterdam street, Ari felt her ass get grabbed. She swung around to see a creepy-looking thirty-something, nearly bald guy, wearing matching leather pants and jacket, staring at her and licking his lips. "You piece of fucking shit!" she screamed, and ran at him, violently smacking him in the head with her purse. The man blocked her assault, grabbed her wrists, and threw her to the ground.

Duncan and Rennie were just a step behind Ari, but they were too taken by surprise to prevent her being hurled down to the bumpy road. But as soon as they saw her hit the ground, the two of them attacked the lip-licking, girl-hitting ass-grabber, together tackling him to the ground, and unleashing heavy punches all over his body, punishing his face, ribs, and groin.

The beating, however, only lasted about ten seconds before five other men, all dressed more or less identically to Ari's assailant, top-to-bottom in black leather, jumped Duncan and Rennie. Focused on kicking the shit out of the ass-grabber, they never saw the others coming. Duncan felt a boot crunch into his ribs, and he knew immediately, without a doubt, that several of them were fractured at the very least.

Rennie was grabbed by his dreads and thrown violently to the ground. Two men began to stomp on his upper body, and he curled into the fetal position, covering his head. Despite his best efforts at protecting himself, Rennie was kicked savagely hard on the top of his head, and even the padding provided by his dreads couldn't prevent him from getting completely knocked out.

Duncan, for his part, had an adrenalin flow surging through his body, taking away the nasty pain he felt from the crushing blow to his ribs. After getting kicked, he rolled off of the guy he was pummeling, and then popped up, ready to do battle with his leather-clad assailants. Unfortunately, with Rennie knocked out, he was forced to face off against five guys all by himself. He balled his fists and put up his dukes, hands in front of his face for protection.

Three of the men rushed him like linebackers. Duncan caught the first one with a right jab, right on the sweet-spot of his jaw; the guy dropped like a sack of potatoes. Without even resetting the position of his body, Duncan sustained his forward momentum, as he threw a left cross at the second guy, again directly connecting with the jaw's sweet-spot. The third guy was right on top of him though, leaving Duncan no opportunity to readjust and protect himself. He was tackled to the ground, where he was defenseless to prevent a stomping by the last two. Their boots broke several more of his ribs, and when his diaphragm was stomped, he had the wind completely knocked out of him.

Duncan was squirming around on the ground, fighting for air, failing to successfully inhale, and consequently panicking. As he writhed in pain and desperately tried to breathe, he looked up to see a boot sole primed to stomp on his head.

Chapter 37

Duncan and Matty G waited at the bus depot with their moms. They had both been selected to attend a month-long sleep-away camp for top-notch ball players from all across the nation, and their Greyhound would be leaving in fifteen minutes.

The two of them had just finished fifth grade. They were so relieved that next year they would be going to multiple classes, each subject having a different teacher. Now, they would only be stuck with any given teacher for fifty-five minutes, and then the bell would ring. A school day would now be divided into seven periods, a situation the boys greatly preferred to being stuck in the same room all day with the same teacher. Sometimes, if you got lucky and got one of the few really cool teachers in the school (like the one the boys had shared in third grade, Ms. Gardner), it could be great having just one teacher and being in the same room all day. But the one they had had this past year, Ms. Worzel, was a mean, crotchety, Oscar the Grouch, of a woman. After having a year-long taste of her bad medicine, to Duncan and Matty G, moving on to middle school was just what the doctor ordered.

The Nike Elite Hoops Camp was specifically for middle-schoolers, those going into sixth, seventh, or eighth grade, and Matty G and Duncan had been dying to go for several years now. This was their big chance to show their stuff to actual scouts for the first time. What also made the boys want to go so fervently was that the camp would have several really big-name NBA players show up to do some clinics, sign some autographs, give the boys a thrill, and generally enhance the camp's rep simply with their presence. Both Matty G and Duncan were certified idol-worshippers, and their gods were those of the hardwood and blacktop. No one knew who might appear this year. This was going to be the elite camp's eighth summer in operation, and they had new surprise guests every year. Last year, the massive Dikembe Mutombo had made an appearance, as did Chris Webber and Jason Kidd. These were not light-weights of the NBA, and it was wildly exciting to the boys that they might have the opportunity to meet stars of that caliber.

Naturally, Duncan and Matty G were dominant at camp. Before "Woops and Oops" came to define their tandem, the boys both played with youthful finesse, displaying finer ball-handling skills and court-vision than any of their peers. Once puberty set in, Matty supplemented his finesse-game with athleticism and power, while Duncan added speed and cunning to his. But at ten-years old, their raw skill alone set them apart.

G drove the lane repeatedly, finishing with seemingly effortless circus-shot layups. Duncan shot abnormally long three-bombs with staggering efficiency, and orchestrated fast-breaks with court-long passes and coast-to-coast runs.

The way that Matty G and Duncan played was no case of man-children amongst boys. They were just as small as the rest of the kids, so there was no size advantage or any other physical attribute that could explain the disparity in talent between them and their peers. Everyone who saw them play at the camp agreed that they were both special, and that they would continue to be throughout their lives. They just *had it*.

The more time that Duncan spent at the camp, the more he kept feeling a stronger and stronger sense of déjà vu. He didn't even know what déjà vu was, but that was what he was feeling, like everything he was doing, he had already done.

When they first got to the camp, Duncan felt like Duncan. He was ten years old and really wasn't thinking about much besides playing basketball. But by the end of the second week, he was feeling a bizarre sensation, like he was living in someone else's body, and that he had no control over what this person was saying or doing. And he was remembering things. Things that never could have happened. He was only ten. But he felt like he had lived so much more life than that. It was so confusing. He just wanted to play basketball.

During the third week of camp, the NBA players came. Duncan and Matty G were stunned to find that this year's crop were the best in the history of the camp: Kobe. Shaq. And, not to be believed, His Airness, Michael Jordan himself, graciously made a *three-day* appearance. Most of the kids were completely awestruck. When Michael spoke to them, they just mumbled and stuttered incoherent muttering sputterings.

At the time, Michael was still in the league, playing with the Washington Wizards. Though past his prime, he was still a force to be reckoned with. But how he played now was irrelevant. He was the greatest player of all time. He was probably the most famous man in the entire world. He did what no one else could do, the way he could fly through the air, drive the lane, shake, bake, and shake again. For most of the kids, they might as well have been meeting God himself. Number 23: greatest there ever was…greatest there will ever be.

Then there was the magnanimous, hugely entertaining, hugely huge Shaquille O'Neal, who seemed to constantly have a kid sitting on each of his shoulders. He was always telling jokes, laughing, and goofing around with the kids, who felt far more at ease with him than they did with MJ. Sure, Shaq was a legend. But he was a more accessible legend. Michael was not of this Earth.

Kobe was also cool with the boys. Though not as much of an Alpha personality as his Lakers teammate, he was revered by the kids just as much as Shaq, and his easygoingness and ever-present gracious smile made him very popular and easy to talk to. The boys had all watched he and Shaq win back-to-back-to-back NBA championships, and the dichotomy of the two made for an interesting and amusing experience for the campers' boggled minds.

Michael separated the boys out into two teams for a scrimmage, one coached by Shaq, the other by Kobe. The three superstars wanted to see what kind of talent they were working with. These kids were full of such immense potential, and it was nice to see what kind of raw ability they had when it came to improvising on a squad with unfamiliar teammates. But Michael didn't know Duncan or Matty G, and he put them together on the same team. From the opening tip, Michael Jordan, Shaquille O'Neal, and Kobe Bryant, three of the greatest basketball players to ever bounce a ball, knew that they were seeing something special. Duncan Lipton and Matty G were the future. They were chucking up all variety of circus shots, 360-layups, and long bomb three-pointers, all set up by elaborate tic-tac-toe passing. Their defense was ice-cold, both of them getting multiple steals. Duncan even had two blocks. This was before Matty G's growth spurt, so he had yet to become a mainstay at the top of the stat sheet's blocking column. Duncan was already on the rise though. And he had ups like a kangaroo.

After the scrimmage, the boys' heads were as level as they could possibly be, after being profusely praised by everyone. That is to say, their heads may have been getting just a wee bit big for their shoulders. They were raised right though, and managed to at least put up a front of modesty. But it was utter domination, and it was perfectly clear to all that these two were going to do big things in the world of basketball.

When the boys walked back to locker room, a voice hollered after them, "G! Lipton! Hold up!" They turned around, and there was Michael Jordan, calling out their names. They looked at each other and smiled beaming, cocky smiles that said, *Yeah, boy. Talkin to MJ. Bosses.*

As they approached MJ, the boys felt swallowed up by the 6'6" living legend. They fell silent and just stared at their idol. "That was pretty amazing today, fellas," he said. "I'm not gonna lie to you; I've never seen kids your age doing anything like that. Seriously, I've hardly seen anybody doing anything like that. You two are crazy."

Matty G couldn't speak. Duncan said, "Thank you, sir."

"It's just a shame what happens."

"What do you mean?" asked Duncan. But somehow, he knew exactly what Michael was saying. And he knew that he wasn't ten. And he knew things that he didn't know he'd ever known he'd known he'd known he'd known.

"You know what I mean, Dunks," said Michael.

"No," said Duncan, sheepishly. "Oh no." His head shook slowly back and forth. His eyes were wide and searching.

Matty G looked back and forth between Duncan and Michael, who were locked in heavy eye contact. "Uh, uh, what are you guys, uh, talking about?" he asked. But there was no response from either of them.

Michael was smiling, a smile that spoke of pity, concern, well-wishing, and faith. Duncan, on the other hand, had tears running down his cheeks. "No, this isn't…" he choked out. "Oh no, G, oh no. We're not ten, dude. FUCK!"

"What?" Ten-year-old Matty G was befuddled. And he was ignored.

"Duncan," Michael said, "Listen to me now. You're gonna fight, you hear me?"

"Who?"

"Not who, Dunks. What…" Pointing at Matty G, Michael said, "He's gone. And there ain't nothing you or anyone can do about that except hold him in your heart and in your head." Duncan looked at Matty G, who looked as confused as a deer in headlights. Duncan started bawling. "You're almost there yourself, man," Michael continued at Duncan. "You gotta fight this. Don't give in, Dunks. It's gonna be hard, but you're gonna pull through. You can do this, little man. You were meant to be great. And you're NOT gonna let some motherfuckin little gang of Dutch motherfuckin leather-boys ruin *your* motherfuckin LIFE!"

For the first time in over three months, Duncan woke up.

Chapter 38

The dream seemed longer than any dream Duncan had ever had before. But when he woke up, it was as though he'd had a normal night's sleep. He had no sense of the vast amount of time that had lapsed between getting his face stomped on and waking up in the hospital.

His body was limp and weak, a feeling he wasn't used to. And he could tell immediately that he'd lost weight. He tried to prop himself up on his elbow, and in doing so let out an achy groan. Outside his room there was a sudden stir. "Did you hear that?" someone said.

A large black nurse, wearing a nametag that read "Mr. Paul", peeked his head in the room. "Wellllll," he exclaimed, "look who decided to join the party! Mr. Duncan is back with us, ladies and gentlemen!" Duncan heard some excitement coming from outside his door, and in rushed nurses, doctors, everybody.

"I'll call his mother," one nurse said.

"What the fuck is going on?" Duncan asked no one in particular.

"You've been in a coma," said Paul. You've been out cold for the past three months.

"Three months?" Duncan asked.

"Three months" said Paul.

"Three *months*?"

"Three months."

Wow, Duncan thought. *That's a new one.* "What happened to me?" he asked Paul.

You got in a fight in Amsterdam. You and your friend, you guys got jumped. One of them stepped on your head, and you've been out ever since.

"Jesus," Duncan breathed.

"Jesus is right," said Paul. "The good Lord had your back, my friend."

Duncan was pretty amazed by this news. He had only played one game with the Blue Devils, breaking out as the team's big star. He had been looking forward to making a name for himself in the Netherlands, and further raising his stock for next year's NBA draft. This was clearly going to be a setback.

Rennie, Duncan thought, suddenly recalling the circumstances that precipitated his coma. "What happened to my friend, Rennie?" he asked. A downcast expression washed over the massive nurse's friendly face, which seemed to darken with the disappearance of the gleaming white teeth, behind thick, frowning lips.

"I'm sorry," Paul said. "Rennie didn't make it."

"No," Duncan whispered. "Oh no."

"I'm really sorry," Paul repeated, as he took Duncan's blood pressure and comfortingly gave his hand a squeeze. "He was already gone when the medics got there."

Duncan was immediately overwhelmed with grief, and started to cry. Paul held his hand and squeezed his thumb hard into Duncan's palm. "The Lord has his plan for everyone," he said, but as Duncan was not one to have any religious faith, this was no consolation.

"Fuck," Duncan said. "Fuck, fuck, fuck, fuck."

"Yeah," said Paul. "It's a drag, man. It really is. But he's in a better place now." Duncan didn't respond, just dug his palms into his wet eyes, and Paul, seeing that the young man could use some time alone, told him that he would come back soon, and politely excused himself from the room.

Alone, Duncan's tears flowed even more freely. He could barely believe what had happened. *I've been in a fucking coma for three fucking months,* he thought. *Three fucking months! And Rennie's dead. First Matty. Now Rennie. I'm a liability as a best friend.* He lay in the narrow hospital bed, sobbing, reflecting on the amazing, one-of-a-kind relationships he had had with each of them, and punished himself emotionally by trying to somehow cast some blame on himself for how they had lost their lives. It was Duncan who had first introduced Matty G to Xanax. And it was his idea to go to that particular area of Amsterdam to eat with Rennie and Ari, after his first game. These facts filled him with regret. Rationally, in the back of his head, he knew that neither of the incidences were his fault, but the pain of the news of his friend's death, coupled with the physical and emotional vulnerability he was feeling as a result of so much time in a coma, took him to a dark place.

Fifteen minutes later, Duncan's mother rushed in, followed by his father after another twenty. It was the middle of the day, so it took some time for Mr. Lipton to get there from work, once Mrs. Lipton phoned to give him the news that their son had woken up.

As his ecstatic parents smothered him in hugs and kisses, Duncan struggled to make sense of reality. It seemed like it was only yesterday that he had dominated his first game as a professional basketball player. But it had been three months ago. He was now tired, weak, stiff, and confused. And he was clueless about the extent of the damage to his body, which made him clueless about what kind of recovery process he was in for.

The doctors had their tests to run, and he had to retrain his legs to walk again, but in under two weeks Duncan was back home.

Chapter 39

Tucker Mobley thoroughly licked the outer leaf of a Dutch Master cigar. He removed the leaf, cracked the cigar down the line with his thumbs, and emptied the tobacco guts into the small trashcan under his desk. His friend, John Weinhaus, sat next to him, carefully breaking apart a nugget of good weed, which smelled like a skunk that had found its way into a bag of orange rinds.

Across the room, Corey Pager sat on his bed with an open copy of *The Daily Word*, State's school newspaper. He had it opened to the crossword puzzle, which he stared at intently, as he twirled a Bic pen around in the fingers of his left hand. "Jesus," he said. "These c-words are so fuckin hard on Thursdays."

"Bummer," said John.

"Yeah...*major* bummer,"Tucker said sarcastically. He and John had a chuckle at Corey's expense.

"Fuck you, jerks," Corey replied. He threw down *The Word*, scattering a couple of the pages across the floor. "I'm too impatient for this shit."

"And too dumb," said John.

"Yeah," said Tucker. "Way too dumb."

"You guys are so fuckin stupid," Corey said. "I'm goin to have a smoke outside."

"Good luck with that," said John.

"Yeah, best of luck, buddy," said Tucker. Neither of them looked at Corey as they made their snotty remarks, and Corey walked out of the room rolling his eyes.

"I'm fuckin sick of that dude," said John.

"I bet," saidTucker. I'd lose my fucking mind if I lived with that guy."

"Oh, if only you knew…" said John, sighing and shaking his head side-to-side. "If only you knew."

John and Corey were freshmen roommates at State. Tucker lived four doors down the hall, on the fourth floor of Metzger Hall. They were in their first semester, and overall the two friends had definitely been enjoying State. But John couldn't stand living with Corey.

Corey was an only child from an exorbitantly rich family from the South. His accent was an oddly posh southern drawl. He was obese. He wore shirts that didn't quite fit properly, hugging his fat belly. He ate John's food. He frequently neglected to use deodorant. Conseqently, he smelled awful.

"Yeah, well, I can fuckin imagine," Tucker replied, meditating on the idea of how much it would suck to be Corey Pager's roommate. "That dude smells like a fuckin turd mountain." He and John had a laugh, one of many which the two immediate friends had shared at Corey's expense over the course of that first semester. Dorm-rooms at State were tiny, making living with an odiferous individual virtually unbearable, and the fact that Corey so drastically degraded the tiny space's air quality made John *resent* him. He already didn't like Corey's style, accent, or personality, but he was pushed over the edge of dislike into the abyss of hate by the lingering presence of his roommate's pungency.

John finished breaking up the weed, and put it into the waiting inner blunt leaf. Tucker expertly rolled up the inner leaf, and then smoothly twisted the outer leaf around it. He flicked his lighter, and hovered the blunt over the flame to dry off his saliva. "Mmm, mmm, mmm," said John. "Looks delicious."

"Thank you, good sir," said Tucker. "The doctor has operated. It has been a successful operation."

Tucker and John walked outside to smoke their blunt. They would have preferred to smoke in the dorm room, but Bridget, their Resident

Advisor, took her job very seriously, and had already written up two other kids on the hall for smoking. One of them had been smoking a cigarette, and was punished by being forced to work forty hours in the dining hall. The other one of them had been smoking pot. The police were called, and the kid had gotten tossed out of school, only one week into the semester. Consequently, John and Tucker smoked their weed off in the woods near their dorm.

As they walked out the front of the building, they saw Corey finishing his cigarette. "Hey guys," Corey said.

"Mmph," replied John, as though it was a chore just to say hello to his obnoxious, rotund roommate.

"Where are you guys going?" Corey asked.

"To go play fuckin tummy sticks in the fuckin bushes," said Tucker. "I bet you'd like to watch, wouldn't you?"

"I knew you two were fruits," Corey replied.

Faking a flamboyantly gay affect, Tucker said, "You know it, big boy. And you're next, you little Krispy Kreme. The only reason I come around your room and hang out with John is I've really just been waiting to get to your doughy ass. I'm gonna cover you in chocolate syrup and just lick you from top to bottom, and then use grape jelly to lube up your ass before I pummel it." John laughed his ass off, as Tucker, grunting obscenely, made pelvic thrusting motions."

"You make me fuckin sick," said Corey. "I'm gonna puke."

"Oh," Tucker replied, "I love it when you talk dirty to me."

Disgusted and annoyed at being blown off by his roommate and his accomplice yet again, Corey rolled his eyes and marched inside, back to he and John's fourth-floor room.

Laughing, John and Tucker headed into the woods. As they smoked, they discussed whether or not they should pledge a frat. John's older brother had recently graduated from State. "If I have one regret about my time at State," he had told John, "it's that I didn't join a frat. I could have gotten so much more pussy." That made a big impression on

John, who was an enthusiastic pussy fan. He was not exactly a ladies man, so he was willing to consider any leg-up he could get on the competition.

"Dude," John said to Tucker, "my big bro just graduated from this place, and he said that his big regret is not joining a frat. He told me that getting pussy is ridiculously easy if you're in one, and the girls who go to the parties there are the hottest ones in school. I say it's a no-brainer."

"Yeah, that makes sense," replied Tucker. "I've just heard that a lot of frats make the pledges do all sorts of weird gay shit to get into the frat. I'm definitely not down with weird gay shit."

"Nah, dude," John said, "my brother said they don't do that shit anymore. Kids have gotten way cooler about it. There was some shit that went down at the University of Vermont, with the hockey team, I think, where they made the freshmen do the elephant walk."

"What the fuck is the elephant walk?" said John.

Tucker laughed. "You've never seen a picture of elephants walking in a line?"

John thought about it. "Oh, shit," he said. "That's fucked up. I wouldn't do that shit."

"Fuck no," said Tucker. "But I figure, I wanna try it out."

"The elephant walk?" said John.

"Fuck you, Weinhaus. Nah, I'm talking about pledging. I figure I'll just take the risk. If they try to make me do some gay shit, I'll just fuck some kids up."

"Sounds like a plan, Mobley," said John.

When they were finished smoking the blunt, they went back inside, where they found Corey lying on his side, reading the second Harry Potter book. John scoffed, and Tucker rolled his eyes. John went to his desk, sat down, and logged onto Facebook, where he saw that he had two new friend requests. They were from girls in his Spanish class. Cute girls who didn't need help studying. *Right on,* he thought.

Tucker, who was bored easily and required consistent mental stimulation throughout the day, decided to peruse the copy of the Daily Word that Corey had thrown on the floor earlier. The first thing that caught his eye was the sports section. "Holy shitballs," he said. "Yo, Haus, you're not gonna believe this." John looked away from his computer screen, and took the paper that his friend handed him. When he saw the headline, his jaw dropped and his eyes grew wide. It read: *Duncan Lipton Is Coming To State!!!*

Chapter 40

Once drafted into the NBA, or playing any kind of professional ball, a player is no longer eligible to play college basketball in the US. Unlike the NBA, there can sometimes be exceptions made when it comes to playing overseas. Sometimes what constitutes "professional" is a gray area. Duncan played his one game as a pro overseas, and, after reviewing his case, the NCAA decided that the extenuating circumstances of his situation should make him still eligible to play in school.

After he was released from the hospital, it took him about six weeks of rehab and intense sessions in the weight room, six days a week, to get his weight back up, and to get his body feeling something like it used to. His doctors advised him to begin a pilates regimen as well, to improve the flexibility he had lost during his period of immobility. His prognosis was good, but the experts insisted that a full recovery would take some time.

Duncan's healthy young body recuperated quickly though, and in short order it was clear that he would be able to play basketball again soon. That meant that a decision had to be made about where that basketball would be played. The Liptons came to a family decision that it would be in Duncan's best interest to be close to home while still rehabbing. And, aside from reasonable proximity to his doctors, he quietly conceded that perhaps he had done enough adventuring for a while.

Luckily, the Blue Devils' owners were incredibly understanding, and were gracious enough to void his contract, owing to the unfortunate circumstances. To show good will and appreciation of Duncan's immediate impact, they even paid him as though he had played ten games, rather than just one (under the table though, so that there wouldn't be a chance of his college eligibility getting messed up).

Everything that happened in Amsterdam took place in early July, shortly after Duncan's high school graduation, and his coma lasted three months until he woke up in early October. That gave him the rest of October to get his body straightened out, and to plan his next move. The NBA draft would not be held until next June 24th, and Duncan needed to keep on playing competitive basketball, in order to keep his skills sharp and maintain his competitive edge. He wanted to be close to home, and being the social butterfly that he was, he decided that one year of playing college ball really couldn't hurt, and that it was more than likely that he would have a ridiculously good time, especially since, with no intention to graduate, he could dedicate just enough time to his schoolwork to pass his classes with the minimum GPA he needed to be academically eligible to be active on the hardwood.

Although he was considered to be a definite first-rounder right out of high school, Duncan's injury now caused some scouts and coaches to question whether he would be able to live up to the expectations created by his stellar, statistic/artistic performance in high school.

Duncan's agent, Lee Bernstein, pressed upon him that playing college ball was, if not necessary, then a very good idea, in order to prove that the stomping he had endured in Amsterdam had not adversely affected him for the long haul, and that he was still worth such a high draft pick. (Had it not been for the relatively new rule that you had to be at least nineteen to play in the NBA, he would have entered the draft immediately instead of going to Amsterdam. Instead, he was now in the position of having to continue to prove himself.)

Duncan wasn't worried though. If there was one thing that he knew he could do, it was play basketball. And he knew that he could do *a lot* more than just play the game. On the court, his cup runneth over with confidence, and he had every reason to feel that way. His whole life, he had been the best, and he certainly didn't expect anything to change now. He didn't rub it in anyone's face; outward modesty had always been one of his strengths. There was no need to brag when everyone already knew about his accomplishments. Inside, though, he maintained a powerful, unshakeable confidence that he was going to run shit. In no way, shape, or form was he going to allow playing college basketball to hinder him from attaining his lifelong dream of playing in the NBA.

For college, Duncan, who could have started at point guard for almost any top tier school, decided on State because it was only a forty-five minute drive from his parents' house, and it was the closest school that was perennially ranked among the top twenty-five teams in the nation. He had also been charmed by State's young coach, Richard Flynn. When it came to wooing the best player in the state, Flynn thought, some research was required to find out just what made Duncan Lipton tick, and what he truly wanted out of a school, team, and coach. Consequently, Coach Flynn had a very different approach to recruiting this particular player than his contemporaries.

What Flynn found out through the grapevine was that Duncan was a bit of a marijuana enthusiast. More or less, a pothead. It just so happened that Flynn himself did a bit more than dabble with the herb. His smoking had cooled down since his younger years, but he still took a daily spliff or two to the face.

During his recruitment visit, the coach and Duncan had gone to a local outdoor court to have a shoot-around, where they discussed what it would be like for Duncan to attend State, and to play basketball there. Duncan liked Coach Flynn, more than most of the other coaches trying to recruit him, and he thought that State would probably be a good fit. But when Flynn busted out a fat spliff, and sparked it up, right on the ball court, Duncan was *smitten*. Being that there was no one in sight, Flynn liked the idea of sparking up on the court, his intention being for the act to be emblematic of his philosophy that fun and basketball success did not have to be mutually exclusive.

That was all it took. Duncan decided that Coach Flynn was the coolest, and there was no one else he wanted to play for. As long as he lived up to the hype on the court and performed in the classroom, he wasn't going to catch any heat from his coach for his extra-curricular activities. And thanks to "The Stuff", a fruit punch-flavored detox drink, and a heads-up from Flynn himself, random drug tests would never be an issue.

Duncan was recognized as the best high school player the state had seen in a very long time, and, consequently, he was paid a lot of attention by the media, as he was regularly questioned by reporters regarding the status of his career direction. So that the newsmen would not consistently hound him, a press conference was held, at which he declared that he had made a decision to attend State for at least a year, before entering the draft.

The next day's sports pages, in newspapers all throughout the country, showed pictures of Duncan and Coach Flynn shaking hands with huge grins on their faces. All of the articles detailed the circumstances under which Duncan had come to this point, including the beating he had endured in the Netherlands, his three-month coma, his stubborn determination to continue to play his favorite game, and his refusal to give up on his dream to play in the NBA.

People other than just sports fans became interested in his miraculous recovery and success in overcoming this difficult setback. Coupled with his unique, singular athletic ability and creativity, Duncan's comeback made for quite the human-interest story. People who had never even heard of him before found themselves feeling proud of this remarkable young man's strength in surviving, recovering, and having the will and drive to resume the pursuit of his dream.

And just like that, even before the first game of his freshman season, Duncan Lipton captured the imagination of sports fans across the country, who couldn't wait to see if he would live up to the hype and become America's boy.

When people believed in him, Duncan hated to disappoint. He rarely did.

Chapter 41

ESPN was all about Duncan Lipton's first game as point-guard for State. SportsCenter made a big deal out of it. They talked about him on Pardon the Interruption. They talked about him on Around the Horn. ESPNews had clips of his poorly-filmed high school games, playing a few times every hour. Jim Rome even had a few words to say.

"College Superstar" was basically Duncan's title to lose. As of yet, those who had witnessed his game agreed that the kid was truly an artist. Hype like this hadn't been this intense since LeBron James, five years earlier. LeBron came into the league, straight out of high school, three years before the rule making nineteen the minimum age for draft eligibility had been implemented by the Commissioner, David Stern. But Duncan was very different than LeBron was at his age. LeBron was a miraculous physical specimen and a basketball phenom at eighteen, but he had yet to really develop a good jump-shot, and he and his game were rough around the edges.

Duncan's game, in contrast, was balletic, his dribbling fluid and smooth, his jump-shots graceful and effortless, his passes crisp and on-target. There was nothing anyone could teach him to improve his shooting or dribbling. He could do it all, with incredible proficiency. He had spent countless hours on the driveway and in the gym, perfecting how to control the ball, as though he had it on a string, like a yo-yo. He had it down to a precise, effortless science. So, the question on everyone's mind was whether Duncan could take those skills to the next level. But for those who had seen him play in high school, or watched the videos on YouTube or ESPNews, optimism abounded, and expectations were through the roof. Those who doubted that he would live up to the hype were few and far between.

And those doubters were usually cynics and haters with no frame of reference, having never even seen him play.

The night of the first game, Duncan felt a sensation that he had never experienced before in the context of playing sports: butterflies in his stomach. The last time he had even felt nervous like that was when he had to recite a short monologue in the school play, when he was fifteen and in the tenth grade. He had lost a bet to Matty G, the terms of which dictated that the loser had to be in the performance. Although it wasn't his thing to act and be in with the drama crowd, Duncan had ended up really enjoying the experience, and gaining a lot of respect for his fellow thespians. The butterflies were not a result of stage fright; they were there because he wanted his small contribution to come off well, and not mar the quality of the play.

These butterflies, however, were different. These were butterflies of doubt. This was the first time that he was going to be on national television, and there had been so much hype that he was suddenly feeling a little bit of the pressure. He jumped up and down in place, cracked his neck, and thought about the mechanics of his jump-shot. *Just do what you always do, Dunks*, he thought. *You're money, doggy. Money, money, money.* But he couldn't help feeling just a little bit unsure of himself.

After a little pump-up speech and dry-erase board strategizing from Coach Flynn, Duncan and the rest of the State Soldiers ran through the tunnel, and out onto the court. A ball-boy passed Duncan a ball off the rack to start up the pre-game shoot-around. The moment that he touched it, his butterflies were gone. He smiled at the ball, kissed it, then turned around and hit a fade-away jumper. He was standing five feet outside the three-point line. *I'm feelin' it*, he thought. *Oh, shit. Watch out! I am feelin' it tonight!*

State was playing against MGU. They were ranked, preseason, as number five in the nation. State was ranked twenty-second. MGU's center was 7'2", an absolute Goliath, named Blake Waycaster. State's center, Michael Charmatz, was only 6'11", totally massive, but tiny in comparison to this monster facing him in the opening tip-off. Waycaster easily won the tip, and the ball went back to MGU's point guard, David Brautigam, who confidently dribbled up the court, weaving the ball back and forth between his legs.

Brautigam, Duncan's defensive assignment, prepared for MGU's opening attack. He brought the ball up, and faked once to the right, then tried a quick crossover to the left, to get past Duncan and penetrate the lane. But Duncan was too quick. He tipped the ball, sending it bouncing toward the sideline. Although the ball was moving quickly, he lunged after it, and threw a backhanded scoop pass to his teammate, Sean O'Neill, the shooting guard. Duncan quickly recovered, and called for the ball. O'Neill shot him a laser pass, which he caught mid-air, and floated to a reverse layup.

State's crowd went completely bananas. One play. One play, and it was plain to see that Duncan Lipton was the real deal. The rest of the game went something like this: In the first ten minutes, Duncan showcased his ability to run the fast break, scoring twenty points and dishing out seven assists. In the second quarter (really, the final ten minutes of the first half), he slowed the game down by orchestrating intricate passing sequences that lead to his teammates being wide-open. He scored no points, but had ten assists. In the first ten minutes of the second half, he had ten points and five assists, as he eased back and provided his teammates with an opportunity to showcase their skills as well. In the final ten minutes of the game, he had fifteen points and three assists. The last fifteen points were all scored behind the three-point line.

For the game, Duncan scored forty-five points and dished out twenty-five assists. He was ten points shy of the school scoring record. The assists record, however, he decimated. The previous record had been *seventeen*! He smashed it by *eight* assists.

This was the night that Duncan Lipton became a celebrity.

Chapter 42

There were definitely plenty of people who had heard about Duncan and his prodigious ability to play basketball. He was, after all, projected to be a first-round NBA draft pick once he turned nineteen and became eligible. But most sports-fans didn't have access to footage of his high school games. He was a folk hero, someone whose exploits were often talked and written about, but rarely seen.

The season-opener against MGU changed all that. Duncan was no longer the best-kept secret on the hardwood. Now that he was visible to the public, he immediately was on his way to becoming a legend. He gracefully displayed an un-teachable, natural, balletic fluidity on the court. He was a handsome kid, well spoken, and modest during the post-game interview, graciously praising his teammates and noting that he couldn't have had the twenty-five assists had his teammates not scored the ball. And the story of his comeback from a three-month coma made his achievements all the more impressive. His new fans were emotionally impacted by his genuine presentation of seldom-seen will power and the strength of character he had needed in order to pull himself through his ordeal.

He was now recognized, congratulated, and praised everywhere he went. At State, sports were not taken lightly; students were fanatical about the school's teams, and, accordingly, they collectively fell in love with their new star. Considering just how many "Staters" were athlete-worshipping sports fanatics, Duncan's brilliant performance elevated him to hero status on campus. If State were a monarchy, the king would have knighted him by halftime. He was just that good, and he was just that guy.

After that first game, Duncan's days were full of pats on the back and "Way to go!"s from Staters he'd never met before. Everybody at school knew who he was. He was a legit BMOC. He was getting "the eye" from half the pretty girls he walked by, many of whom were more than happy to add Duncan Lipton to their contact list, and to be at his beck and call for late-night booty. As far as he was concerned, he was pretty much in heaven, just living *the life*.

Being that he spent very little time on schoolwork, and basketball (or basketball-related functions and activities) really only occupied no more than five or six hours of each day, Duncan was left with plenty of time to have fun. Having fun meant a variety of things to him: spending time with a nice young lady, reading, playing the drums at the music school if he got a chance, poking around on Facebook, playing pool and ping-pong at the student center, and playing other sports recreationally.

Basketball was far from the only sport that Duncan had some proficiency in. He absolutely loved the game; it was his favorite and the one he was best at. But he loved athletics in general. Because he was so important to the basketball team in high school, Coach Stager had insisted that neither he nor Matty G be on any other school teams. "Basketball is a year-round commitment, boys," Stager would always say, strongly advising all of his players to spend at least two hours playing basketball, and another two hours doing cardio and lifting weights, during the off-season.

Though the coach did consider off-season devotion to be important, it wasn't the real reason he didn't want the two boys playing any other sports. They were unstoppable, and Stager knew that playing other sports wouldn't hamper either of their playing abilities. The real reason he didn't want them playing other sports was that he was afraid that one or both of them would get hurt, completely ruining the team's championship aspirations. It was preventive medicine against the dreaded possibility of a losing season.

Stager actually felt bad about his personally instated team rule, which forbade any of his players to participate on any other athletic teams. Some of the less-played kids on the team were pretty good at other sports, and probably could have done well had they had the chance. But he couldn't make a rule applicable to only two of his players because there was no way that either Duncan or Matty G would have accepted that kind of restriction without informing their parents, who were the kind of people who would make a very big deal of the situation, and swiftly involve the school principal. So, Stager made all his players choose between basketball and all other sports.

Not being allowed to play any other team sports was always kind of a bummer to Duncan who, during the Fall football season, would go to all of the Eastfield home games, and entertain the fantasy that he could be out there utilizing his speed and jumping ability to play receiver, or, perhaps, employing his reputation as a natural leader to play quarterback. Being a point-guard, he thought, was a whole lot like being a quarterback. Illustrating the concept, point-guards are often referred to as "floor generals", and quarterbacks as "field generals", the implication being that leadership is a necessary skill for one to have success at either position. But it just wasn't a possibility, and Duncan grudgingly accepted the fact. Basketball was it.

Well, whether Duncan would have gotten hurt or not, no one would ever find out because Coach Stager succeeded in keeping his point-guard off any other playing surfaces. Now, in retrospect, Duncan couldn't help but feel gratitude. The life he was living was just what he wanted, and it was all due to his ability to effectively play basketball. He graciously obliged fans who asked him for his autograph. As he walked around on campus, random students were giving him daps, high-fives, and pounds. Faculty were shamelessly asking him to pose with them in hearty-handshake, back-patting photos. The girls, to say the least, were treating him well.

And one day, in the back of his Intro to Communications class (during a discussion on whether or not the porn industry was, more or less, responsible for the success of VHS and the downfall of Beta-Max), Duncan made two new friends named Tucker and John.

Chapter 43

Intro to Communications was a large lecture-hall class full of nearly three hundred horny kids in their late teens and early twenties. It was an easy, introductory class that put labels on concepts that most people were familiar with, but didn't discuss in technical terms. The professor was a small man in his early thirties, with long, curly dark brown hair, named Dr. Jordan Goldberg. Dr. Goldberg would often have students break into small discussion groups of five or six, and on the day of the Beta-Max vs. VHS discussion, Duncan ended up in a group with Tucker Mobley and John Weinhaus. He was sitting in the aisle seat at the back left (from the teacher's perspective) of the auditorium.

"Fellas," Duncan said, nodding to the two boys seated closest to him, and then nodding to the two girls sitting in the row right in front of them, "Ladies. How you guys doin?" He beamed a big smile at his four group-mates.

"Good," said a chubby, bespectacled girl named Kim. The other girl, a cute, innocent-looking redhead named Shauna, repeated Kim's sentiments.

"Chillin, chillin, dude," said Tucker.

"Agreed," said John, nodding.

Duncan introduced himself, and the others followed suit.

"Aren't you the basketball player?" Shauna asked, blushing a little bit.

Blushing himself, Duncan responded, "That would be me." It had been less than a week since the big season-opener, and Duncan was still getting accustomed to being recognized. He wanted to just blend in, but he was definitely getting a kick out of people all over campus knowing who he was, even in his huge classes, some of which, like Intro to Communications, were easily more than ten times the size of his largest classes at Eastfield.

"I watched the home-opener on TV," Shauna said. "You were really good."

"Wow." Duncan's face lit up. "Thanks," he said sincerely. "Thanks a lot."

"Yeah, man," Tucker chimed in. "That was badass."

After a little more hoops chatter, Kim steered the conversation toward what they were supposed to be discussing, why Beta-Max video players didn't stand the test of time and were made obsolete by VHS. It turned out that in adopting VHS tapes as the means by which it distributed its multi-billion-dollar-a-year entertainment to home viewers, the porn industry had played a large part in rendering Beta-Max players, though essentially no better or worse than VCR players (which played VHS), useless to the millions of people who chose to have their player be the one which allowed them to pop in a skin flick. Dr. Goldberg asked the class to discuss, in small groups, whether or not they believed that porn could have played such a pivotal role in the players' rivalry, given that it was not fact per se that porn was indeed responsible for the success of VHS and the downfall of Beta-Max.

The small group was divided into two camps: the girls vs. the boys. The girls were both small-town eighteen-year-olds and neither had ever actually seen a porn film before. But they were adamant in their refusal to believe that dirty movies could have played such a pivotal role in determining the fate of the now-obsolete casette player. The boys, on the other hand, held the exact opposite belief. Tucker and John (who Tucker told Duncan to call Haus, as that was his longtime and preferred nickname) were both nineteen. Duncan was eighteen. They were horny teenage boys who had each spent more than their fair share of time on the internet, looking at RedTube, PornHub, Brazzers, MilfHunter, and the myriad other hardcore websites readily available.

Tucker, to the disgust and rolled eyes of Kim and Shauna, made the point that if one internet service provider, all else being equal, gave him access to porn and the other did not, then it was a no-brainer as to which one he would choose. It made perfect sense that others made the equivalent decision in the seventies and eighties.

Though the conversation started off academic, seeing that the girls were made uncomfortable by the topic of porn, Tucker seized the opportunity to make them even more so by engaging the other boys in a graphic porn discussion that left them in tears from laughing so hard, after he informed the group that there was only one thing he did better with his left hand than his right, and that was because he needed his right hand to operate the mouse. All five group-members were beet-red: the boys from their hysterical laughing, the girls from squeamish embarrassment.

After class, Duncan walked out of the auditorium with Tucker and Haus. They were still giggling from the conversation and how uncomfortable it had made Kim and Shauna. As the boys were about to part ways, Duncan said, "So, what are you fellas up to the rest of the day?"

"Prolly gonna smoke a blunt," said Haus.

"More like *definitely*," said Tucker.

"Interesting," said Duncan, with a sly grin.

"Would you care to partake?" asked Haus. He and Tucker looked at Duncan expectantly as he thought about the offer.

"Well, I have practice in a few hours," Duncan said. "But, I suppose I have a little time to kill. Fuck it. Why not?"

"Indeed," said Tucker.

The three of them walked across campus to Haus's dorm. Once inside, Tucker removed a vanilla Dutch Master cigar and a twenty bag from his backpack. He sat down at Haus's desk, unleafed the Dutch, broke up the weed, and began to fashion a blunt. As he did so, something loudly banged into the door of the dorm room. Startled by the sudden unexpected noise, Tucker spilled the broken-up weed onto the carpet. "Shit!" he said.

"What the fuck was that?" Duncan said, kneeling down with Tucker to salvage most of the weed that wasn't too badly stuck in the carpeting. As he did so, he looked up to find the answer to his question: an obese young man wearing an ill-fitting pink polo shirt, khaki cargo shorts which unpleasantly ended well above his knees, and a bloody nose.

"Goddamn it, Corey!" shouted Haus. "What is your fucking problem, you tub of spuds? Why did you slam into the fucking door?"

"Sorry, John," said Corey meekly. "I was rushing, and I, uh, I tripped."

"You're such a fucking retard, Corey," hissed Haus. "I can't believe… of all the twenty-five thousand people in this fucking place, I get stuck living with the fattest…ugliest…clumsiest…most retarded fucking retard in this whole fucking school!"

Duncan watched in amazement. He had only just met Tucker and Haus in the class that had ended less than half an hour earlier, and the three had been getting on well, pretty much laughing the whole time. So, seeing this flip in Haus's personality came as something of a shock. Duncan didn't know who Corey was, and he didn't know what the big deal about tripping into the door was. Haus seemed like a completely different person from the affable kid he had just been joking with in Communications. He looked at Tucker to try to get some kind of nonverbal clue as to what was going on.

But Tucker was looking at the other two boys, and a sneer was playing around his lips. "Seriously, Pager, you've got to be the dumbest sack of shit alive," he contributed.

Corey hung his head in shame. He had grown accustomed to verbal tirades from the two bullies during his brief time at State, but it stung every time all the same. He said nothing and walked over to his desk to get a tissue for his nose, which had been bloodied by his stumbling into the door.

Tucker finished rolling the blunt, and he, Haus, and Duncan left the room. As they entered the stairwell to go outside the dorm, Duncan asked, "Who was that?"

"My fucking roommate," said Haus, "Corey. He's a fucking imbecile."

"Seriously," added Tucker.

"What's so bad about him?" Duncan asked.

"Everything," said Haus. "He's fat, stupid, gross, annoying…the list never ends with the kid."

"Hmm," said Duncan. He had never been a bully nor been bullied, but he had known some bullies in high school, and had always found that kind of behavior to be rather abhorrent. He recognized it immediately. The fat, silly kid upstairs looked harmless and hardly deserving of being yelled at like he just had. The experience of seeing his two new friends act so callously was leaving a sour taste in his mouth.

"Forget about him," said Haus. "He's not worth remembering."

Chapter 44

Corey Pager stared at himself in the full-length mirror next to his bed. He did not like what he saw. He could hardly even blame his roommate and his vindictive friend for being so mean to him. *I am a tub of spuds*, he thought. *God, I'm such a fucking loser!* He knew that his outfit was ridiculous. He knew that he was way overweight. And, as he silently berated himself, he began to cry. Suddenly, he kicked the mirror, more or less shattering it, sending shards of glass all over the floor. Realizing that he was definitely in for a merciless verbal assault once Haus saw what he had done, he started bawling. But, with the presence of mind to know that a clean floor was better than one covered in shards of glass, he grabbed a dustpan, and started sweeping up the mess. When he was done, he threw the glass in the trash, sat down on his bed, and continued to weep as quietly as he could manage.

Duncan took a big pull off the expertly rolled blunt, fashioned by Tucker. "What do you think?" Tucker asked.

"Bangin'," Duncan coughed out.

"Word," Tucker said, smiling. He was chuffed at the fact that a celebrity athlete of Duncan's status appreciated his handiwork.

"What time do you have practice?" Haus asked, looking at his watch, which read 1:16pm.

"Like 4," Duncan replied.

"True," Haus said. "You got plenty of time."

They finished smoking the blunt, and Duncan thanked his new friends before heading off to get changed for practice.

"What a fuckin cool guy," Tucker said to Haus, as Duncan walked away . "I thought he'd be more, like, straight-edge, ya know?"

"Yeah," said Haus, "he's definitely one of us."

They walked back upstairs to the dorm room Haus shared with Corey. Haus opened the door to find Corey whimpering on his bed, his face pressed into his pillow.

"What the fuck are you doing, Pager?" Haus said unsympathetically.

"Nothing," Corey blustered into the pillow. "Leave me alone."

"Leave *you* alone? This is *my* fucking room. Go be a baby somewhere else, pussy."

Not wanting to face any more verbal abuse from the two bullies, Corey pulled himself together, stood up, and, without another word, walked out of the room.

"You think maybe we were a little hard on him before?" Tucker said, once Corey was gone.

"Seriously, I don't give a shit about that kid," said Haus. "He just takes up space in my living area. And way too much of it at that. I wish he'd just kill himself and be done with it."

Tucker couldn't help but feel the pangs of guilt that Haus was obviously devoid of. Sure, Tucker was a bully, but he had a conscience. Haus, on the other hand, seemed to completely lack one, at least when it came to his treatment of his roommate, so Tucker dropped the subject. He suddenly felt restless, like he should go somewhere and do something. "Dude, I'm gonna split. I'll catch ya later," he said.

"Where you goin'?" asked Haus. "You givin' me the ol' 'smoke-n-run'?"

"It was *my* weed, son," Tucker said.

"This is true," Haus laughed. "Alright. Be cool."

"You too, homes," Tucker said, giving Haus a dap.

Once Tucker left, Haus laid down on his bed and turned on the TV. There was a rerun of Jersey Shore on MTV. It was one of his favorite shows, so he decided to watch it. On the episode, Vinny made a lame attempt at getting with a hot dancer named Ramona by calling her and asking her to come along on a double-date as his "sympathy date".

Haus was disgusted. *What a pussy*, he thought.

Within ten minutes, before the episode was over, he was asleep.

Duncan had almost made it back to his apartment when he realized that he had left behind a book that he was going to need for his Communications homework at Haus's dorm. Since he still had almost an hour to go before the start of practice, he decided to walk back to the dorm and pick up the book. He would be tired after practice; he wouldn't want to go anywhere then. He figured that he would be pleased with himself, at that point, for having made the trip earlier.

When he approached Haus's building, Duncan saw a girl swiping a card to enter the front door. "Hold up!" he shouted from a short distance, so that he wouldn't have to wait for the next student to leave or swipe him or herself into the building. He started to jog over towards the girl, who showed a faint irritation at being held up. That was, until she realized whom it was she was holding the door for. "Thanks," Duncan said.

"No problem," the girl replied, blushing.

"I didn't wanna get trapped out here," Duncan told her. "I'm just going to see my buddy, John Weinhaus, on the fourth floor."

"Oh, Haus?" the girl said.

"Yeah, that's him. You guys friends?"

"Yeah," the girl said, though thinking, *He's a total asshole.*

"Cool," said Duncan, noticing for the first time that this girl was really cute. "What's your name?" he asked.

"Erika," the girl said. "I'd ask yours, but…"

"But what?"

"I already know it."

"Oh," Duncan laughed. "You saw the game on TV?"

"Yes I did… Duncan," she giggled.

"Cool," he said. They looked at each other for a moment, and then Duncan gave a nervous laugh, and said, "Well, I gotta run. It was really nice to meet you, Erika. Thanks for letting me in."

"You're welcome," she said.

Duncan turned to walk toward the stairs, but Erika's voice stopped him. "Hey, wait a second," she said. He turned around to see her taking one of her notebooks out of her oversize shoulder bag. She also took out a pen, and wrote her number down on a loose-leaf sheet of paper. "We should hang out some time," she said, ripping the piece of paper out.

Surprised and happy at this unexpected development in his return to the dorms, Duncan said, "Yeah, definitely. I'll call you."

"Good," she said.

"*Very* good," he replied. "Later."

"See you soon… Duncan Lipton," she said demurely. Duncan went upstairs where an even more unexpected and much less welcome surprise was waiting for him.

Chapter 45

As John Weinhaus slept, Corey Pager quietly entered the room and closed the door. He stared at his sleeping roommate, with a creepy half-grin, as he fondled the Swiss-army knife in the front-right pocket of his khaki cargo shorts. He imagined what it might feel like to sink the three-inch blade into Haus's neck. He had to stifle a laugh at the pleasurable thought, lest he should wake his tormentor.

Corey had been told by his parents and teachers and guidance counselors and by his shrink, and by his small group of friends… that college would be different. They all told him that no one would bully him in college; kids would be more mature and accepting; bullies practically don't even exist in the "real world". They all told him that there would be a zillion other freshmen there, and he could be friends with any and all of them. New Beginnings. That's what *everyone* told him. So, after years of being harassed by the jocks and other "cool" kids throughout middle and high school, Corey had been ecstatic to go to college. But, so far, his first semester at State had taken a huge, cruel dump on his expectations.

The day that Corey moved into his dorm, he found Haus already there, putting his belongings away in the dresser drawers and on the shelves of the left side of their small shared bedroom. The buzz-headed boy was standing with one of his friends, laughing heartily, as he attempted to fold clothes. It was a difficult task to accomplish, while gesturing animatedly with his hands to accompany a story that was clearly sexual in nature.

Not one to possess a bounty of social grace, Corey had interrupted Haus's story. "Hi, guys. I'm Corey," he said, extending his hand in the boys' direction. Instead of shaking Corey's hand, Haus had stared him up and down. As he did so, a sneer creased his lips, and he reached out to shake Corey's hand. But instead of shaking it, he did a more complicated dap that he knew a nerd like Corey wouldn't be comfortable doing. Just as Haus expected, Corey gave him a sloppy, uncoordinated greeting that made him feel socially inferior, just as Haus intended.

"Uh huh," Haus said, slowly "I'm John. You can call me Haus. This is Tucker."

"What's up?" Tucker said, unenthusiastically, not extending his hand or even looking at Corey. "Haus, let's go do that, uh, ya know…" And the two had abruptly left the room.

From that moment on, Haus had gotten progressively worse in his treatment of Corey, always making snide remarks about Corey's weight, dress, awkward manner, forgetfulness, or any other personal characteristic he might find disagreeable. Corey, for his part, was used to being made fun of, and took it all with a grain of salt. For a while. But that attitude had really only lasted him the better part of a month. He was getting fed up with being made fun of, but he was at a loss for ideas when it came to figuring out what to do about it. He had never fought back before when he was being bullied. It had never really been an option. But it *felt* like an option now, even though, with little to no practice when it came to retaliation, he was having a hell of a time figuring out what exactly that option entailed.

As Haus slept, Corey rationally came to the decision that stabbing his roommate in the neck with his Swiss-army knife was not going to lead him down a particularly sunny path, so instead he decided to take a shower. He disrobed, momentarily exposing his naked shame to the open air, and as he was about to wrap a towel around himself, the door to his dorm-room was suddenly thrown open, and there stood Duncan Lipton.

"Oh shit. Sorry," Duncan said, immediately closing the door and cringing in equal measure at the sight of the unpleasantly nude Corey

Pager and the resulting painful twinge of awkwardness.

"What the fuck!" Duncan could hear Corey shout.

"What the fuck!" Duncan could hear Haus shout.

The door burst open, and Corey, wrapped in his beige towel, bustled down the hall to the communal men's room. He left the door open, and Duncan could see an irritated Haus sitting on his bed, rubbing his eyes. "What the fuck just *happened?*" Haus said, seeing Duncan standing in the doorway. "I fall asleep for two seconds, then I wake up and that tub o' spuds is butt-ass naked in the middle of the fucking room... screaming!"

"Jesus," Duncan said. "I forgot my notebook here, dude. I just came back to get it. I should've knocked. I think your roommate was going to take a shower. I came in and he was naked." Duncan couldn't help but giggle; Corey was a strange sight in the flesh.

"Ah, shit," Haus laughed too. "Here's your notebook, dude. Sorry you had to see that."

"It was my own fault," Duncan replied, taking the notebook. "I don't know how the hell I'm gonna sleep tonight, but..." They shared a laugh at Corey's expense.

"Alright, man," Haus said a few seconds later, "you should probably get outta here. Wouldn't wanna be late for practice."

"Serious," Duncan said. "Later, bro."

"Later. Oh, shit, wait a second," Haus called out as Duncan was about to turn on his heels. "We didn't exchange numbers before." Quickly, they gave each other their digits. "I'll give you a call tomorrow," Haus said. "There's gonna be a solid party at my boy's house on Elk St."

"Is that girl Erika from downstairs gonna be there?" Duncan asked.

"Erika Westley?"

"I don't know."

"Brown hair. Blue eyes. Like 5'7"?"

"Yeah," Duncan said.

"You *want* her to be there?" asked Haus.

"Fuck yeah, I do!" Duncan said enthusiastically.

"Then I'll see what I can do, brother."

"Right on. You're a good man." And Duncan meant it, forgetting his distaste for how he had seen Haus treat Corey.

"Alright, all-star," Haus said back. "Get your ass to practice so that we have something to celebrate tomorrow night." Duncan gave him a look that said, *Do you know who I am?* They laughed, dapped, and parted ways, Duncan to practice, Haus back into his bed for a mini-nap.

By the time Corey returned from the shower, Haus was already out cold. *Thank God*, Corey thought. He was mortified at having been seen in the buff, and the last thing he wanted to hear right then was a verbal barrage about how fat, useless, retarded, and (insert derogatory adjective here) he was.

He dressed quickly, picked up his backpack, and went to the library to study for a math test that he had to take the following day. Studying in the room was out of the question, for the ire of the waking Haus was not something that he wanted anything to do with at the moment. Instead, he opted for the solitude of a second-floor library cubicle, where he wouldn't have to deal with anyone bothering him.

When he arrived at his preferred cubicle on the second floor, he removed his textbook, notes, calculator, and pencils from his backpack. Before sitting down, he looked around and took note of the fact that there was no one else around at all on the second floor. That was just grand as far as he was concerned, seeing as his relations with the human race as of late had been substandard. Some peace and quiet, he thought, would do him well.

He thumbed through the pre-calc textbook to the assigned practice problems. He started to work on the first problem, but quickly found that he had little to no idea what the hell what was going on. Cruel as they may have been, Haus's accusations of Corey's intellectual shortcomings were fairly accurate, and the fact that Corey suffered from undiagnosed attention deficit disorder only exacerbated the problems he had in school. How was he supposed to do the practice problems when he had absorbed next to nothing in class?

As he stared at the numbers and letters on the page, he was suddenly overwhelmed with despair and self-pity. He thought that he was useless, pathetic, stupid, weak, and, worst of all, helpless to change any and all of these negative characterizations of himself. Consequently, he began to cry.

But just as Corey started to do so, he suddenly felt something brush his left leg and he jumped out of his seat in surprise. He looked down, and there, looking up at him with sympathetic yellow eyes, was a beautiful, purring, cinnamon-colored kitten. "Oh my god!" he yelped. The kitten tipped her head to the right, and looked expectantly at Corey. "What are you doing in the library?" he said. The kitten, being a kitten, had no answer for him. Corey leaned over and picked her up. She immediately began a storm of purring that set Corey's troubled mind at ease. "How did you get here, little thing? Do you have a collar?" No answer. No collar.

Corey's mother was a cat lover, and Corey had grown up with a number of cats throughout his life. From this experience, he was able to surmise that this little one was probably only about two months old. And this was the sweetest cat he'd ever met. He sat down at his cubicle and rested the kitten on his big belly. She immediately curled into a little fur-ball and closed her eyes, happily purring away as Corey happily stroked her luxuriously soft fur. "You're so pretty," he whispered.

After about half an hour of silently enjoying the company of her new friend, the kitten started to quietly meow. "You hungry, little girl?" Corey asked. The kitten meowed again, which Corey took as an affirmation. "That sounds like a yes to me, pretty girl," Corey said. "Let's get you something to eat." He wrapped the kitten in a gym t-shirt from his backpack, so no one would be able to see her, and walked out of the library, straight to the dining hall.

Since it wasn't yet dinnertime, the dining hall was relatively empty, and Corey chose a table in the corner, so no other early diners would be able to see him from behind. Carefully holding the wrapped kitten in his left arm, he assembled an assortment of food on his tray from the vast buffet. He got some breaded chicken breast stuffed with broccoli and cream, pizza, fries, lentil soup, vegetable samosas, cantaloupe slices, chili, and some fettuccine alfredo. He brought it back to the table and discretely put the kitten on the tray, so she could try out the goods. She went straight for the fettuccine alfredo and nibbled to her heart's content. Corey laughed, "Well, I guess we know what you like, huh, little one?" Playing on the name of her apparent favorite dish, he decided to name the kitten Frayda. The rest of the food, he greedily overindulged in himself, as was his way.

When they were done, Frayda curled up and fell asleep, wrapped in Corey's t-shirt. Corey had no intention of finding out where the kitten had come from. She was his now, and that was that. This presented a new problem for him: how to keep her a secret from Haus.

Chapter 46

Amadi B'Wale caught the rebound. Being that he was seven feet tall, this was relatively easy for him. Duncan was already sprinting down the court when Amadi came down with the ball. Amadi saw this and launched a quarterback-style pass, which Duncan caught for an easy breakaway to the basket, finished by a smooth dunk. The score was 67-65, in favor of State over MT. The crowd went crazy at State's home arena. MT inbounded the ball and, in one last-ditch effort, their shooting guard heaved the ball from center-court. It clanged off the back of the rim, and the win went to State. Again, after scoring 34 points, including the winning basket, Duncan Lipton was the hero. The crowd rushed onto the court, and Duncan was scooped onto the shoulders of his teammates and fans alike.

After the game, Duncan went back to his apartment. He showered, went to the dining hall for dinner, then went back home and prepared himself to go out. He was excited to hang out with the girl he had met, Erika. He had a good feeling that Haus would come through for him by figuring out how to get her to the party.

Sure enough, after having dinner, his phone rang. It was Haus: "Yo, wusgood, all-star?" he said.

"Chillin', chillin'," Duncan replied. "On my way back to the apartment to get ready. That party still goin on?"

"Oh, doggy, you know it. And guess what."

"What?" Duncan said.

"Erika Westley's making an appearance. And I'm not gonna lie. She seemed pretty psyched when I told her you were hoping she'd be there."

"You told her that?" Duncan asked, a little irritated at having his spot blown up.

"Yeah man," Haus said confidently. "No need to beat around the bush. And you're a fuckin hero, man. It's in the bag."

"Word?" said Duncan.

"Word," said Haus.

"Awesome," Duncan replied. "Well, I'm gonna get ready. I guess then I'll come and meet up with you at your dorm, and we can head over to the party."

"Sounds good, all-star," Haus said. "I'll see you around 9."

"Cool," said Duncan. "Peace." He hung up the phone and contemplated his good fortune. Considering the loss of his friends, and how badly he had been beaten in Amsterdam, things were really looking up for him. And tonight, he was going to get to hang out with a beautiful girl that he had his eye on. *I'm a lucky dude*, he thought. *One lucky dude.* And for a moment, it made him sad to think about how Matty G and Rennie couldn't be around to enjoy this life with him, but he was nonetheless grateful that he had had the pleasure of knowing and being friends with two amazing guys like that. And he was making new friends here at school, meeting people, making his way toward his life's goal of playing in the NBA. *Yeah, man. One lucky dude.*

Around 9pm, Duncan stood outside Haus's dorm, waiting for him to come downstairs. Haus came down, wearing a pair of jeans, Nike Air-Max sneakers, and a tight-fitting gray t-shirt. He also sported a backwards Navy Blue Yankees hat. "What's good, all-star?" he said, giving Duncan a dap.

"Chillin', chillin', man," Duncan said. "So, where's this party at?"

"On Elk St.," Haus replied. "Ten minute walk. We just gotta stop by the Frazier dorm and pick up Tucker, right over there." He pointed to a building that was part of the same complex of four dorms that his own building was part of. "He's chillin' with some girl."

"Cool," Duncan said.

They walked over to the Frazier building as Haus called Tucker to tell him that they were outside. Just as they walked up, a smiling Tucker exited the building. "Helllllllo, gentlemen," he said, laughing, then giving daps to Haus and Duncan in succession. "Beautiful night, isn't it?"

"What the fuck are you so happy about?" Haus asked, laughing along with the giddiness evident in his friend's face.

"Oh, you know," Tucker said. "got an A on my Chem test, then poked Sally about fifteen minutes ago. Life's good, motherfucker!"

Haus laughed and said, "Well good for you asshole, but my night's just beginning. Me and all-star over here still need to get laid."

"Well," said Tucker, "I'll see if I can help the cause, seeing as I'm pretty much tapped out for the day."

"Good," said Haus. "Maybe you could put in some good words for me with Sally's friend Jenn. I've wanted that bitch since the day I got here."

"I'll see what I can do, buddy," Tucker replied. "Let's get goin'."

Duncan and his two new comrades walked over to the party. When they arrived, it was just past 9:30, way early for a college party. Later arrivals were presently pre-gaming in their respective dorms and apartments.

When they got to the door, they were greeted by one of the house's occupants, a 20-year-old guy name Dave, with long brown hair, a bright green long-sleeve polo, baggy jeans, and a pair of Timberlands on his feet. "Oh shit!" Dave said. "Duncan fucking Lipton! At my fucking house! Awesome!" Duncan smiled warmly, though somewhat bashfully. He definitely was enjoying the positive attention that he was getting, though he was still unused to the concept of being a celebrity.

Dave ushered Duncan, Haus, and Tucker into his house and called out to some guys who were doing shots in the living room, "Guys! Guess who's here!"

"Who?" replied one of the boys, just before downing a shot of tequila. When the kid looked up and saw Duncan, he immediately started to cough on the hard liquor. "Oh shit!" the kid said. "Dude, you were just on Sportscenter." He pointed to the TV, which was displaying college basketball highlights on ESPN. "Gimme the remote," the boy said to another guy across the room. Then, to Duncan, "We got the DVR, dude!"

The boy rewound the TV broadcast only about four minutes, and there Duncan was. He stared at the screen. *Wow, that's a new one*, he thought, very pleased at the sight of himself on TV. He had missed seeing himself on SportsCenter from the previous game, as he hadn't been watching, so this was the first time he had seen himself on video, other than game film and home videos taken by his dad. This was the real deal. The big time. Duncan could hardly believe it. On the screen rolling down the side, it said "Lipton drops 34 on MT."

Everyone in the room introduced themselves to their local star, and Duncan could barely remember any of the names being told to him, but he was gracious and classy when it came to such matters, and he easily ingratiated himself to the crowd.

Around 10:00, a big group of girls came in, and Duncan saw her. Erika Westley. His heart skipped a beat, and he took a swig of the Coors Light can he held in his hand. Then, their eyes met, they both smiled, and Erika walked right up to him. "Hi," she said.

"Hi," Duncan replied with a sheepish grin. There was something about this girl that Duncan couldn't quite put his finger on. He felt something electric, like what he felt when he had first met Tessa. Erika licked her lips, not seductively, just because they were dry, and Duncan found it to be very charming and cute.

"I was at the game," she said.

"Oh yeah?" Duncan replied.

"Yeah," she said. "You were okay."

Duncan laughed, "Just okay?"

"Maybe a little bit better than okay," she laughed back. Immediately, she took his hand, and said, "let's take a shot." She removed a small bottle of raspberry flavored Smirnoff vodka from her purse, and found a couple shot glasses in the house's kitchen. She poured out two shots and handed one to Duncan.

"What shall we toast to?" Duncan asked.

"To us," she replied. And in her eyes, Duncan saw the purposeful seduction that her lips had not shown a moment before. They downed their shots, and, not missing a beat, Erika took Duncan's hand and guided him upstairs, where they immediately slept together before ever engaging in any kind of real conversation. Not one to beat around the bush either, Duncan was instantly enchanted with this exciting, incredibly forward girl. When they were done, they walked downstairs and rejoined the party, which had more than tripled in size since Duncan had first arrived. They danced, kissed, held hands, and generally acted like a couple, which was just fine by him. This was his kind of girl.

After about an hour, Erika told Duncan that she felt like leaving and asked him if he wanted to smoke some weed. Duncan was enthusiastic in his reply that he would love to, and that he knew just where they could get some. "Hmmm," Erika said, "let me guess: Haus?"

"Of course," Duncan replied. "He's the man."

Erika gave him a somewhat quizzical, skeptical look, and said, sarcastically, "Yeah, sure," but Duncan, who was at this point full of vodka and tequila, didn't pick up on the sarcasm.

"Let's find him," Duncan said, and they walked to the basement where they found Haus engaged in a serious game of beer-pong. "Yo, Haus, doggy," Duncan said, giving his friend a dap, "can me and Erika get a little chronic?"

"Yeah, dude," Haus said. "But the stash is back at my dorm. I wanna leave anyway, so just wait 'til we lose and I'll walk back there with you guys."

"Beautiful," Duncan replied. While they waited for Haus to finish up, a bunch of Duncan's fellow students came up to him and congratulated him for the dominant way that he'd been playing, and for scoring more than half the team's points against the hated rival, MT. Graciously, Duncan accepted their praise, and looked at Erika, embarrassed, and with that sheepish grin that spoke of his pride and humility in one easy facial expression. Understanding what that expression meant, Erika found it completely charming, and she squeezed Duncan's hand supportively.

When Haus and his teammate lost at beer-pong, he turned to Duncan, who was canoodling with Erika in the corner, and said, "Alright, all-star, you ready to go?"

"Hell yeah!" Duncan said, excited at the prospect of getting some nug, getting high with Erika, then getting a tour of Erika's dorm room.

They walked back to the dorm, and upstairs to Haus's room. It was earlier than he would normally be back on a party night, so Corey was not ready for his roommate's arrival. The door was unlocked, so he never had time to hide his new friend.

"What the fuck is that?" Haus said to him, as he saw Corey sitting on the bed with his kitten.

Corey, slack-jawed, surprised, and frightened didn't know what to say.

"What the fuck is that, Pager?" repeated Haus.

"Um, I, um…," Corey blustered.

"Why is that thing in my fucking room?" Haus was irate. Drunk and annoyed at the fact that he had to come home to find his loathed roommate taking up space was bad enough. But now he had brought a pet. A cat, no less. Haus hated cats. He hated their aloofness, their independence, their attitude. To top it off, he was even slightly allergic.

Haus truly *hated* cats. Especially cats owned by *people* he hated. Like Corey.

"I found her in the library, Haus," Corey said. "She was hungry. I couldn't just leave her there." Haus gave Corey an icy stare.

Erika, however, had another take on the situation. "Ooooh," she cooed, "that is so sweet. Can I hold her?"

"Sure," Corey said, immediately struck by the positive impact of a friendly female presence. He held out the kitten to the beautiful girl he'd seen occasionally around the dorm. Whereas before she had never paid him any attention, she was now sitting right next to Corey on his bed, playing with his kitten, and he was more than pleased that she was doing so. He looked at Haus, who was fuming, but felt nonetheless protected by Erika's presence.

For his part, Duncan didn't know what to make of the situation. He looked at his friend, who was literally red with anger as he stared at his hated roommate, and thought, *What the fuck is his problem? It's a fucking kitten.* Duncan liked dogs *and* cats. He preferred dogs, as he had found was normal amongst most people he had talked to in his life about the subject, but he had nothing against cats. They were soft and cute, and the fact that they were often aloof made friendly cats all the more endearing. This was clearly a very friendly cat, so he thought that Haus's reaction was a little inappropriate, and he correctly surmised that his anger was based far more on his dislike of Corey than any practical reason for not wanting a cute little kitten in his room.

"Dude," Duncan said to Haus, "what's the big deal, man? It's just a kitten."

Not looking at Duncan, Haus replied, "There's a fucking cat in my fucking room. A fucking *cat!*" Haus was drunk. Duncan just noticed it for the first time, and he could see a fire blazing in his new friend's eyes that he had not seen before. He had a reckless look, like he could snap at any second.

Meanwhile, Corey was trying to ignore Haus by sharing the playful little animal with this nice girl on his bed. "What's her name?" Erika asked.

"Frayda," Corey replied.

"Oooooh, Frayda!" Erika gushed. "That is such a pretty name.

How'd you think of that?"

"Well," Corey said, "after I found her, I took her to the dining hall and got a bunch of food. She liked the fettuccine alfredo the best, so I thought Frayda was a good name."

"Oh," Erika said, "you are so cute. What's your name?"

Corey was just about to reply when all of a sudden Haus bounded across the room and punched him square in the jaw.

"Oh my god!" screamed Erika. "What are you doing?!?!"

Haus said nothing as he violently grabbed the kitten out of her hands, threw it on the ground, and in one swift motion stomped on its tiny head, killing it immediately.

"Nooooooo!!!!" wailed Corey.

"Holy shit!" Duncan screamed. "What the fuck?!?!"

Erika and Corey were both crying as Corey bent to pick up the dead kitten. "You asshole!" Corey screamed. "You fucking asshole!"

Haus stood there with a malicious sneer on his face. "Bring a fucking cat into my fucking room," he said. "*That's* what you get."

Duncan was stunned. He couldn't believe that his friend just did such a sick, twisted, evil thing. But what happened next was on a whole new level of madness.

Corey picked Frayda up, gently placed her on the bed, and then slowly turned to face Haus. His face was full of rage. Suddenly, he began to scream. It was a primal, barbaric scream that came from deep within his soul. It was a scream that had been waiting years to emerge from this tender, sensitive, reserved person. It was a scream that could only precipitate violence.

Corey reached into the front right pocket of his cargo shorts and took out his Swiss army knife. With quickness one wouldn't expect from such an ungainly boy, he flashed open the largest blade, then charged at Haus. Haus, being much quicker and more athletic than Corey, was able to get out of the way of the knife that was speeding toward his face. But it sank deep into his shoulder. He fell to the ground with Corey's large body falling on top of him. Corey had no intention of leaving the knife in Haus's shoulder. He quickly removed it and stabbed at Haus again. Haus blocked with his right arm, swinging the knife to the side. This time it hit him in the right part of his chest. Had it been the left, the blade might have hit his heart. But he was lucky; the blade only sank into his pectoral muscle.

Duncan reacted as fast as he possibly could to the attack. Sure, it was sick and twisted that Haus had killed Corey's kitten, but he wasn't going to stand by as the guy got stabbed to death.

Duncan was standing by the door, next to which sat Haus's rec-league baseball bat. He grabbed the bat, what amounted to a heavy wooden club, and rushed at the boys grappling on the floor. As soon as he was close enough to connect, he swung as hard as he could at Corey.

It all happened so fast that Duncan's effort to aim at Corey's shoulder was unsuccessful, and the heavy wooden bat connected solidly with his jaw. The large boy flopped backwards, off of Haus, and landed next to his bed. His eyes had rolled into the back of his head. He was twitching. Erika was screaming, "Help! Help! Somebody please, pleeease!"

Duncan looked at Haus, who was down on the blood-flecked yellow carpet, writhing and moaning.

He then looked at Corey. The demented sight of Corey's twitching, shaking body caused him to promptly pass out and drop to the floor.

Chapter 47

"Yo, Dunks! What up, playboy?" Kobe said.

"Hey, Kobe," Duncan replied in a melancholy tone of voice.

"What's the matter?" Kobe asked.

"I don't know, man."

"What you mean you don't know?" Kobe paused. "You know."

"Yeah, I mean, I guess I just miss the way life used to be, ya know? Everything was so simple. I miss Matty G. I miss Tessa. I miss just playing ball for fun. Everything's all fucked up now."

"Why's everything all fucked up, man? What you talkin' about?" Kobe said.

"Don't you know where we are, Kobe?"

"We at home, baby," Kobe said. "On the court." He snatched the basketball out of Duncan's hands, ran towards the basket, crossed over an imaginary defender, and threw down a vicious dunk.

"No, Kobe. *We're* not at home. *I'm* at home, dude," Duncan said, as Kobe hung from the rim.

"Oh yeah," Kobe said. "I guess you're right." And with that, he dropped the ball, walked off the court, and disappeared into thin air like an apparition. Duncan longingly stared at the spot where his idol had just stood, then past it, to the high stone walls that surrounded Northern State Prison, and finally down at his olive green uniform. *I'm home*, he thought. *I'm really home.*

Chapter 48

Inmate number 661066 looked at himself in the tiny mirror he was allowed to keep in his cell. He had been at Northern State for six months, and still, every day, when he awoke and looked at himself, the same word pounded over and over again in his mind: Manslaughter. Manslaughter. That was what inmate number 661066 had been put away for, or better yet, what he was *probably* going to be put away for. And for a long, long time, the prosecutor seemed to think. But the trial had yet to happen. He was being held without bail in a maximum-security facility, due to the severity of the crime and the fact that the judge considered him a potential flight risk, owing to the fact that his parents had the means to get him out of the country if they so chose to do so. The judge had agreed to postpone the trial another six months, due to the testimony of several expert medical witnesses who insisted that it was entirely possible that the victim would survive, and had persuaded him that it was premature to hold a trial for a killing which had not yet occurred. However, the judge had also been convinced that the victim was on very thin ice and that if that ice should crack, an assault with a deadly weapon charge would hardly foot the bill. So the judge was allowing an extra six months to pass before the trial, to find out what inmate number 661066 should indeed be tried for.

Inmate number 661066 was not actually a killer. Not yet anyway. His crime had left the victim in a completely comatose state, a vegetable. But, technically, not dead. For the past six months, the victim had not said a word, and was only able to survive on life support. The doctors were not at all optimistic. And neither was inmate number 661066.

He stared at himself in the little mirror. It was just before 6:30am. Just before role call. "I cannot fucking believe I'm me," he whispered aloud. "Duncan fucking Lipton."

Chapter 49

The heavy buzzer rang out, signaling time for role call. Duncan stood up from where he sat at the end of the small cot in his single cell, rubbed his eyes, and walked out in front of the iron bars that had just automatically moved aside, allowing for his exit.

First thing in the morning each day at Northern State, just after role call, the inmates were trudged down to the dining room for breakfast. Today, there were piles of powdered eggs and soggy toast. It was not ideal, but it would get Duncan through the long morning of license plate stamping that was his assigned duty in prison. He didn't hate license plate stamping, despite its monotony. There was a certain rhythm to it that he found pleasant enough. And it was physical, thus making his less-than-pleasant prison-slop breakfast a necessity. Luckily, he had never been a picky eater.

Despite his disastrous fall from grace, Duncan was, all in all, handling his situation well. There were a few inmates at Northern State whom Duncan had known growing up . They were older guys from Hightown, where Duncan had always been popular, thanks to his relationship with Matty G. While there were several inmates he had been previously acquainted with on the outside, it turned out to be a man he had no memory of ever meeting before who would prove to be his most valuable asset in the pursuit of staying in one piece throughout this ordeal. But Duncan *had* met the man before. And he re-met him on his very first day at prison.

Joe Curtis was a middle-aged former Bloods gangbanger, who had been a good friend and basketball teammate of Matty G's dad, Ernest G, once upon a time. Much like his son and his "nephew" Duncan,

Ernest G was just one of those guys whom *everybody* liked, and his non-judgmental mindset and basketball skills earned him a number of friends whose pursuits away from the basketball court were often highly illegal (to put it nicely). Ernest never cared that Joe was in a gang, and Joe certainly didn't care that Ernest wasn't. They shared some good basketball games and some good laughs, and Joe remembered him fondly. He had been deeply distressed when he learned of Ernest's passing some years earlier. Had he not been recently incarcerated, he never would have missed the funeral.

When Duncan first arrived, Joe had just finished his eighth year of incarceration for the murders of two members of the Crips gang, the Bloods' sworn enemies. At this point, he was a seasoned veteran of prison life and a highly respected Bloods elder, an OG (Original Gangsta) known not to be trifled with. Though he had put his gangbanging days behind him, within the walls of Northern State, he was a member of the Bloods' upper echelon.

"What up, li'l Lipton?" Joe said to Duncan, upon seeing him in the prison dining area on his first day there. Duncan kept his head down. He had been advised by MSNBC's *Lockup* program and a number of movies to ignore other prisoners and keep to himself, that keeping a low profile would better his chances of avoiding physical confrontation. Accordingly, he avoided any kind of response to Joe talking to him. He didn't know how this guy knew who he was, and he didn't want anything to do with him. Inmates were allowed television time in prison, so because of his brief collegiate success and the sensational disaster that led to his incarceration being aired over and over on ESPN, there were plenty of guys at Northern State who knew who Duncan was from the moment he arrived. This guy trying to get his attention in the dining hall, he figured, probably was just calling him out, bringing his presence to the attention of the other inmates who knew who he was.

But that was not the case. As Duncan walked away, the voice

continued, "I knew Ernest, little man. Good friend of mine."

Duncan's head spun to look at the low-voiced, smiling, black man. The man had a puffy, heavily graying afro, and a pair of matching mutton-chops. "Ernest *G*?" Duncan said.

"Ernest motherfuckin G! Name's Joe Curtis," Joe said, holding out his hand for Duncan, who was walking over, looking quizzical, with a half-smile.

"Nice to meet you," Duncan said, giving the older man a firm, respectful handshake.

"This ain't exactly the first time we meetin', youngsta," Joe said.

"What do you mean?" Duncan asked.

"I knew you and Matty G when you was real little kids."

"Word?" Duncan said.

"Word," Joe laughed. "Played a little ball with ya. 'Bout nine, ten years ago, I'd say."

"Wow," said Duncan. "That's great. It's really nice to re-meet you, Mr. Curtis." Duncan had played a lot of basketball with a lot of different people. He wasn't sure, but he thought that he might remember Joe's face. Whether he did or not, he could use all the friends he could get in that crazy place.

"Joe'll be fine youngsta. But you's a classy muthafucka, son. I like that." He laughed out loud, "*Mr*. Curtis, if you please! Been a long fuckin time since anybody called me that."

Knowing Joe kept Duncan safe while he was locked up. Being a handsome, eighteen-year-old white kid should have, under normal circumstances, been a death sentence, but Duncan was able to float on the protective cloud of a powerful man doing a solid for his late friend. He couldn't help but wonder if protecting Matty G in middle school had granted him karmic preservation. Whether it was karma, luck, fate or…whatever, Joe Curtis was a godsend, and Duncan didn't know what to think except that the powers that be deserved thanks, whatever (or whoever) they were.

For the most part, Duncan avoided other prisoners, but he spoke freely with those he knew from Eastfield, and they and Joe made sure that his back was watched.

However, as well as he was taking his incarceration, he found himself often in a melancholic state. He didn't regret what he'd done; he was trying to save his friend from being *stabbed to death*! But he achingly wished that he'd hit Corey somewhere other than the dome with that bat. *Anywhere but the dome!* He didn't really hold out much hope for the kid's survival, and, consequently, he didn't really hold out much hope for his stay at Northern State being cut short. He had more or less resigned himself to this fate, that he would be locked up for something like a decade, that he would never play professional basketball, and that he wouldn't have sex for a very, very long time.

It was the basketball that ate at him the most. He was *so* close to the NBA draft. With one swing of a heavy wooden bat, Duncan had laid waste to any hope of ever accomplishing what he and his best friend had dreamed of as far back as his memory could stretch, long before they were old enough to know that it was a dream worth having. Woops and Oops, the two-man team that could have been a conqueror of worlds, instead was tragically lost, left to remain as nothing more than a beautiful, albeit wasted opportunity, floating in the ether.

With the brutally boring time that he was forced to spend alone in his cell, Duncan resumed a hobby that had lay dormant in him since he was about nine years old: writing poetry. While locked up, he had spent some of his free time releasing his troubles onto paper. His first poem, titled *Stuck in Here,* he wrote five days into his sentence:

Stuck in here, stuck in here
Shit is so fucked up in here
Just wanna get fucked up in here

Up in here. Up in here.
These brick walls got me stuck in here
Nobody gives a fuck in here
'Bout who I am, or why the fuck I'm here
Up in here. Up in here.
Can't believe that I got stuck in here
What the fuck was I thinking?
Seriously. What the fuck? What the fuck? What the fuck?
Seriously. What the fuck?

It took Duncan half an hour to write the poem, and he read it
over and over again, examining just how accurate the words were.
He had forgotten about rhyming at the end, which was forgivable
(and poetic, he thought), considering his regularly prosaic days and
unpoetic regrets.

When his mind wasn't occupied, Duncan harped on the fact that
it was extremely difficult to imagine a worse place than Northern
State. Though he did his best to avoid eye contact with anyone, he
would often catch old creeps staring at him. He would quickly look
away, doing his best to conceal the emotions of disgust and fear, which
he wore like a mask. Every day he thanked the powers that be for the
presence of Joe Curtis. He really didn't know what he would do if Joe
weren't there to protect him from the dregs of humanity, who would
surely love nothing more than to take out their sexual frustration on
Duncan's virgin rear-end.

There was one guy in particular, a scumbag everyone called Fat
Elvis, who Duncan caught staring at him far too frequently. Fat Elvis
was a convicted pederast, a serial rapist of young boys, and was in
the midst of a thirty-three to life sentence for kidnapping and raping
a twelve-year-old boy, who had successfully identified his masked
attacker by recognizing the giant brown splotch of a birthmark that
ran down his left arm. The guy was a completely disgusting creep, and

Duncan was none too pleased at the fact that almost daily he would glance up to see Fat Elvis, who looked disturbingly similar, though far more obese, to late-career Elvis Presley, licking his lips and staring at him like he was a Christmas ham. Always, he would look away as quickly as possible, but the momentary eye-contact was unavoidable, as Fat Elvis's ogling was constant.

Duncan took his frustrations to paper one night, composing another poem called *Fat Elvis*:

> About this creep, What am I to do?
> Damn it, Fat Elvis, God damn it, fuck you!
> A grease ball, a dough ball, pureed into goo
> Fuck *this* shit, Fat Elvis, God damn it, fuck you!
> You sick fucking freak, you belong at the zoo
> The rapist exhibit, for all to view
> You freak, you animal, you sicko, you shrew
> You're a dead man, Fat Elvis, God damn it, fuck you!

Fortunately, due to the influence of Joe Curtis, nothing ever came of Fat Elvis's creeping, but it gave Duncan the willies nonetheless. At a certain point, he was so sketched out by the daily stare-down, he went to Joe with his complaint at breakfast.

Duncan got his powdered egg mush and went over to the table where Joe sat with two other inmates. "Hey, Joe. How you doin, man?" Duncan said.

"Chillin out, little brother. Just another day in the pen, nah mean?" Heads nodded around the table, some solemnly, some baring the small smile that acknowledges the profoundly life-altering detour that is prison. A guilty smile.

"Yeah, man," Duncan replied. "Listen, Joe, I got a problem. You know that Fat Elvis guy?"

"Fuckin creep," Joe said.

"Yeah, man. Well, I catch his fat ass staring at me every day, man. He's creeping me the fuck out."

"You think he wants a piece of that ass, huh?"

"I don't know what the fuck he wants," Duncan replied. "I just know that I don't want him giving me that creepy stare-down every time I look up. Who knows what the fuck he wants."

"I know what he wants," said Joe. "He wants a piece of that ass. But he ain't gonna get it, little brother, don't you worry. And he ain't gonna be checkin you out no more neither. Mark my words." He gave Duncan an emphatic dap and that was that.

The next day, when Duncan went to breakfast, the right side of Fat Elvis's face was purple and his right eye was swollen shut. The obese lout didn't even glance Duncan's way.

After six months of being locked up, Duncan was none too worse for the wear. He regularly had to combat excruciating boredom and the depression of uncertainty and disappointment, but Joe Curtis kept him safe. Exercising in the yard kept him as fit as the day he came in, and writing his little poems kept him somewhat mentally active. He was even starting to find a certain degree of acceptance of his circumstances, and dealt with it as bravely and nobly as he could.

As he stamped his twenty-second license plate of the day, one of the corrections officers, Officer Carmody, came over to him. "Lipton," he said, "you got a visitor."

"Is it Thursday?" Duncan asked. Thursday was when he was allowed visitors, and he had lost track of time. He was not one to mark days off on a calendar with X's, particularly because there was no tangible end in sight since he had still yet to be tried.

"Yeah," Carmody said. "It's fucking Thursday. Let's go."

Duncan followed the officer to the visitation room. There, behind the bulletproof glass, holding the telephone receiver that allowed him to speak with his client was Duncan's lawyer, Marcus Schott. Duncan picked up the receiver. "Hey, Mr. Schott," he said.

"Hey, Duncan. How ya doin', kiddo?" Mr. Schott always called Duncan "kiddo" (He actually called almost every person younger than himself "kiddo".).

"I'm okay, I guess," Duncan replied. "This place is insanely boring though."

"I can't even imagine," the lawyer replied. "Well, my young friend, I have some news for you. Some very, very good news indeed."

Duncan held his breath and stared expectantly at Mr. Schott. The lawyer cleared his throat. "Corey Pager woke up, kiddo," he said.

Duncan could barely believe his ears. He was momentarily silenced. His eyes grew wide and his head nodded forward, as if to say, *You're kidding*. But the lawyer was not joking. "That's not all," he said, taking a deep breath, then smiling a huge, cheek-to-cheek, toothy grin, displaying a full of set of dentist-whitened, gleaming chompers.

Duncan could barely stand the suspense. "What else?"

"He's talking. As soon as he was told what happened, he insisted on dropping the charges against you."

Duncan's jaw dropped open. He said nothing. He had resigned himself to this boring, wasteful existence, and simply couldn't believe what he had just heard.

"We'll have you out of here in a few days," Mr. Schott said.

And just like that, before the week was out, Duncan Lipton was a free man.

Chapter 50

"Goddamn, it's great to have you home, kid!" hooted Duncan's dad, long before they even got home. In fact, he said it as he wrapped Duncan in a powerful embrace right outside the prison walls. The middle-aged man bounded joyfully like a kid to the car, and opened the passenger-side door for his beloved son.

"Thanks, Dad," Duncan said, his head slumped forward, though a wry smile played around his lips. He knew that he should be ecstatic at the end of this nightmare, but he was nonetheless overcome by a sense of melancholy. He thought that he had lost his chance to ever play pro ball, that he had lost Tessa, the only girl who ever cared about him, and images of Corey Pager's writhing body still haunted him. But he knew that he should be happy, and he did his best to force that feeling to emerge. It had just been so long since he had felt it, since he had felt like his former carefree, confident, cheerful self that he hardly knew how to regain his footing on that emotional high-ground. Seeing his dad as excited and happy as he was certainly aided his emotions. He loved his dad, and he was sure that there was going to be a grand welcome-home dinner at home, prepared by his mom, who was no slouch in the kitchen.

Mr. Lipton pulled the car off of Harley St. onto their cul-de-sac, Candace Pl. There were more cars than usual parked on the street…a lot more, and Duncan immediately realized that this would be more than a private family get-together. Duncan looked over at his dad who broke into a huge grin. "Surprise!" he chuckled.

"Wow, Dad. I figured we were gonna keep it kinda low-key," Duncan said.

"There are a lot of people real happy that you're home, buddy," his dad said. "So many people asked me about you, we had to throw you a little thing. You don't mind, do you?"

Duncan didn't know if he was ready for a big reception, but he didn't want to disappoint his dad, so he said, "Nah. It's great. Thanks."

Mr. Lipton ruffled his son's hair and gave him an adoring smile. "C'mon, kid," he said, "let's go on in."

Upon opening the front door, Duncan was greeted by all the people that he could have possibly hoped to see. The first person to run up to him, naturally, was his mother, who showered him in hugs, kisses, and tears. "Oh, Duncan!" she cooed. "Oh, my little Duncan!" Duncan couldn't help but find that kind of funny, considering his mother was only 5'4", nearly a foot shorter than he was. But the sentiment was touching, and he couldn't help but tear up while he and his mom squeezed the daylights out of each other.

The next person to heap greetings and physical contact on him was Mrs. G. "Duncan, baby," she said. "I thought I lost you like my other babies. I'm so happy you're home, honey pie. We're gonna have to catch up." And, as was her way, she smothered him in her ample bosom.

"Thanks, Mrs. G," he replied, once he came up for air. "It's really nice to see you too. I thought about you all the time while I was away." Mrs. G beamed at her son's best friend as though he were her own child.

Right after Mrs. G released him from her maternal embrace, pretty much his entire former basketball team, twenty-one of the guys he had played with throughout his high school career, rushed him with huge smiles, hugs, high fives, daps, and every other imaginable kind of greeting. They were all happy beyond measure that their brother, as they thought of him, was home. The enormous Ike Eze, demonstrating the team's love for their leader and friend, wrapped him in a bear-like embrace that made it delightfully difficult to breathe. It was all love, and Duncan's melancholy washed away as he felt it.

After each of his teammates, Mrs. G, his parents, and a few other friends had finished wrapping him in hugs, Duncan was startled to see, standing in the corner of his kitchen, the one person he had longed to see more than anyone else: Tessa. She was dressed in skintight black leggings with furry white Ugg boots and a light pink baby-T from the Gap. Her hair was in a ponytail, though one strand had escaped and loosely dangled in front of her right eye. She wore around her neck a silver chain from Tiffany's, the kind that Duncan found to have an oxymoronically classy trashiness that he had always thought represented well the duality of Tessa's sexiness behind-closed-doors and her well-groomed public self-presentation. He had given her that necklace for Valentine's Day, and it always made him think about the famous rap lyric by Ludacris, "I want a lady in the street but a freak in the bed," because of the memorable bedroom experimentation that the gift had helped to facilitate.

But at that moment, the details of Tessa's ensemble escaped Duncan's train of thought. All he saw was her radiantly welcoming face, and it was the ultimate sight for sore eyes. She was the most beautiful girl he could imagine, and the tears of joy running down her smooth cheeks washed away the stain on his soul, the product of his months of imprisonment. As he slowly walked over to her, they stared into one another's eyes. Neither said a word. They just beamed cheek-aching smiles at each other, staring disbelievingly until they came together. Tessa's breasts pressed against Duncan's abdomen, and their eyes locked at a forty-five degree angle. Silently, with tenderness born of the fondness of absence, regret, second-chances, and good old-fashioned love, Duncan gently wiped away the tears from both of Tessa's cheeks with his thumbs.

"Duncan," she breathed quietly.

"Shhh," he said, and lightly kissed her forehead.

Her heart pounding a mile a minute, she closed her eyes, wrapped her arms around his waist, and savored the magical feeling of the only boy she had ever loved gingerly pressing his lips to her skin. When he withdrew from her forehead, she looked back up to meet his eyes, and they both smiled more broadly than either of them ever had before.

When they kissed, neither of them could remember having ever been so happy.

Chapter 51

Elmer Brent was a man who made quick decisions. He was seventy-eight years old and impulsive, and despite the often negative implications of that personality trait, it was that very quality which had resulted in his becoming a self-made millionaire in his early twenties. In his particular case, it was not strategically playing the odds that made him such a rich man. It was instead playing *against* the odds that had resulted in his biggest moneymaking career moves. He would do something that logically made no sense, bet on a virtually unknown entity that he just had a "good feeling" about, and somehow he would end up with a winner.

His detractors viewed his "business strategies" as nothing more than "gambling". So, in the estimation of many of his contemporaries, Elmer Brent was, simply put, one lucky son-of-a-bitch.

When Brent was twenty-three years old, he bought a rambling 2500-acre ranch in Texas. The reason for this purchase was that a friend had informed him that there were people who had made millions in Texas just because their land was sitting on top of an underground mass of "black gold", as crude oil was often affectionately known, for its black color and incredible ability to make the lucky bastard sitting on top of it a very wealthy individual. Despite his knowing next to nothing about where oil was actually located, he was so enamored with the phrase "black gold", he more or less picked the first ranch he could find and just hoped for the best. He hired experienced Texas drillers to search the relatively small ranch. What the drillers told him after several days of surveying the land and testing the drill in different areas was that his entire ranch sat atop one of the biggest oil reserves ever discovered on private land in the state. In fact, the discovery even made several of his *neighbors* overnight millionaires, as the reserve flowed far into other properties as well.

Brent, who leaned to the political left, often felt uncomfortable in Texas and kept his time spent there to only the necessary minimum. He was more than happy to sell his land to the highest bidding oil company, and ended up with almost a half-billion dollars. With that kind of money, he could have just about anything he wanted, and as an avid basketball fan, born and raised in a suburb just outside Los Angeles, what he wanted was to own the Los Angeles Lakers. Although the franchise wasn't actually on the market at the time, for the price that he was willing to pay, the team turned out to indeed be for sale.

Chapter 52

Tessa was getting dressed, and Duncan was watching. As he did so, he thought about Fat Elvis and reflected on how different his life would have been at that very moment had Corey Pager not woken up and blessed him with the proverbial get-out-of-jail-free card. Time passed in slow motion as he savored every millisecond. The sight of his beautiful girlfriend (who had graciously and enthusiastically taken him back), half-naked, the morning after, was pretty much the polar opposite of the drab, gray, brick walls, bleak emptiness, and sexless solitude that greeted him each morning upon waking up in his 6x8 cell during his stay at Northern State.

Staring at the love of his life, the-one-that-got-away (but returned), Duncan, at that moment, was in full revelry, and basketball was the furthest thing from his mind. In fact, as sweet relief washed over him, he did just about no thinking at all. The beautiful feeling was all-consuming, rendering active thought unnecessary.

As Duncan stared, Tessa turned to him and blushed. "Duncan!" she said playfully, "I'm not *decent*."

Duncan didn't respond verbally. A slow, unhurried smile crept across his lips. Tessa batted her eyelashes and bit her lower lip. "Hi," she whispered.

"Hey," he smiled back. "'Sup?"

That made her giggle. "Nuttin'," she said. "Sup witchoo?"

"Nuttin'"

"Nuttin'?"

"Just about."

"Well, *that's* something."

"Isn't it though?"

"It really is."

"I know."

"I'm glad you agree."

"Me too."

Tessa walked to the bed, her jeans on, though her shirt had yet to make its way over her bra. She leaned down, her long brunette hair falling in Duncan's face. He pushed the impeding strands aside, and tilted up to meet her full lips, which were slowly dropping towards his own. Kissing her tasted, at first, like sugary strawberries (her lipgloss), and when their mouths opened and their tongues intertwined, that flavor gave way to the freshness of sweet mint (her gum). *Delicious*, Duncan thought. *Unbelievable*. And never being one to forget to stop and smell the roses, he silently contributed to his mind's running commentary: *I cannot fuckin believe I'm me.*

A few months earlier, waking up to this was unimaginable. While he was imprisoned, the idea of mornings like this one had become beautiful, yet distant, memories. And mornings such as this had become nothing short of impossible. But as it was wont to do, Duncan's luck defied the odds, and he yet again found himself in a position of uncommon comfort. And joy! Exhilaration! And this time it was better than ever because now he was familiar with the feeling of his luck running out. It made the cake that much sweeter when he had it and ate it too. *Yum.*

"Baby," Duncan said, locking eyes with Tessa, "I..." His voice trailed off, and his eyes looked away from hers, past her, settling on the ceiling, which for the first time he noticed was painted the blue of a perfectly cloudless late-spring day.

"What, honey?" Tessa said, a note of concern ringing in her voice, as Duncan's expression changed slightly from a handsome, lazy smile into one of distant thoughtfulness.

"Baby," he continued, "Baby, I'm... I'm so sorry." And with those words came a sudden and unexpected stream of tears, accompanied by muffled sobs.

"Oh, Duncan," Tessa said, cradling his head in her velvet-soft arms, "Oh, baby, shhh. It's okay, honey. It's okay."

Duncan allowed himself to cry for several moments in her sweet, forgiving embrace before attempting to continue with what he had to say. "Baby," he said, "I've put you through so much. I can't believe you're still here for me. I don't deserve any of this. I don't deserve *you*."

Tessa flashed an easy, comfortable smile, and said, "You're probably right, Sir Dunksy Woops-A-Lot. But that doesn't matter. I love you. I love you so much, and nothing matters anymore. I don't care about when you left in high school, after Matty died. I don't care about Amsterdam. And I don't care about you being gone these past months. It just doesn't matter. All that matters is this."

Their lips grazed each others' in the most tender, gentle kiss the couple had ever shared. Tessa then wiped the tears from each of Duncan's eyes with her thumbs, and lightly pressed her lips against his warm forehead. He opened his reddened eyes and remade contact with her big baby-blues, then wrapped her in a firm embrace, from which neither of the lovers left for more than ten minutes of truly golden silence.

Chapter 53

Elmer Brent sat in his office, staring at his computer screen. He was doing research. The NBA draft was three months away, and although he largely left the decision-making on draft prospects to his employees, he had grown very emotionally attached to his team, and over his decade of ownership had come to give his input on who should should be drafted more and more each year (often to his underlings' chagrin).

The Lakers were in the midst of another successful season, led by Kobe Bryant, who was playing at the top of his game. Consequently, they would again be picking late in the draft. This, however, did not bother Brent. As his love of the pro game increased, he watched more and more college ball to see what he could find in college players that would translate into their professional success. The NBA is full of successful late picks, undrafted players, and relatively unheralded players. It is also full of horror stories of failed early picks.

Brent was far more interested in the fact that lesser prospects could have remarkable success. He looked at a recent late pick of the New York Knicks, Landry Fields, as a shining example of a diamond in the rough. Had the Knicks not picked up the unheralded player out of Stanford, he might have gone undrafted, and maybe ended up being a star overseas, rather than the starting 2-guard in the biggest basketball market in the world. But someone in the Knicks' front office had a good eye, and Brent's current passion was cultivating that eye in himself.

And so, he was doing research. The internet, along with tons of game-tape "auditions" that had been sent to and procured by the Lakers, provided him with ample information. But he was yet to see anything that really jumped out at him. There was one player, an

Asian-American kid at Harvard named Jeremy Lin who intrigued him, but he wouldn't be in this year's draft and still had some work to do to prove himself worthy of an NBA career.

That day, Brent had risen, as was his habit, at 5:45 am, had his chef make him a light breakfast of oatmeal and a hardboiled egg, and promptly began his research a little before 6:30 am. This "hobby" of his, as time-consuming as it was, seemed to make time fly. Never a basketball player himself, Brent was fascinated by the physical talent of these young men, and found great pleasure in living vicariously through their achievements. But he was very selective about just whom he wanted to be living vicariously through. Accordingly, much time had to be spent. It was not until about 2:30 pm, shortly after lunch, when he came across an article on ESPN.com that he found truly fascinating.

The headline read, "Promising State Star Imprisoned After Putting Student in Coma". The story was about a young man named Duncan Lipton who, shortly after having an amazing debut for State University, had beaten a fellow student into a coma with a baseball bat. Initially horrified, Brent found himself impressed with the young man only moments later when the story quoted one John Weinhaus as saying, from his hospital bed, "Duncan only did it to save me. Corey stabbed me and Duncan hit him to save me. He didn't try to hurt him. He really didn't. He was just trying to help me. Duncan's like the nicest guy ever, man. I can't believe they locked him up. I really can't believe it."

All his life, Brent had been a man to rely on his instincts, and he found that the tone of the John Weinhaus quote rang true to him. Not knowing what to expect, he was instantly intrigued about this Duncan Lipton. The rest of the article described Lipton as having more than impressed in his debut game and the follow-up. Dick Vitale, after only the first game, was on ESPN calling Duncan a "diaper dandy", his signature term for an excellent freshman basketball player.

It took a couple of phone calls to get his hands on the full game-tape, and by around 7 pm, Elmer Brent was staring at his television screen with his jaw on the floor. This was the best thing he'd seen all day... by far. *Where the hell is Duncan Lipton now?* he thought. A quick Google search immediately provided him with the answer he was hoping for. The kid, Corey Pager, had woken from his coma and corroborated what his victim, John Weinhaus had said. He insisted on the charges being dropped and Duncan had been released back to his parents' house in Eastfield.

Brent was ecstatic. He went to WhitePages.com and found the number for the Lipton house in Eastfield. He picked up his phone in Los Angeles, and dialed the number. The phone rang three times before a young woman answered the phone. "Lipton residence," she said.

Chapter 54

"Duncan," Tessa said, "there's somebody on the phone for you." She held her hand to the receiver. "It sounds like an old man," she whispered.

Duncan shrugged, and, with a curious expression on his face, walked from his bed to the phone. "Hello?" he said.

"Duncan, this is Elmer Brent. How are you, young man?"

"Good?" Duncan said tentatively.

"Do you know who I am?" Brent asked.

"Um, no, sir. I don't."

On the other end, the old man laughed. "I'm the owner of the Los Angeles Lakers, Duncan. I'm very interested in you. I was wondering when you might be available to have some lunch with me. There are some things I'd like to discuss with you."

Duncan's jaw hit the floor. He looked at Tessa, who looked back at him with *What's this all about?* written all over her face. His eyes were bulging out of his head, and his lack of any sign of positive or negative emotion gave her something of a fright, considering the events of his life as of late. "Um, wow, um, sure Mr. Brent. I'd love to," he said. "Um, yeah, uh, my schedule is pretty much wide open right now."

"Good, my boy. Very good," Brent said. "Tomorrow then?"

"Um, yeah, yeah, sure," Duncan said, his disbelief continuing to cause his speech to sputter.

"Twelve noon it is then?"

"Twelve noon it is, sir."

"I'll be by to pick you up then, young man. Your address is still the same as the White Pages listing I presume?"

"Yes, sir."

"Was that your girlfriend who answered the phone?"

"Yes, sir."

"She sounds like a dear. I hope the two of you have a lovely evening. Sleep well, my young friend. Tomorrow is a new day, and a big one at that. I will see you at 12pm sharp."

"Yes, sir." Duncan hung up the phone.

"Who was that?" Tessa asked.

"Oh, you know, just Elmer Brent."

"Elmer Brent?" Tessa racked her memory for the name. "The oil guy?"

"Um, I don't know anything about oil, hon, but he says he's the owner of the Los Angeles Lakers and he wants to have lunch with me tomorrow!"

"No...fucking...way!" Tessa said. She ran over to Duncan's laptop, did a quick Google search, and found out quickly that Elmer Brent was most certainly the man she remembered learning about in school, and he was most certainly the owner of the Los Angeles Lakers.

Wow, Duncan thought. *That's a new one.*

That night, Tessa stayed over, and she and Duncan made sure to have the lovely evening the old man had wished for them.

Just before noon, Duncan and Tessa sat on Duncan's bed, holding hands and smiling at each other. Duncan's heart beat with nervous rapidity. "Wow," he said, "I can't believe Elmer Brent is about to come over. Just as he said the words, a horn beeped three times out front of the Lipton McMansion.

"Ooooh, there he is!" Tessa squealed. Duncan sighed, stood up, and looked himself over in the mirror. He was wearing his best suit, and Tessa had given his hair a neat little trim. He looked more than presentable for this important meeting, and his nervousness was giving way to excitement.

"How do I look, babe?" he asked.

"Fantastic!" Tessa said enthusiastically.

"Cool. Let's go."

They walked out the front door and there was a black stretch limo with an appropriately-capped driver standing at the back door. As they approached the limo, Duncan put up his index finger to the driver and said, "One sec, dude," and then walked Tessa over to her Jetta.

Duncan opened the door for her to get in. Before sitting down, she turned to him and gave him a quick kiss. "Good luck Sir Dunsky Woops-A-Lot. Let me know how it goes."

"I'll call you as soon as we're done, baby," he replied.

One more quick peck and Duncan walked over to the limo. "What's goin' on, dude?" Duncan said to the driver.

"Hello, sir," the driver replied. He opened the door, and they shared a brief smile and nod before Duncan sat down in one of the limo's plush leather seats.

"Hello, young man," said the small, immaculately-dressed old man in the back. "I'm Elmer Brent."

"Hi, Mr. Brent. I'm Duncan."

Brent took Duncan's hand and shook it in a firm business grip. "Please my young friend, call me Elmer."

Chapter 55

"Okay, Elmer," Duncan said with a slight chuckle, as he wasn't used to being on a first-name basis with senior citizens. But there was something very youthful about Elmer Brent. He seemed to have a joie de vive that radiated youthfulness, despite his craggy skin and the obvious age in his speaking voice.

"Are you hungry, Duncan?" Brent asked.

"Actually, yeah I am," Duncan replied. He had bypassed breakfast in anticipation of lunch, and due to the mild nervousness he was feeling, he couldn't have eaten anyway. But as soon as he met Elmer Brent, his appetite returned to him in full force.

"Good, good. Well, where shall we go?"

Duncan had expected that Brent would be all prepared with a dining location, but apparently he was leaving that up to his young charge. "Um, well, what are you in the mood for, Elmer? Some place nice, pizza…?"

"Ya know what? I could go for a sub. You have a good deli around here?"

"Do we have a good deli?" Duncan laughed. "Heck yeah. There's this place called Hershey's that I've been going to since middle school. It's everybody's favorite place around here."

"Well, that'll be perfect. I looked up what kind of fine dining there is around here, but I figured you and I would probably be more on the same page with a sub. Am I right?"

"You couldn't be more right."

"Juuuust what I thought. Excellent. Where is it that we're going?"

"South Ave."

Brent rolled down the window separating the back cabin from the driver's area. Toby, Hershey's on South Ave. in Eastfield please."

"Yes, sir," said the driver, and after plugging the information into his GPS, they were off.

"Well," Elmer Brent said, rolling the dividing window back up, "it is certainly a pleasure to meet you, young man. Quite a pleasure." Brent wore a beatific smile, like meeting Duncan was the most blissfully perfect thing he could be doing at that moment.

"It's really nice to meet you too," Duncan said, mildly astonished at the old man's delight in meeting him. After all, he was more or less fresh out of jail, and while he had been a high school star, he had played only two basketball games in college. The NBA was a dream, and while *he* knew that he was good enough to play at that level, he didn't think that many others were thinking the same thing. So, what Brent said next came as a bit of a surprise.

"Duncan, my friend, tell me something. How would you feel about playing basketball for the Los Angeles Lakers?"

"Sir?"

"I mean, hypothetically, how would you feel about playing pro ball... for my team?"

"Wow, um, I mean, sir, that's my ultimate dream in life. I just love playing ball so much, and the Lakers are my favorite team, and Kobe's my favorite player, and I love the purple and gold, and..."

Brent laughed. "I expected as much. Yes, yes, that's what I expected. Have any other teams contacted you yet about the draft?"

"Oh, no, not at all. I wasn't planning on entering. Hardly anyone knows who I am. I mean, I'm sure you know, I just got out of prison. And I only played in two games for State last season before the whole incident. So, I don't think most people really even know who I am, to be honest."

"You're right, Duncan. You are absolutely right," Brent said. "Most don't know who you are...yet. But they will. And by that time, I don't want there to be any competition for acquiring your services, my young friend. I want you on the Los Angeles Lakers. We are lacking in the point guard department, and I feel in my heart of hearts that you are our guy."

Duncan was floored. "Well, I only played those two games. As flattering and amazing as everything you're saying is, how do you know that I'm your guy?"

"Duncan, I don't know if you know how I became who I am today, but I did it on instinct, son. The same thing that I felt when I bought my first oil field, *supposedly* on a whim, that's what I felt the first time I saw tape of your first game with State. When I know... I know."

That was a lot of pressure to have heaped on him in the matter of a couple of minutes, but Duncan knew that this was no crazy old man putting his faith in a silly pipe dream. Because Duncan knew himself. He was Woops. He had always been the best at what he did, and he had always believed he could take his abilities to the next level. And now he had found a kindred spirit who, based on scant evidence, found the same kind of belief in his game that he had in himself. It was a beautiful feeling.

The limo pulled up in front of Hershey's, and Brent rolled the dividing window down to speak to the driver. "Toby, just find a spot nearby. I'll phone you when we're finished."

"Yes, sir," Toby said.

"Can I get you anything while we're in there?" Brent asked the driver.

Toby, obviously used to his employer's generosity didn't miss a beat in requesting lunch. "Yes, sir, that'd be great. Could you get me a ham and Swiss sub with lettuce, tomato, and mayo please?"

"No problem, son."

Duncan was impressed by this little exchange. Here was an epically powerful businessman, selflessly concerning himself with his driver's lunch. Duncan was a sucker for people going out of their way to make small considerations for others. It just made him like Elmer

Brent even more than he already did. He had known the man for all of twenty minutes, and he was duly impressed with his boldness, generosity, and whimsical nature. He silently hoped that he would be something like that when he was an old man.

Brent and Duncan stepped out of the limo, and Duncan noticed that the old man was surprisingly agile in his exit. They walked into Hershey's and stood on line. "So," Brent said, "you've been coming here since middle school, you said?"

"Yeah," Duncan replied. "I love this place. When I was in high school, my friends and I used to walk here every day for lunch when we were freshmen and sophomores, even though we weren't technically allowed off school grounds until we were juniors."

Brent chuckled. "Nothing like breaking the little rules," he said. "I was always a bit of a rogue, if you will, in my younger years. Hell, who am I kidding? I'm still a rogue."

Duncan laughed. "Yes you are, Elmer. Yes you are. You wouldn't be standing on line at Hershey's with me in Eastfield if you weren't, I guess."

"Well put, young man. Well put." They smiled a somewhat conspiratorial smile at each other.

Duncan greeted one of the deli's owners, Mike, at the counter and ordered half a turkey sub with American cheese, lettuce, onions, vinegar and oregano. "And just a little bit of mustard," he said. Brent ordered half a capicola, ham, and prosciutto sub with provolone cheese. "Everything on it," he said. "Extra tomatoes as well, please."

As Mike rang up their order, he said to Duncan, "So, Dunks, congratulations on getting out, man. Everybody's been talking about it. You should hear all the high school kids coming in here. They're, like, what's the word? Ecstatic, man. You're a hero to those kids. What the hell happened, man? I know what the papers said, but I've been dying to hear it from you."

"Ya know what, Mike," Duncan replied, "I'll explain it to you next time I come in, alright? I'm with somebody right now." He nodded his head at the elderly man next to him in line.

"Oh yeah, sure, man. No problem. You gonna be back soon?"

"Highly likely I'll be back for breakfast tomorrow morning. You gonna be here?"

"Oh, you know it, brother. It's been a little while, but don't think I don't remember. Taylor ham, egg and cheese on a bagel, little bit of salt and pepper."

"You got it, dude," Duncan said, smiling. "Always on point." Besides being the best deli around, as far as the food went, it was how they made him feel at home that most endeared the place to him. He turned his head and looked at Brent, who was smiling widely. Brent was silently noting that his instincts were sharp as ever, and that if this young man's game was half as good as his personality, he had found yet another diamond in the rough.

They sat down at a table next to the window. "Well," Brent said, "obviously you're going to have to tell the story again tomorrow morning, but I'd like to hear it myself if you don't mind. What the hell landed you in prison for those nine months?"

Duncan sighed, not at the annoyance of having to tell the story, but rather at the memory of the crazy night that had landed him in jail, and almost robbed him of many years of freedom. "Well, when I went to State, I became friends with this kid, John. And, Elmer, being that you've been so open with me, and so generous with your time, I'll just come out with it. John and I, along with this other kid, Tucker, bonded over smoking weed. They were, like, the first guys other than my teammates that I met at school. They offered, and since I smoked a bunch in high school, I decided to join them. It's not something I'm doing now, but I won't lie, I had more than the odd puff back then."

"I appreciate your honesty, Duncan," Brent said. He found the young man's openness to be a profoundly positive quality. And the fact that smoking weed was a hobby that he had himself taken up in the sixties and continued to occasionally enjoy to this day, made him not look down on moderate pot usage.

"Thanks, Elmer," Duncan said. "I just want everything to be out on the table, ya know? You're putting a lot of faith in me, and I just want you to know who I am and how I ended up where I'm at."

"Believe me, my young friend, those words are music to my ears. Our developing relationship is a highly unique one, and I want it to be frank, open, and mutually beneficial, both personally and professionally, you understand?"

"Yes sir, definitely. Wow. I'll tell ya, this is *something else*. Just yesterday, I was really wondering what direction my life was going to go in. I mean, just getting out of jail was a big surprise, and now it's like everything's comin' up Duncan."

Both men laughed, and Brent said, "Anyway, you were telling me your story."

"Right," Duncan said. "Well, basically I became friends with those guys pretty quickly. But there was this side of John that I thought was really messed up. I mean, he was super mean to his roommate, Corey, the kid who was in the coma. Honestly, I found it really off-putting. I mean, I don't know what the extent of their relationship was, and exactly why John was so mean to him, but it really just seemed like a bullying situation. I've known a lot of bullies in my life, and I was always one to step in and try to help whoever was being picked on, but in this situation I just kept quiet because they were roommates, and I had no idea what the back-story was to their relationship. So, I just kept my mouth shut and didn't say anything to John about it. He and Tucker would say stuff about Corey when he wasn't around, but Tucker didn't join in bullying Corey to his face so much, as far as I could tell.

"Anyway, after a party, less than a week after I had met Tucker and John, I went back with them to John's dorm to smoke. We were also with this beautiful girl that I just met, Erika. So, the three of us get back to John's dorm, and there's his roommate Corey, playing with the cutest fuckin kitten you ever saw in your life, Elmer. Pardon my French."

"Pardoned."

"Erika's oohin' and aahin' over the little thing, but you can just see on John's face, he's, like, *boiling* mad. I'm thinkin', *What the hell is up with this guy?* John takes like two steps across the room and just punches Corey flat out in the face, grabs the kitten, throws it on the ground, and stomps on its adorable little head. Then, he's like mocking Corey. Corey completely flipped out. He just reaches into his pocket, pulls out a Swiss army knife and starts stabbing John. I saw him get John once, and my instinct just kicked in. I saw a baseball bat in the corner of the room, I picked it up, and I swung at Corey. I did it to stop him from killing John. I was aiming for his shoulder, but he kinda moved and I hit him in the head. He was in a coma for months, and I sat in jail for all that time. Then, he woke up, and he was told what happened, and apparently the first thing he did was insist that the charges be dropped against me. He knew that I had been trying to save my friend, and he was glad that I had been there to make sure that he didn't kill John. Can you believe that, man? I put him in a coma for, like, nine months and he gets me off the hook. I'll never be able to repay him. I don't think…"

"Pardon *my* French," Brent said, "but holy fucking shit."

"Oh, don't worry, Elmer. French is like a second language to me." They both laughed, and ate in silence for a moment, each contemplating the insane story. It was the first time that Duncan had actually told the story out loud to anyone other than his friend in prison, Joe Curtis. He almost couldn't believe that he was talking about himself. Brent on the other hand, could very much believe it. Duncan had simply been trying to save his friend. However much of an asshole, pothead, and bully this John Weinhaus may have been, Brent could plainly see that Duncan had been trying to do the right thing. He found it admirable and very congruous with the rest of the impression that the young man had given him over the course of their meeting. "So, yeah…" Ducan said.

"Yeah," said Brent. "You're a good boy, young man. A good, young man-boy. You have much to learn, young Padawan. But you already know so much. Don't forget how much there is to know that you don't know yet. *Yet* is what you make of it, Woops. Yet is what you make of it."

Duncan was amazed at how Elmer was able to give such profound advice and manage to lace it with a *StarWars* reference. He was honored to have him be the Yoda to his Luke Skywalker. The guy *got it*.

Duncan couldn't believe his luck. This brilliant old man just came out of nowhere to give him another shot at making his lifelong dream a reality. This time, he decided, that shot would not be wasted. All the luck in the world wouldn't get him where he wanted to go without a lot of effort, but yet again he found himself in the kind of extraordinary circumstances that, seemingly, only he ever encountered. Under his breath, he said to himself, "I cannot fuckin believe I'm me."

Chapter 56

At the behest of his boss, the magnanimous Elmer Brent, Toby sat and enjoyed his sub in the front seat of the limo, while Duncan and Brent talked more about this and that, that and this, friends and foes, girls and women, sports and beer, learning and earning. When he was done eating, Toby drove them back to the Lipton house.

"Truly, son," Brent said, "it has been a pleasure like few I have experienced to meet you today. I am going to the drawing board to figure out how to make you a Los Angeles Laker. Listen, I already have a great team, don't I? I am not relying on this draft to make or break the team. So I'm going to work with my management team to ensure that you become a Laker. Hopefully, we will be able to keep you under the radar, but I am certain that your performance at pre-draft combines will carry you far. So, in the near future, we might want to discuss how you probably should *perform* at the combine."

Duncan picked right up on Brent's meaning. He needed to tone down his ability at the combines. If he played too well, he might get picked up earlier in the draft. Neither Brent, nor Duncan, wanted that to happen. All Duncan ever wanted was to be on the Los Angeles Lakers. He knew that he was going to have to do his part to get himself there. Actually toning down his ability? He had never done it, always outshining his peers with fiery determination. But, he figured, he had to do what he had to do. *Wow*, he thought. *That's gonna be a new one.*

Duncan would do it though. He couldn't help but be amazed by the faith that Brent was putting in him. The old man had seen him play in only two games, and had only heard about his legendary high school play. There was so little information on his new prospect compared to that of other players, but Brent's track record clearly showed that he knew a good thing when he saw one, and Duncan was not going to question his judgment.

"Now, you go have a nice evening, Duncan," Brent said, extending his hand and gripping Duncan's in a firm, businesslike shake that also had the light quality of friendship and a grandfatherly tenderness that Duncan, whose grandfathers had both passed away when he was very young, identified as sort of filling a personal void.

"You too, E.B."

Brent chuckled. "E.B., *huh?*"

"I think it fits you, man," Duncan said.

"That's what the kids I played baseball with called me when I was nine years old. Everyone I played with called me that. Then, so did everyone in school. All through high school, until I left for college, I was always E.B. Since my best friend passed away fifteen years ago, nobody's called me that. You didn't know that somehow, did you?"

"Nah," said Duncan, "I like acronyms, and E.B. rolls so nicely off the tongue."

Duncan's smile implied no lie to Brent, and the old agnostic found himself suddenly believing in signs from a higher power. "Unbelievable," he said. "Lipton, my young friend, you really are something else. Go have a nice night with that pretty young lady I saw you with when Toby and I picked you up. Make sure you don't stay up late. And make sure that when the phone rings, you answer it. You don't want to miss this call. That much I can guarantee."

"Yes, sir," Duncan said, a huge smile on his face. Brent smiled back at him, and Duncan gently shut the door.

Duncan started to walk up the driveway to his house when he heard Brent's voice. "Hey, Woops!" the old man said.

Duncan turned around to see him slightly leaning out of the opened window. "Yeah?"

"Tonight," Brent said, "on MSNBC there's going to be an episode of the show 'Lockup'. Watch it. You know why."

Duncan half-smiled and nodded. "You got it." The joy of his change of fortune would fuel his fire. That's what Brent thought. But Duncan didn't need any fuel. The fire was already blazing as hot and bright as it ever could. And then some. When it came to basketball, his play always came down to his innate understanding of what it took to win and his pure love of capitalizing on that ability. External motivations didn't factor much into his execution. Getting where he really wanted to go was probably going to require some modification to his game, in the sense that he might need to play less than his best basketball to get himself into that optimal situation, but he could handle that.

Duncan understood Elmer's intent in having him watch *Lockup*. He knew it wouldn't serve the purpose that the old man intended, but he watched the episode anyway, and he quickly found that the footage of life inside the walls of prison brought on an unexpected wave of emotion. The feeling was intense, but it was not any kind of sadness, pity, regret, fear, doubt, or any windstorm of negative emotion. Nor was it the sweet feeling of relief. What he felt instead was an immense, dam-of-the-soul-bursting love for his new benefactor, mentor, and friend, Elmer Brent.

As he watched, Duncan experienced a genuine moment of clarity regarding their budding relationship. Sure, his skill at basketball was what was going to get him to the NBA, but this fateful meeting cemented an unlikely friendship that he *knew* would prove to be based on mutual admiration, unrelated to the respective talents that were the catalyst for their meeting. He had stumbled across a valuable intergenerational bond, and had made a real friend. And, conveniently, it just so happened that this new friend was going to provide him with the opportunity to have just about everything he'd ever wanted. *Soooo convenient*, Duncan thought. As the credits rolled at the end of the show, he smiled and shook his head. Watching the show hadn't been about motivating him to play basketball at all. It was about him seeing the big picture of his life and truly appreciating his freedom.

Chapter 57

"Hi," Tessa softly answered her phone. She was smiling.

"Hey, babe," Duncan said.

"Wellllll," she said, "how'd it go, Sir Woopsy Dunks-A-Lot?"

"Baby," Duncan said. "Oh, baby, baby. Um, as long as I do what I gotta do, I'm gonna end up on the Lakers. They're gonna draft me, babe!"

"You're sure?" She would have hated to see Duncan have his hopes raised and then dashed after all he'd recently been through.

"Yeah, baby, I'm so fuckin sure," he said. "I mean, I think that I have a pretty good eye for honesty, sincerity, character, all that good shit, ya know? I'm telling you, this guy is the epitome of all that is beautiful about all those words. And he just told me that he doesn't give a shit who else is in the draft. Whenever they pick, *I'm* gonna be their guy. Even if they picked first, which they can't because their record's too good, I'd still be first. He said the team is good enough as it is. He doesn't want any high-priced rookies replacing any of his current players. For whatever reason, all he wants is to add me to what he's already got goin' on."

"Oh my God, honey," she said. "Oh, Duncan."

"Yeah," he said. "Now, all I gotta do is make sure that I don't get picked by another team in the first round, before the Lakers have a chance."

Tessa had seen Duncan play about a million and one times, so the idea that such a thing could happen, she knew, was hardly farfetched. Being just about unknown on the national stage, except for his involvement in the debacle that led to his spending nine months incarcerated, Duncan had had no intention of declaring himself draft-eligible. But now he would be expected to perform in pre-draft workouts and the NBA combine to show teams that he was worthy of even being listed among the potential draftees, let alone worth a draft pick. The key to getting selected by the Lakers would be to play well, yet underwhelm the scouts. Then, down the road, the teams that picked before L.A. would discover what they'd missed. But on draft day, the Lakers would undoubtedly be the laughing stock of the league, and the sanity of their septuagenarian owner would come into question.

"Gosh, honey, I hope you can tone your game down," Tessa said, only half-jokingly.

"Me too," he replied.

"But tonight though, big guy, I don't want you to tone your game down at all. In fact, I'm expecting you at full force. I'll be over in half an hour." Tessa didn't even wait for a reply. She just hung up, leaving Duncan on the other end, surprised, excited, and horny.

She quickly did her makeup, put on a cute little outfit, and climbed into her Jetta. Within an hour, her cute little outfit was on Duncan's bedroom floor, and she was asleep in his bed, a post-coital little spoon, with an exhausted big spoon holding her close. Just moments after she drifted off, the big spoon was asleep too.

Chapter 58

The Staples Center, the home arena for the Los Angeles Lakers was completely empty except for three men having a friendly shooting competition on the basketball court. When they dribbled the ball, there were multiple echoes in the cavernous building, and when one of them swished a shot, it sounded like a gust of wind briefly blowing through.

After Duncan knocked down seven three-pointers in a row, his two companions began to express their approval. "Okay, my dude," Kobe said. "Okay. I'm feelin' your stroke, man."

Duncan smiled, took an extra step back behind the arc, and swished his shot. "Thank you," he said.

"That's my *boy*," Matty G said to Kobe. "You see how dirty he is from downtown, bro? He can bury 'em like that with a hand in his face too. Man, fuck it. My boy Dunks can do that shit while you give him a bear-hug and wrap a bandana around his fuckin' *dome*!" The two men laughed, and watched Duncan's ninth shot in a row fall so purely it barely grazed even the *net*, let alone the hoop.

"So…*wet*." Duncan said, releasing another parabolic masterpiece, and cockily licking his lips after the ball swished.

"Son," said Matty G, "you are lights out, kid!"

"Yeah, man," Kobe contributed. "You're gonna fit in real well around here. Real fuckin well."

"Thanks," Duncan replied, as casually as he possibly could.

"Don't thank *me*, Dunks," Kobe said. "I just call it like I see it. Bringing you in sure as shit wasn't my idea. I never hearda ya, and if it were up to me, I wouldn't be gambling on unknowns. This draft class was respectable enough, but Mr. Brent knows what he wants, big man, n' he ain't settlin' for *anything* other than you."

Duncan fired up a tenth shot, and it clanged off the back of the rim, flying high over the backboard. "Got it!" shouted Matty G. He ran to the hoop, and pulled off his basketball jersey to reveal an enormous set of wings, which he used to fly up to the ball. He caught it, then casually floated back down to the court, and dropped it through the rim on his way there. "Oops," he said, and laughed.

"Holy shit," said Duncan. "What the…uh, how'd you, uh…?"

"What, you ain't never seen a nigga with wings?" Matty G said, laughing as he pulled his jersey back over his head.

"Um, no. I have not," Duncan said.

"And you won't for a long time," Kobe said. "We got a lot of work to do. Unfortunately, just you and me."

Duncan didn't know what to say. If he understood correctly what Kobe was implying, it meant that Matty G was not going to be playing with them. He didn't like the idea of playing on a team without his best friend. It had always been Woops *and* Oops. Couldn't the three of them play together?

"Well…can't Matty G play with us too?" With his hands in his pockets, his head tipped forward, and his eyes staring at the ground, Duncan looked and sounded like the little boy he had been when he and G first met.

Kobe wore a grave expression. "Sorry little brother, but Matty G's playing for a new team in a better place now. Unfortunately, we're gonna have to do this without him."

"That sucks," Duncan quietly replied, as Matty G walked up to him and put his arm around his shoulder.

"We woulda made a hell of a squad," Kobe said. "But you and me, Dunks…we're gonna kill it, man. We are gonna blow the roof off this motherfucker!"

Duncan gave a wan smile, and said, "I hope so, man."

"Look around, little brother. This place is gonna be packed. You're gonna sign autographs 'til your wrist hurts. People will be paying *stupid* money for a hot dog and a beer, just so they can see *us*. Man, fuckin Jack Nicholson's gonna want *your* autograph."

The three of them laughed, and Matty G said, "Well, that's just about *as good as it gets*." The goofy reference caused Duncan to roll his eyes and give a half-smile as he shook his head side to side. "Alright, fellas," G said, "I got a game. I'll catch you on the flip, Dunks." Instead of a dap, he gave his best friend a bear hug. Reciprocating, Duncan could feel the enormous wings on Matty G's back straining to break free from the confinement of the embrace. Reluctantly, they let each other go. Matty G gave Kobe a dap, then took flight. When he was halfway to the roof, he turned around and flew back down. He hovered a few feet above Duncan and Kobe, and said, "Ya know, Dunks, I shoulda said it more back when I was, um, around, but I love you, man."

"You're just rockin' with the movie references today, aren't you, dude?" Duncan said.

Matty G laughed. "I was wondering if you'd pick that up."

"Oh you know it, brother."

"But really, man. I love the shit out of you, and I just want you to know that I always will."

"Me too, dude. I really fuckin do."

Matty G flew back down and gave Duncan one more hug. "Tell that pretty Tessa of yours that I said, 'Stay fly, baby booboo.' Just like that. Aiiight?"

"No doubt, kid."

Matty G took flight again and called out, "Kobe, take care of my boy! I'm countin' on you!"

Kobe said nothing; he just smiled, extended his arm, and pointed at Matty G, who disappeared into thin air as he flew through the roof. He then turned to Duncan and said, "Alright, son, I'll see you sooner than you think."

"Cool," said Duncan.

"You and me got some business to take care of." He took Duncan's hand and shook it in a firm, manly handshake, then promptly vanished into thin air, right before Duncan's eyes.

Duncan woke up a little after 8am. Tessa was still asleep, but Duncan wanted to talk. He lightly shook her. "Baby," he said. "Hey, baby. Wake up."

Tessa woke up, and looked at him groggily. "Hi, love," she said.

"Good morning, baby. Sorry to wake you up. I just needed to tell you about my dream." Duncan told Tessa all about the dream he'd just had with Kobe and Matty G. "Oh yeah, and G wanted me to tell you something. He said, 'Stay fly, baby booboo.'"

"Oh my god," Tessa said. She started to sniffle and held Duncan's hand tight. She wrapped him in a strong embrace, which they held for a long time until there was a knock at the door.

"Come in," Duncan said.

It was his mom. "Hi, honey," Mrs. Lipton said.

"Hey, Mom. What's up?"

"Sweety," she said, "get dressed. There's someone here to see you."

"Really?" he said. "This early? Who is it?"

Mrs. Lipton's face lit up in an ear-to-ear grin. "Honey, you wouldn't believe me if I told you."

Chapter 59

Duncan went downstairs, immensely curious. *Who could make Mom's face light up like that?* he wondered. He walked into the kitchen to find two men sitting at his kitchen table. One of the men he had spent several of his waking hours with the previous day. The other man he had spent much time with in his dreams, including the previous night.

"Duncan," said Elmer Brent, "I have someone I want you to meet." Motioning to the man rising out of the kitchen chair and extending his hand in greeting, Brent said, "This is Kobe Bryant. Kobe, meet Duncan Lipton."

Duncan's eyes bulged slightly at the sight of his favorite basketball player standing in his kitchen, and he couldn't help but give a little chuckle at this early-morning shocker and unlikely arrangement. But he managed to keep his cool, and say, "Hey, man. Nice to meet you."

"It's nice to meet you, too," Kobe said. "Elmer's told me a lot about you, man."

"Wow," Duncan said. "What a trip."

Kobe laughed, and said, "He pretty much chewed my ear off about your story on the flight over." He flashed that famously cocky grin at Brent, who smiled back. Returning his gaze to Duncan, he said, "I feel like I know you already."

Duncan shook his head from side to side. "Elmer," he said, "you are *something else*." The three men laughed, and Brent stepped forward to shake Duncan's hand.

"Well, my young friend," Brent said, "I want the protégée to meet his new mentor, and vice versa. We have important work to do, gentlemen, and I don't want to beat around the bush. I believe in my heart of hearts that this is the combination that is going to lead this team where it needs to go. So, I'm not going to waste any time, and neither are the two of you."

"Yes, sir," Duncan said, his tone conveying his understanding of the gravity of this business venture for Brent. The man had something to prove. His reputation was on the line. His instincts were famous in the business world, and, to him, sports was yet another business for him to put his stamp on with his instinctual prowess. To Brent, business was the game that basketball was to Duncan and Kobe.

And Duncan was the vehicle for Brent's success; he knew that. But he didn't view his role as though Brent were using him. He believed in everything the man said, and he felt a beautiful relationship growing between them. Still, he had to recognize that his basketball talent was the catalyst for the relationship's formation, and the optimization of that talent would be a major factor in the relationship's continuation. That meant he was going to have to put in the kind of effort in the gym and on the court that reflected just how important it was to him that his dream come true. If he wanted to prove to Brent that he wasn't making a mistake by believing in him, it was time for him to put in the hard yards.

"Duncan," Brent said, "are there any basketball courts nearby?"

"Yeah," Duncan replied, "just up the block."

"What do you say the three of us head up there, and take some shots?"

"Sounds great. Let me go change real quick."

"No problem. Kobe and I will go wait in the car."

"Cool...oh wait, hold on. Kobe, my girlfriend's upstairs. You mind if she comes down and meets you? We're both, like, crazy big fans. I'm trying to keep my cool, ya know?" Duncan grinned. The three men laughed, and he continued, "But, seriously, dude, I've been watching you just about forever, and my girl's gotten all into the Lakers while we've been together. It'd mean a lot to her."

"She still in bed?" Kobe asked.

"Yeah, she should be," Duncan said. "She's probably sittin up, nibbling on her fingernails, wondering what the hell's going on downstairs. My mom was super excited, but she didn't say that it was you guys who were here. She was all secretive."

"Cool," Kobe said. "We'll surprise her then. Breakfast in bed." Kobe nodded at a brown paper bag on the kitchen table. "We brought bagels. And cream cheese."

"And lox," Brent said. "I thought it would be appropriate, considering your family's… I saw the thingy on the door."

"Yup," Duncan said. "Nail on the head. My mom will love it. Tessa loves that stuff too."

"Perfect," Kobe said. "Plates? Knives?"

Duncan showed Kobe where the utensils and plates and whatnot were. Kobe fixed Tessa a sesame bagel with lox and cream cheese, and Duncan escorted him to his room, where he expected Tessa to be waiting. Kobe gently knocked on the door. There was no response. He knocked a little louder. Still nothing. All of a sudden, the bathroom door behind them opened. Tessa walked out, wearing nothing but a towel. She let out a little shriek. "Oh my god, Duncan, you scared me," she laughed. "Who's your friend?" The hallway outside Duncan's room and the bathroom was rather dimly lit at the moment, and Tessa, who was somewhat nearsighted, had yet to put in her contacts, after her shower. She walked towards them, and said, "Hi, I'm…" She stopped in her tracks. "No fucking way," she said.

"That's a beautiful name," Kobe said.

"No fucking way. Kobe Bryant is in the Liptons' house. No fucking way."

"Nice to meet you…no fucking way," Kobe laughed.

"Oh…god," Tessa said, regaining her composure. "I'm sorry. My name is Tessa. Hiiii."

Tessa blushed as Kobe took her hand and shook it. "Hi, Tessa," he said. "My name's Kobe."

"Ya don't say," Tessa joked. "I'm sorry for being, uh, weird I guess. I'm just, like, a really, really big fan of you and the Lakers, and seeing you in the hallway just really took me by surprise."

"Oh, no worries, no worries," Kobe said. "Believe me, I've seen way worse."

"I'll bet. Say, could you boys give me just a couple of minutes to put some clothes on, and I'll come downstairs, okay?"

"Sure, babe," Duncan said.

"No problem," Kobe replied.

As Duncan and Kobe walked back downstairs, Kobe said, "Looks like you got a winner there, Dunks."

"Thanks, man," Duncan said. "I love her."

"That's what's up. There's nothing like a good woman to keep your feet on the ground."

Shortly after Duncan and Kobe rejoined Brent in the kitchen, Tessa came down wearing what Duncan knew to be yesterday's clothes. Regardless, she exuded youthful beauty and happiness. "Hi, guys. How are you?" she gushed. The men smiled at her lovely, friendly presence.

"Tessa," Duncan said, "this is Elmer Brent."

"Hi," Tessa said. "It's so nice to meet you, Mr. Brent."

"The pleasure is all mine, young lady. Please, call me Elmer."

"Okay, Elmer," she giggled. "I actually learned about you in history class. When you first called Duncan, I was like, 'I think I've heard of that guy', so I looked you up on Wikipedia, and it was you. We learned about how you found that amazing oil field in Texas."

"Yes, ma'am. That was me. I just follow my nose, and hope that it leads me in the right direction. That's what I'm doing with this fine young man over here," Brent said, gesturing at Duncan.

Tessa said, in a surprisingly serious tone, "It's leading you in the right direction, Elmer. It definitely is."

"I believe you," he replied.

After they ate, Tessa went home, and Duncan, Kobe, and Elmer went to the nearby basketball court to have a shoot-around. "Kobe's been teaching me a few moves," Brent said, as they stepped onto the court. Duncan bounced the ball lightly to the old man, and Elmer Brent, surprisingly lithe and athletic for a man his age, drove to the basket and made a clean lay-up. The joy on his face was like that of a child.

"You see that, man?" Kobe said. "Ol' boy couldn't even *dribble* when I first got my hands on him. Look at him now! My pride and joy." He and Duncan chuckled, as Brent threw a pass out to his prospective point guard.

"Alright, young man. Let's see what you've got. I've been hyping you up, you know," Brent said.

Unblinkingly, Duncan took one step outside the three-point line and tossed up a high-arcing beauty that swished trough the net, leaving the rim untouched. He left his arm up, with his hand pointing at the basket in a follow-through motion.

"Ooooooh," Kobe said. "Sweeeet, man!"

"Very nice," said Brent.

"Do it again?" asked Kobe.

"I don't know," said Duncan. "Maybe it was just luck." He took the ball and did the same thing, again swishing his shot, the ball not even grazing the rim.

"You remind me of me," Kobe said, and laughed. He was impressed, and he was looking forward to making the most of this opportunity. The Lakers needed a quick point guard with a clean jump shot, and this kid, Kobe thought, just might be the man for the job.

Brent was impressed too. This was the first time either he or Kobe had seen Duncan shoot in person, and he was feeling increasingly confident in his decision to pursue the young man, and give him a second chance to have the basketball career that, considering his circumstances, he likely would have missed out on.

Brent watched Kobe and Duncan shoot around for about half an hour, very pleased at how his star and his prospect were getting along. *This is going to be very good*, he thought. *Very good, indeed.* "Alright, gentlemen," he said. "That's enough. I have some meetings to attend to in Los Angeles. I wanted you two to meet and get to know each other. I think that we have more than accomplished that mission for today, wouldn't you agree?"

"Absolutely," said Kobe. He turned to Duncan, and said, "You're livin up to the hype so far, young buck. I think we're gonna do big things. *Biiiiiig* things."

Duncan smiled. "Me too," he said.

Toby, Brent's driver, drove the three men back to the Lipton residence to drop Duncan off. "Take it easy, Dunks," Kobe said, as the car pulled up to the McMansion at the end of the Candace Place cul-de-sac.

"You too, dude," Duncan said. "It really was a pleasure meeting you."

"Likewise, little brother."

"Alright, Duncan," said Brent, "you be good, stay out of trouble, and I'll see you in two weeks at the combine."

Duncan extended his arm to give Brent a handshake. "You got it, E.B.," he said, giving the old man a firm shake and a wink. "See ya then."

Chapter 60

When Duncan decided to enter the draft, he caused something of a stir in the media. He had made a name for himself based on the incredible potential he had displayed in only a couple games at State. But, considering he'd been in prison, no one knew when (or if) they might hear from him again. People could hardly believe that he was coming back to basketball. And he wasn't just coming back; he was trying to make a move straight to the top. He had been at rock bottom, and now he was gearing up to scale the mountain. Forget trying to go back to college. He was going for the big time.

Though the media was intrigued by Duncan's declared eligibility, the boardrooms of nearly all NBA franchises left him out of their conversations about which players they were interested in drafting. The kid had played in only two college games and one pro game. In *Amsterdam*. Sure, he had a stellar high school career, but that meant just about nothing to the NBA brass.

Often, a player from a small school shows up to an NBA combine and really impresses scouts and team executives. Colleges recruit kids based on high school performance, but some kids are late bloomers, whose talents don't come to fruition until they are already playing for a program that is usually overlooked by NBA teams, which favor the more prestigious programs: the Ohio States, the Kentuckys, the Michigan States, the Georgetowns. The point of the combine is to give a chance to unheralded mid-major players (and even D-III players) to showcase their skills against the kind of competition that the NBA will provide. If a player performs particularly well, he will be invited to work out privately for individual teams that are interested in him.

This was where Duncan needed to be careful. He didn't want

too much attention heaped on him at the combine. He wanted to fly under the radar, so that the Lakers would be the only team interested in him. Elmer Brent wanted it to be a big surprise to the world that the Lakers would pick Duncan Lipton. He did not want there to be any competition for the young man's services. Should Duncan impress other teams at the combine, and subsequently at private workouts, the Lakers might be unable to get him, at least not without trading a valuable player and/or a good deal of cash to get him on draft day. But Brent was confident that he and Duncan had clearly established what he needed to do at the combine in order to help guarantee that he would be a Los Angeles Laker by the end of the first round of the draft.

Duncan caught the opening tip of his first scrimmage at the combine. He started dribbling up the floor, and, at the first sign of defensive pressure, passed it off to the small forward. He continued to play tentatively, and although he did none of the spectacular things that he was capable of, he still presented himself as a court savvy point guard. He didn't want to appear like he had absolutely no clue what he was doing, so he racked up a number of assists, and he shot a couple mid-range J's and some three-pointers at the line. He made sure, however, to miss a few of them. He had to constantly remind himself to tone it down. He knew that he would be able to take over each of the scrimmages that he played in, and it took every ounce of self-restraint that he could muster to stop himself from doing so. He had committed himself to this plan with E.B., and he was not going to let the man down.

Brent sat in the rafters, with the Lakers' general manager, head coach, two assistant coaches, and two other scouts. They had all been briefed on the situation with Duncan, and, considering how little information they had on the kid, they were skeptical enough to wonder if their owner, who was getting up there in years, was losing some of his marbles. They knew that the kid was supposed to be toning his game down, but he looked so real playing out there. It hardly looked like he wasn't trying. Either he wasn't as good as the old man thought he was, or he was one hell of an actor. Other than Brent, the sentiment was that the kid was probably not quite as good as everyone hoped he'd be. Little did they know, the opposite was the case, and Duncan was playing his role perfectly.

If the other teams' brass felt the same way that the Lakers' did about him, acquiring his services on draft day would be no problem at all. The feeling that Duncan was going to be a star, though, was presently held by only Elmer Brent. Unfortunately, the other Lakers executives didn't know what Brent knew, so amongst the higher-ups in the organization, it was not a popular plan of action for them to put Duncan on the team. That being the case, it was a damn good thing that Duncan had the relationship he did with the owner.

If Brent were out of the picture, it was, at this point, highly unlikely that Duncan would become an NBA player, at least for the upcoming season. He purposely failed to make much of an impression on other teams that he could have potentially played for, as he put all his eggs in Elmer Brent's enticing basket. But Duncan knew that had Elmer not come along and convinced him that an NBA career was within reach, he probably would have never ended up at the combine in the first place. In fact, Brent had to pull some strings behind the scenes to even get Duncan's name on the eligibility list to get into the combine. Duncan had put basketball so far on the backburner, that he most likely never would have pursued the NBA on his own.

So, had Brent never been in the picture, it was highly unlikely that he would have ever had the chance to become an NBA player. That caveat made up Duncan's mind when it came to putting his faith in the wealthy and charming old man who had put his faith in him. There never really was an option for him when it came to how he performed at the combine. He went along with Elmer Brent's plan, and consequently his NBA fate was in Elmer Brent's hands. That was just where he wanted it to be, he thought. He thought.

Chapter 61

"I don't get it," said Sherif Simon. Sherif was the general manager for the Los Angeles Lakers, and had been for the past twenty-three years. At fifty-eight years old, he was a kind, friendly gentleman, around whom women had been known to say, " I thought chivalry was dead." He opened doors, shared his coat when it was cold outside, and regularly put others' needs before his own personal considerations. He wasn't argumentative, and he was rarely angry.

But there was one thing that really got Sherif heated. Hearing, seeing, or reading anything negative regarding his Los Angeles Lakers could flip a switch in him that brought out a side that the world could rarely see. The boardroom was where that side would show itself, and he would put his foot down to quash any perceived slight against the team that was more or less his life.

"I just don't get it. Why this guy?" he said.

"Because," Elmer Brent said, "he's the best. He's my guy, and I want him."

"Did you see this fucking kid at the combine, Mr. Brent?" (Brent didn't mind cursing, but he made sure that his underlings addressed him as Mr. Brent. This was business, and he didn't want any of his employees confused, thinking that they were his friends on a personal level. He could hire, fire, replace, and overrule anyone, and to establish the point, he guaranteed a certain level of respect by introducing himself as "Mr. Brent". His relationship with Duncan, he believed, called for a much more friendly tone, and so he put himself and his young charge on a first-name-basis.)

"I did," said Brent.

"He hardly did anything! How can you possibly want him as our first-round pick? I didn't hear anyone say a word about this kid until now. We could probably pick up Paul Spears with the twenty-ninth pick! He's flying under the radar, I'm telling you, Mr. Brent. We'll be able to get him. I'm certain."

"That's interesting," Brent said.

"Or Ada Ukwuoma. If Spears is gone by then, we could pick up Ukwuoma. I am telling you, he's a little rough around the edges, but we can polish them up. He's only nineteen."

"Also interesting. Well, I am certainly not averse to picking either of them up, preferably Spears, with one of our draft picks. But it's going to have to be our second pick. So, hopefully, one of them will be around when we pick fifty-first."

Sherif's jaw hit the floor. He couldn't believe his opinion wasn't even getting heard. As if this old man even knew anything about basketball! Ha! The responsibility of deciding on whom the Lakers picked in the draft had been primarily his for more than two decades. During Brent's tenure as owner, he had never forced a pick upon him like this. He had always left the final decision up to him. But this situation was different. The old man was putting his foot down. He had decided that the Lipton kid was going to be the Lakers' first draft pick, and there was nothing Sherif could do about it.

But Sherif loved the Lakers, and it was more or less the only topic that could bring out the ire in him, what one might call his dark side. So, even though in his head he knew that that there was nothing that he could do to stop Brent from deciding who the Lakers drafted, his heart decided to put up a fight that rationality knew could not be won. "Why the hell do you want this kid so bad?!?!" he screamed. This is fucking insane! Are you losing your fucking mind? This could be the onset of dementia!"

There was a collective gasp amongst the other executives at the meeting. No one had ever heard someone get so out of line with Elmer Brent. They collectively considered the possibility that this might be the end for Sherif with the Lakers.

Brent maintained his calm though, and said, "You are losing yourself, Sherif. You've worked for me since I took ownership of this team, and I very much value your opinion and the work you do. But you will not speak to me like that again. You get a get-out-of-jail-free card *this* time. But you will never do that again. Do you understand?"

Sherif paused for a moment; his heart raced as he considered his options for what he could say next. As much as he felt like he was right, that it was absolute insanity to use the Lakers' first pick on a completely unproven kid, he still found the presence of mind to choose the most prudent option, the one most likely to allow him to keep his job. He chose to apologize. "I'm sorry, Mr. Brent. I don't know what came over me. It's just…god, I care so much about this team. I feel like we'll be throwing away an important pick. I really just lost it there. I'm very sorry. I just don't understand what this is all about. But, it's your team…of course."

"What this is all about, Sherif," Brent said, "is that Duncan Lipton is the best player in this draft class, and he is the player that I want on the team. And, as the owner, I have decided he *is* going to be on the team. There will be no ifs, ands, or buts about it, and I suggest that you get used to the idea."

"Yes, sir," Sherif said.

"Good. Now that we're clear, I have some other business to attend to." Brent got up, and walked out of the room, leaving behind a boardroom full of amazed executives. They couldn't believe the owner was putting all his stock in a 19-year-old kid, who had almost no track record in high-level competition, and who had clearly had a mediocre performance at best in the combine. They also couldn't believe the audacity of the GM, Sherif, in saying what he did to Mr. Brent. The fact that he still had his job blew the minds of everyone there.

Chapter 62

The day Duncan got back from the combine, he and Tessa were spooning in bed. The young couple couldn't believe their luck. Fate had brought them back together when it looked like their relationship wasn't going to make it, and what was going on between Duncan and Elmer Brent was just the icing on the cake of a beautiful time for the two of them.

"Duncan," Tessa said.

"Yeah?" he replied.

"I'm so happy to have you here with me, baby. I don't know, I just...I really thought it was over between us. Like, when I got back from Amsterdam, I was just so mad at you. I didn't want anything to do with you ever again, I thought. I mean, we didn't talk for *so* long, Duncan."

Tessa had not even been aware of the concussion that Duncan had suffered. The Liptons didn't want the press getting involved in Duncan's hospital stay, so they kept it completely secret. Many people wondered where Duncan was, and what he was doing, but the Liptons kept their lips sealed. Consequently, Tessa was never given any second-hand information. And she certainly, at that time, didn't go looking for it. When Duncan resurfaced, and made his decision to attend State, she had been made aware by friends of friends that he was going to go to school, but she didn't actively seek any information about him. When he went to prison, the news was a town-wide story of tragedy and the picture of sensationalism. She could do nothing to avoid it.

When Duncan got locked up, it had been, to Tessa's young mind, a very long time since she had spoken to him (roughly four months) and she felt too distant from him - and angry with him at the same time - to write him while he was in jail. But somewhere along the line, during his nine-month imprisonment, the absence of Duncan made Tessa's heart grow fonder, and all her feelings of love toward him were rekindled. So, when he returned home from prison, she decided to be there to welcome him, and hoped that he would be as willing to have her back as she was willing to have him. Neither of them could have hoped for anything better than the other's response when he returned.

"I'm happy too, baby," Duncan said. "I really am. I didn't think I'd see you again. I thought you had it up to here with me, to be honest."

"I did," she said. "But I missed you so much."

They kissed, and held together for a long time, just enjoying a peaceful moment, when the phone rang. "I'll get it," Duncan said. He picked up the phone. "Hello?"

"Duncan? Is that you, young man? It's your good friend, Elmer Brent."

"Hey, E.B.," Duncan replied, "How are you?"

"I'm fantastic," Brent said. "Absolutely fantastic, thanks to you!"

"Thanks to me?" Duncan asked.

"Yes, thanks to you, Duncan. The way you sold yourself short in that combine was marvelous. No one will even be thinking about drafting you, I must say. And if they are, they have a poor eye indeed."

"Thanks, Elmer. I really, really, really toned it down for you there. I even let one of my passes get picked off. That was embarrassing, man!" Duncan joked (though only half-jokingly).

"Well, my boy, you did damn good. Damn, damn good. I'm proud of you."

"Thank you," Duncan replied, sincerely.

"Next order of business, I'm going to take you out to dinner to celebrate and discuss your future with the Lakers. Some time next week. I will be in touch. I need to check my schedule, and we will arrange a day. And bring that beautiful girlfriend of yours. I think she'd make delightful dinner company."

"No problem at all," Duncan said. "Thanks, E.B. That sounds great."

"Alright then, young man. I will speak to you next week."

"Awesome…boss," Duncan said. They both chuckled over the line. "Have a good week."

"You too, son," Brent said. Duncan went to hang up the phone, but as he pulled the receiver away from his ear he could here Brent say, "Wait, wait, Duncan. One more thing."

Duncan put the receiver back up to his ear. "Yeah, Elmer?" he said

"Yeah," Brent continued, "Just one more thing. Don't tell anyone besides your girlfriend and your parents about any of this. This is hush-hush. I don't want anyone to know that I am showing interest in you because it will bring unwanted attention, and who knows? Maybe we're doing something against the rules!"

"Don't you worry," Duncan said. "Our lips are sealed." And just as he said it, he could hear the chorus of the Go-Go's song playing over and over in his mind, and he bobbed his head along with it.

"Very good," said Brent. "Very good. Goodnight, Duncan."

"Goodnight, E.B." Duncan hung up the phone, and, for a moment, stared at the receiver and smiled. Then, he turned around, and looked at Tessa, waiting on the bed expectantly. "Sorry about that, hon," he said.

"Sorry about what, babe? You've gotta talk to Mr. Brent. What did he have to say?"

"He was just saying that he was really happy with how I didn't make myself look too good at the combine. He's convinced that that's the only way that I won't get picked up earlier in the draft. And he's probably right, to be honest. I could've schooled those guys out there. But I never would've been there without him, ya know? So, I had to do what I had to do to make sure that I end up on the Lakers. I did the right thing, didn't I?"

"I think so."

"You do?"

"Yeah. You were, like, totally lost before he came along. There's no way you would've gotten an invite to that combine anyway. You had to go along with his plan. It just makes sense for both of you. You did the right thing, baby. Definitely."

Duncan felt relieved. "Thanks, babe," he said, " I don't know why, but for a minute I was doubting myself. You're right. I had to tone it down. If I played too good, I could end up on another team. And I sure as shit don't want that. And even worse, I'd be letting Elmer down. He's been so good to me, ya know?"

"Yeah, I know."

"He wants us to go out to dinner with him next week. You'll come, right?"

"Of course I'll come, Sir Dunksy Woops-A-Lot."

"Good," Duncan said, smiling. "Very good."

Tessa grabbed his shirt, and pulled him close. "I love you," she said.

"I love *you*," he replied. He picked her up, carried her over to the bed, and they spent the next hour proving it to each other.

Chapter 63

It was late May, and the draft was in late June. Duncan and Elmer just had to sit tight until then. Presently, they were sitting at a nice Italian restaurant in Eastfield called Ferraro's. Tessa, who looked radiant in a spaghetti-strapped indigo dress and matching eye-shadow, accompanied them. Duncan, for his part, was no slouch either, wearing a navy-blue suit and a gold tie. Brent, of course, looked impeccable as always, as he finished regaling the young couple with one of his many tales of overseas business ventures and adventures.

"Enough about that sort of thing," Brent said. "Tessa, I'm curious about you, young lady. What is it that you are involved in these days?"

"Well, I haven't really made any big plans just yet, as far as school goes. Right now, I'm teaching tennis lessons to little kids. I've been doing that every summer for a few years now."

"That's lovely," Brent replied. "I play a bit of tennis myself. Wonderful game. Do you enjoy giving instruction?"

"Oh yeah, I do, definitely. I love the little kids. I get kind of attached," she chuckled. "It's hard to let them go at the end of the summer, but they usually come back, so that's nice."

"You're a sweet girl. Do you have any aspirations as far as attending college?"

"Well, I'm gonna wait to see what happens with Duncan. We've been through a lot lately, and I don't want to be far from him again. So, if everything goes according to plan…"

"Don't you worry, my dear. Your boyfriend, I can assure you, will be a Los Angeles Laker come July." He put his right arm around Duncan's shoulder and gave him a strong hug as Duncan beamed. "I suggest you apply to UCLA. I happen to know some people on the admissions committee there."

"Tessa's grades and test scores will get her into just about anywhere she wants to go," Duncan said. "She's a wiz." He squeezed her hand as she blushed.

"Is that so?" said Brent. "Well, that's very impressive indeed. Should you require some assistance in that area for whatever reason though, I would be more than happy to help."

"Thank you, Mr. Brent," Tessa replied. "That's really, really nice of you."

"My pleasure, my dear. My pleasure. But really though, have you seen UCLA's campus. It's magnificent."

"No, I haven't," she said. "I've never been to LA."

"Well, I think I'm just going to have to fly the two of you out so that you can check it out, and so that Duncan can see the Staples Center... his new home."

Duncan and Tessa smiled at each other. Things were really starting to look up for them. All through high school, they'd had it good, but when things went wrong in their relationship, they *really* went wrong. Now, Duncan had a magnanimous benefactor whose purpose in life, at this time, was to make sure that Duncan wanted to play for his basketball team. And it wasn't just that he wanted Duncan to play for his team. He wanted Duncan to *want* to play for his team. There was an incredibly important distinction to be made there. Brent really cared about Duncan's wellbeing, and Tessa could see that. It strongly endeared the old man to her.

"That's really very kind of you, Mr. Brent. I'd love to see UCLA. I've heard really good things about it, and it would be so close to Duncan. I think that's a really wonderful idea."

"Excellent," said Brent. "I'll arrange a tour. What's your schedule like?"

"Well," she said, "I work Monday through Thursday, so I have Friday, Saturday, and Sunday off."

"A weekend tour it is!" he said, enthusiastically. "I imagine we'll be able to do that within the next two weeks or so."

"That's amazing, Mr. Brent. Thank you so, so much."

"Please, my dear. Anything for the two of you."

Tessa smiled, and said, "If you'll excuse me for a moment, boys, I need to use the restroom." Both men watched her as she walked away.

"That's a fine young lady you've got yourself, my boy," Brent said, as he turned to Duncan. "I can't believe how much she reminds me of my Eileen."

"You never mentioned that you were married, Elmer."

"I *was* married, Duncan. She passed away about twelve years ago now. She was my high school sweetheart, just like Tessa is to you. I love her dearly, but sadly breast cancer took her away from me."

"I'm so sorry to hear that," Duncan solemnly replied.

"Oh, yes, well, what can you do?" Brent said, forcing a smile. "Unfortunately, nothing. But seeing Tessa and talking with her, it does bring back some happy memories for me. Some happy memories indeed."

Duncan wasn't quite sure what to say, so he remained silent for a moment.

"Oh, dear," Brent said. "Look at me, dragging the festive mood down."

"No, no, no," Duncan replied. "It's not like that, Elmer. You just got me thinking about how I lost Tessa before. I mean, you don't know the whole story, but I lost her when we went to Amsterdam, and I didn't get her back until I got back from jail. I'm like, the luckiest bastard in the world. I can't believe she ever came back to me, but thank God, she did."

"You're right, my boy, I don't know the specifics of your situation. But please believe me, there were numerous times where I erred, and I was lucky enough to have Eileen return to me. I don't know why she ever took me back sometimes, but she always did. She was the greatest woman in the world, and for whatever reason she felt the same about me. I very strongly get the impression that you have quite the similar situation."

"You are right. Definitely right," Duncan said. "We just love each other. It's a miracle that she's stuck with me through some of the shit I've done, through some of my screw-ups. But, hey, we're here now, and that's what matters."

"Right you are," Brent said. "Now, let's talk a little basketball. Once you're drafted, I'm turning you over to Coach Jackson. I may own the team, but I do not feel as though it is my place to interfere with his coaching. That would only cause highly unnecessary and counterproductive tension. But, basically, the way I see it is that you will be an understudy to Derek Fisher for the time being, and, I imagine, before any of us knows what has hit us, you will be the starting point guard. How does that sound to you?"

"Honestly, Elmer," Duncan said, "just being a professional basketball player is such an amazing concept to me, there's pretty much nothing that I could find objectionable after I get drafted. I'm sure that whatever Coach Jackson thinks is best...is best. The guy has eleven championship rings. I don't really see how you can argue with that, ya know?"

"Exactly," Brent said. "That's why I hired him. Even though he only had six at that time. It didn't really take too much instinct to know that he was the man for the job. I mean, sure, he had Michael Jordan for the first six titles, but did Michael Jordan win a championship without Phil Jackson? No. I should say not."

"He's the best," Duncan said. "I can't believe I'm gonna be playing for him."

"It's going to be a match made in heaven, my young friend. Please believe that to be so."

"Oh, I can hardly wait."

"Excellent."

Just then, Tessa returned from the bathroom. "Sorry to keep you waiting, boys," she said, smiling radiantly.

"No problem, babe," Duncan said. "We were just talking some hoops."

"Just business, my dear," Brent contributed. "I am so very looking forward to having your young gentleman playing for my team, I can hardly contain my enthusiasm!"

Tessa laughed. "Well," she said, "we're very much looking forward to him being a Laker too. This is so huge for him. He's always and forever wanted to be on the Lakers. He and his best friend, Matty G, used to pretend to be Shaq and Kobe when they were little kids. Actually, their dads were even Lakers fans, even though they lived nowhere near Los Angeles. Before he passed away, Matty G's dad, Ernest G, used to call Duncan "Li'l Magic", right honey?"

Duncan chuckled. "Yeah, he did."

"So, yeah," Tessa continued, "this is extremely exciting for everyone. I just want what's best for Duncan, and I can see that this is clearly it." Her smile made both men's hearts flutter, Duncan's with love and attraction, Brent's with nostalgia.

On the limo-ride back to Duncan's house, Brent reminded Tessa that he was going to arrange for a tour of the UCLA campus for her, hopefully within the next two weeks. She was incredibly grateful, and when she and Duncan exited the limo, she gave Brent a tender kiss on the cheek. "Thank you for everything, Elmer," she said. "You're a sweet man." She squeezed his hand, and flashed him her heart-stopping smile. It would be the last time that he would ever see it.

Chapter 64

Brent called Duncan later in the week to tell him that he had arranged a tour of the U.C.L.A. campus for Tessa in two weeks. He said that he would have a limo come pick them up at his house, and then they would take his private jet to Los Angeles. Duncan was ecstatic and grateful that not only were things working out for him, but now Tessa's hopes and dreams were also being accommodated in the mix.

Sure, Duncan knew that more or less all the women of southern California would be at his beck and call once he was on the Lakers, but through his adventures and misadventures, he had learned that, as far as women went, there really was only one that he wanted to be with. So, the fact that Brent was doing his best to make this transition fruitful for Tessa too, only made Duncan love the old guy more.

He was at home, watching SportsCenter on ESPN three days before their trip was scheduled when he heard his favorite anchor, Neil Everett, say the worst thing that he could imagine. A picture of Elmer Brent popped up on the screen behind Everett, in front of a Los Angeles Lakers logo. "Elmer Brent, owner of the Los Angeles Lakers," Everett said, "died yesterday at his home in Los Angeles. The cause of death was determined to be a heart attack. Brent, originally a Texas oil-man, bought the Lakers twelve years ago, and was determined to see his team succeed. He was responsible for the hiring of Phil Jackson, and played an important role in luring Shaq from Orlando and signing Kobe Bryant right out of high school. His funeral is scheduled for tomorrow in Los Angeles. Elmer Brent was seventy-four years old."

Duncan's jaw, as it was so prone to do, rapidly made its way to the floor. "I don't fucking believe it," he said. "I don't fucking believe it. I don't fucking believe it." He held his head in his hands, and started to cry. The first feeling that went through him was sadness that he would never see this great friend and mentor again. Brent had been so good to him, so considerate of his needs, so considerate of his girlfriend. He was just a good person, Duncan thought, and it was horrible that he had to lose him. He had had quite enough of losing his friends to death's permanent grip.

But very quickly, Duncan thought of himself. Was there some kind of plan for him to get drafted in the event that something like this should happen? Duncan was sure that Brent would have informed team executives of the plan to draft Duncan with their first pick, but would they carry through with it? Duncan had performed poorly at the combine. He had impressed no one. Would they still go along with their late owner's wishes? With no way to contact anyone with the answer to his question, Duncan was left in limbo, filled with the sadness of another friendship lost to death and the uncertainty just hoisted on what had only moments ago seemed to be a very certain future indeed.

Chapter 65

Elmer Brent's funeral was something of a circus. Duncan, who still had plenty of money from his and Matty G's accidental heist, flew Tessa and himself out to LA to try to attend. It was a rather naïve notion that they'd be able to get in. When they arrived, security would not allow them to enter, and so they ended up amongst a throng of media and well-wishers who had gathered outside the church where the service was being held. Not knowing whether it was more appropriate for them to be in the crowd or just to leave, they decided to wait out there until the service was over, out of respect for the old man whom Duncan had come to form an unlikely and beautiful bond with.

When the service was over, Duncan and Tessa recognized many faces exiting the church. Basically, the entire Lakers organization was there, even players who had once been Brent employees, though no longer were. Massive and unmistakable, Shaq somberly exited the church, standing next to his former coach, Phil Jackson. Then, about a minute after spotting Shaq and Coach Jackson, Duncan saw Kobe. He wore sunglasses, so it was impossible to know what he was seeing, but all of a sudden, Kobe lifted his arm, and pointed directly into the crowd at Duncan. He mouthed the words, "I got you." Duncan nodded. Kobe nodded back, then stepped into a limo waiting for him at the curb.

Chapter 66

Duncan spent the next three weeks dealing with the agony of uncertainty, until finally the day of the draft arrived. Being an unheralded member of those declared eligible for the draft, Duncan had not been invited to attend the proceedings, so he sat with his parents and Tessa in his family's Eastfield living room. All the expected draft choices were made in the first twenty-eight selections. Then, it was time for the Los Angeles Lakers to pick. The NBA Commissioner, David Stern, went to the podium. Duncan gripped Tessa's hand almost as tightly as Mr. Lipton gripped that of his wife. Stern, a squirrely man in a gray suit and red tie opened up a card and said, "With the twenty-ninth pick in the NBA draft, the Los Angeles Lakers select…Paul Spears."

As the small contingent of Lakers fans at the ceremony went crazy for the well-rounded small-forward out of UNLV, Duncan hung his head in his hands. He didn't cry. He felt too numb for that. Tessa, on the other hand, did. Her heart broke for Duncan. He had been so incredibly close to living his dream, and now, along with Elmer Brent, it was gone from this world.

"C'mon, baby," Tessa said quietly. "Let's go upstairs." Duncan nodded, took her hand, and followed her up the stairs to his bedroom, and quietly closed the door.

Downstairs, Duncan's dad said to his mom, "Shit."

"Yeah," she replied. "Shit." Then they hugged, and went into the kitchen to fix themselves a drink and start making dinner.

"God damn it," Mr. Lipton said, as he chopped up peppers for the salad, "what an awful, horrible tease. The kid was this damn close!" He held his thumb and pointer-finger nearly together to illustrate the point.

"I know," his wife said. "Believe me, hon, I know. It's so sad."

"It's a fucking travesty is what it is," Mr. Lipton said. "And a tragedy, for that matter."

As they continued to fix dinner, the sound of the TV in the living room wafted into the kitchen. They were paying scant attention to it, but they could nonetheless hear Stern's voice announcing the draft selections and the accompanying fan cheers and boos. About an hour after the Lakers made their disappointing twenty-ninth pick, it was their turn to use the second-round pick that had been included in a trade made two seasons earlier.

No one in the Lipton house had any expectations for something good to happen for Duncan with that pick. But no one in the Lipton house could hear the phone call that took place fifty minutes earlier between Kobe Bryant and the Lakers' general manager, Sherif Simon. The call went like this:

"Sherif Simon here."

"Mr. Simon, this is Kobe Bryant."

"Kobe, how are ya? What do you think about Spears, huh?"

"Oh, Spears is alright, Mr. Simon. But that's not who you were supposed to pick, and you know it."

"What do you mean?"

"I mean that I went with Mr. Brent to meet Duncan Lipton. I shot around with the kid. And I know that you were supposed to get him with our first pick. Those were Mr. Brent's wishes, and now, you're taking advantage of his passing to serve your own agenda. So, let me make something really fucking clear for you, right now. If you don't pick Lipton with the fifty-first pick, I will not be a Laker next season."

"You can't just go back on your contractual obligations like that, Kobe."

"Of course I can. You know how fucking rich I am? You think I give a shit about that money? You think my babies won't eat if I don't play next season? If you think that, you are sadly mistaken. What I care about, Mr. Simon, is honor. And since you have shown yourself to be lacking in that department, I'm gonna take up the mantel where Mr. Brent left off. Just fucking test me. Take Lipton with that pick, or I'm done. I've gotta do what would make my boss proud. I don't know how I'll live with myself otherwise."

"What the hell is this all about? Why do you guys think the kid is so good? I've seen him play. He's not that fucking good!"

"He *is* that good. Pick him. Otherwise, shit's gonna get ugly."

With that, Kobe hung up. Sherif stared at his phone disbelievingly. *Well*, he thought, *I'm not about to take responsibility for the Lakers losing Kobe Bryant. Fuck it.*

Mr. Lipton walked out of the kitchen, and passed through the living room on his way to the bathroom. At that moment, it just so happened to be the Lakers' turn to pick. Commissioner Stern walked to the podium and said, "With the fifty-first pick in the NBA draft, the Los Angeles Lakers select…" The commissioner paused for a moment, and looked at the card in his hand with a combination of mild shock and amusement. "Duncan Lipton."

The crowd's lukewarm and confused response did nothing to dissuade Mr. Lipton from losing his mind. "Oh…my…god!" he screamed. "Duncan! Duncan! Get down here! Duncan!"

Duncan, thinking there was some kind of emergency, ran down the stairs. "Dad?" he said, running into the living room. "Are you okay?" Across the room, he saw his father pointing at the television screen. On it was Duncan's picture, next to a Lakers logo and a sign that designated him as being the fifty-first pick in the NBA draft. Had he been able to pick his jaw up off the floor, he would have said, "I cannot fuckin believe I'm me."

CPSIA information can be obtained
at www.ICGtesting.com
Printed in the USA
BVHW032317280620
582495BV00001B/97